Denmark, Past And Present...

Margaret Thomas

Nabu Public Domain Reprints:

You are holding a reproduction of an original work published before 1923 that is in the public domain in the United States of America, and possibly other countries. You may freely copy and distribute this work as no entity (individual or corporate) has a copyright on the body of the work. This book may contain prior copyright references, and library stamps (as most of these works were scanned from library copies). These have been scanned and retained as part of the historical artifact.

This book may have occasional imperfections such as missing or blurred pages, poor pictures, errant marks, etc. that were either part of the original artifact, or were introduced by the scanning process. We believe this work is culturally important, and despite the imperfections, have elected to bring it back into print as part of our continuing commitment to the preservation of printed works worldwide. We appreciate your understanding of the imperfections in the preservation process, and hope you enjoy this valuable book.

THORVALDSEN

*(From a drawing from life by Major Sophus Schack,
in the possession of the Author)*

Frontispiece]

DENMARK,
PAST AND PRESENT

DENMARK
PAST AND PRESENT

BY
MARGARET THOMAS
AUTHOR OF
"A SCAMPER THROUGH SPAIN AND TANGIER,"
"TWO YEARS IN PALESTINE AND SYRIA,"
"A HERO OF THE WORKSHOP," ETC.

ILLUSTRATED

"Skaal to the Northland! Skaal!"

LONDON
ANTHONY TREHERNE & CO., LTD.
3 AGAR STREET
CHARING CROSS
1902

DEDICATED

TO

MY DANISH FRIENDS

CONTENTS

PART I

THE CITIES AND THE COUNTRY

CHAP.		PAGE
I.	FOREWORD	1
II.	THE JOURNEY TO COPENHAGEN	7
III.	COPENHAGEN	11
IV.	INTRODUCTION TO NOTES ON TRAVEL	27
V.	ROSKILDE	29
VI.	FREDERIKSBORG	38
VII.	FREDENSBORG	44
VIII.	HELSINGÖR	53
IX.	ODENSE	59
X.	VEILE	65
XI.	SKAGEN	70
XII.	AALBORG	79
XIII.	VIBORG	82
XIV.	AARHUS	100
XV.	SILKEBORG AND THE HIMMELBJÆRG	105
XVI.	FARUM	111

PART II

INSTITUTIONS, LITERATURE AND HISTORY

CHAP.		PAGE
XVII.	THE DANISH PEOPLE	117
XVIII.	MANNERS AND CUSTOMS	128
XIX.	COPENHAGEN—INSTITUTIONS	157
XX.	COPENHAGEN—THORVALDSEN'S MUSEUM—PAINTING, SCULPTURE AND ARCHITECTURE	170
XXI.	COPENHAGEN—MUSEUMS	184
XXII.	THE ROYAL PORCELAIN MANUFACTORY—MANUFACTURES AND TRADES	203
XXIII.	MODERN DANISH LITERATURE	213
XXIV.	ANCIENT SCANDINAVIAN AND OLD DANISH LITERATURE	254
XXV.	THE DANISH LANGUAGE	271
XXVI.	FOLK-STORIES	276
XXVII.	SKETCH OF THE HISTORY OF DENMARK	287
XXVIII.	AFTERWORD	300

LIST OF ILLUSTRATIONS

THORVALDSEN	.	*Frontispiece*
THE MARBLE CHURCH, COPENHAGEN	.	*To face page* 16
VIEW ON THE LANGELINIE, COPENHAGEN .		,, 18
THE EXCHANGE, COPENHAGEN . .		,, 20
ROSKILDE CATHEDRAL . . .		,, 32
GATEWAY OF FREDERIKSBORG CASTLE	.	,, 38
FREDENSBORG CASTLE . . .		,, 44
KRONBORG CASTLE		,, 54
COURTYARD OF KRONBORG CASTLE	.	,, 56
THE GEDHUS		,, 90
ROSENBORG CASTLE		,, 136
PROFESSOR NIELS R. FINSEN . .		,, 160
HOLMEN'S CANAL AND THORVALDSEN'S MUSEUM, COPENHAGEN		,, 174

PART I

THE CITIES AND THE COUNTRY

" Leave thy home for abroad an' wouldst rise on high
   And travel whence benefits five-fold arise—
The soothing of sorrow and winning of bread,
   Knowledge, manners, and commerce with good men and wise.
And they say that in travel are travail and care,
   And disunion of friends, and much hardship that tries."

Alf Laylah Wa Laylah
(Burton's Translation).

DENMARK, PAST AND PRESENT

CHAPTER I

FOREWORD

> "Good sense is needful
> To the far traveller,
> Each place seems home to him.
> He is a laughing-stock
> Who, knowing nothing,
> Sits 'mid the wise."
> *The Havamal of Odin the Old.*

WITHIN thirty-six hours' easy journey of London lies a country whose inhabitants are akin to us in race and closely related in language, customs, and religion, whose literature resembles our own, and whose love for the perilous adventures of the ocean is as passionate as that of our own island folk, yet of which the average Englishman knows less than he does of Egypt, the Soudan, Australia, and of many another still more remote land. It is indeed somewhat strange that while tourists have overrun and spoiled the more distant kingdoms of Norway and Sweden, they have almost completely overlooked the allied country of Denmark, which remains, comparatively speaking, a virgin land, undeteriorated by the extravagances of the millionaire, or the vulgarity of the casual tripper; and of which most of the inhabitants maintain to this day, in all their integrity, the plain and simple customs of their grandfathers, uncontaminated by the vice and luxury of richer populations.

Lying far removed from the vortex of European politics, conspicuous only by its absence from the councils of nations, unambitious of a slice out of Africa, and indifferent as to the future possessor of Constantinople, China, or Jerusalem, Denmark is like the house of a man who is absorbed solely in his own affairs, and profoundly uninterested in those of his neighbours. Unchronicled in the "Story of the Nations" series, untraversed by the adventurous Baedeker, we can turn to the pages of Murray alone as a guide to this almost undiscovered region,* which nevertheless possesses a romantic history, a fascinating literature, remarkable antiquities, specimens of a style of architecture to be found there only, magnificent forests, tranquil lakes, and many other attractions of special interest to the natives of England, Scotland and Ireland, with all of which countries it has been at one time or another most intimately connected.

* Mr Edmund Gosse has written on the literature; and Mr J. B. Atkinson on the Art of Denmark.

Foreword

The Eddas and Sagas of the Vikings are rich in chronicles of our own nation. The stories of the conquest of England by Danish kings, of the burning of London Bridge by Olaf the Saint, of the discovery of America by the hardy Norse warriors five hundred years before the advent of Columbus, and of many a wild foray and fight on our island shores, can never be read with indifference by anyone claiming to belong to the race of the Anglo-Saxon.

According to the Heimskringla Saga, when Eirik held Northumberland as a fief from King Athelstan, Danes and Northmen often plundered the Saxon kingdom, and under King Harold, Viking raids were frequent on our coasts. "The kingdom of Northumberland, comprehending the present counties of York, Durham, Northumberland, Cumberland, Westmoreland and parts of Lancashire, East Anglia also comprehending the Isle of Ely, Cambridgeshire, Norfolk and Suffolk, Essex, Middlesex and part of Hertfordshire, were so entirely occupied by Danes or people of Danish descent, that they were under Danish, not Anglo-Saxon, law." * Four successive Danish kings from 1003 to 1041 reigned over the whole of England, viz., Svein, Canute the Great, Harold Harefoot and Hardicanute.

The bulk of the yeomanry of England is of Danish origin, principally from Jutland and Slesvig; in fact, "a very considerable part of the present population of the midland and northern

* Laing.

counties of England may with certainty trace their origin to the Northmen and especially to the Danes. As we proceed north, we find numerous names of towns and villages having their termination *with* (forest), *toft*, *beck*, *tarn*, *dale*, *fell* (rocky mountain), *force* (waterfall), *haugh* or *how* (hill), *garth*, together with many others. The inhabitants of the north will at once acknowledge these endings to be pure Norwegian or Danish." *

Carlyle, himself almost a typical Norseman, says, "To know the Norse religion consciously brings us into closer and clearer relation with the Past—with our own possessions in the Past. Unconsciously and combined with higher things, it is in us yet, that old Faith withal."

Saxo Grammaticus, the great Danish historian who flourished in the twelfth century, gives us frequent glimpses of the British Isles in his learned and curious work *Gesta Danorum*.

Shakespeare drew largely on Norse literature for his immortal creations. "The ghost in 'Hamlet,' the apparition in 'Macbeth,' the fairies in 'A Midsummer Night's Dream,' and 'The Tempest,' are closely painted after their Scandinavian originals."

It is an old English superstition that Pulsatilla or purple Pasque flower, which grows plentifully about the Fleam Dyke near Cambridge, flourishes only where Danish blood has been spilt.

There is not another of the minor countries of

---

* Worsaae.

Foreword

Europe which can claim names so illustrious in literature as this little kingdom. To mention only a few, Holberg, Ewald, Oehlenschläger, Heiberg, Grundvig, Ingemann, and Andersen, are writers of the very highest rank.

In science Denmark has given the world the great astronomer Tycho Brahe, and to Oersted we owe the discovery of electro-magnetism which led to that of the electric telegraph.

In the realm of art too she claims a high position. Thorvaldsen, Bissen, and Jerichau in sculpture, Bloch and Kröyer in painting, and Gade the pupil of Mendelssohn, Hartman whom Wagner admired, and Heise the great song-writer in music, are names with which criticism has no more to do.*

The adoption of the Volsungensaga and of the Thidreksaga as the theme of some of his operatic dramas by the great music-magician Wagner, has awakened intense interest in the North, while the fact that our Queen, "the sea-king's daughter from over the sea," the charming and ever-popular Queen Alexandra, is a Dane, has woven a new

---

* The music of Denmark deserves greater study and more knowledge than I am able to devote to it. The popular songs and hymns are striking in their tunefulness and simplicity. In the compositions of Heise, Hartman and Weyse the airs are not such as one hears and carries away but yet are tender and elegant; in those of Heise above all, the accompaniments enrich and enforce the words like those of Schubert. Probably none but a Dane, or at least a Scandinavian, could do complete justice to their purity, simplicity, and the unexpected turns of their phrases. He has put music to poems by Byron, Moore, Burns, Longfellow and Tennyson. Hartman, the teacher of Queen Alexandra, died in 1900, at a very advanced age; the works of Gade are known wherever music is known at all.

tie of relationship between the English and her own countrymen.

To this little kingdom of Denmark, grand in its simplicity, sturdy in its independence, rich in memories and associations, I propose to introduce the reader, and to create with pen and pencil a book which, if not an exhaustive description of the country, shall at least be useful as a guide during a visit to its hospitable shores, and a souvenir afterwards. I think I have said enough to prove how interesting the subject should be to all who call themselves British and American, and to the natives of that Greater Britain beyond the seas, some of whom have so bravely fought and died for the Motherland—our Colonial fellow-subjects.

CHAPTER II

THE JOURNEY TO COPENHAGEN

THE only portion of the kingdom of Denmark which is part of the continent is Jutland, the rest is made up of the islands of Iceland, Fyen, Lolland, Falster, and a number of smaller ones including Bornholm in the Baltic Sea. The Danes have never proved themselves good colonists, but Greenland, Iceland, and the Faroe Islands belong to them. It is proposed to sell the last of the numerous Danish colonies in the Antilles, St Croix, St Thomas and St John, but as the majority of the people and the present king are opposed to the movement, the bargain may not be concluded for some time yet.

There are many ways of getting from England to Copenhagen; the traveller may go *viâ* Ostend, Flushing, Calais, or the Hook of Holland; and if he be particularly enamoured of the dubious delights of the ocean, he may cross the North Sea to Hamburg or Esbjerg, and so thence by rail to his destination. The quickest route is *viâ* Ostend and Hamburg and across the Baltic from Kiel to Korsör; in this way the journey may be done in thirty-four hours, the sea passages from Dover to Ostend occupying about three, and from Kiel to Korsör seven hours.

There is another and longer route by rail from Hamburg to Nyborg and across the Great Belt by steamer to Korsör. In the depth of winter this passage is sometimes frozen, and mails and passengers are then conveyed in large boats which are drawn by men across the ice. The distance is seventeen miles.

The first question many intending visitors to Denmark will ask me is, I know, "Shall I take my cycle with me?" The answer is, "Most certainly," for it is almost an ideal country for the cyclist. To this practical information I may add that a very useful Intelligence Office for travellers where English is spoken, "Den Danske Turistforening Bureau," has been established at 7 Ny Ostergade, Copenhagen, for the purpose of giving information gratis, about travelling, sight-seeing, pensions, hotels, etc.

I am not fond of travelling direct from place to place, I like to linger by the way and while as it were stretching out my hand to grasp the distant rose, gather also the wild flowers which grow around my feet. Therefore I usually break my journeys by visiting places not exactly on the route. I have even pursued my devious way from England to Jerusalem *viâ* Nîmes, and to Rome by way of Innsbruck.

On my last visit to Denmark I took in some of the old Flemish cities: Bruges, where the music of its carillon seems to live forever in the air; Ghent, with its matchless Van Eycks; Malines, and Antwerp, where he who would judge Rubens must undoubtedly go—old-world places which have been so often described that I shall only mention them here.

The traveller, if so disposed, may also make a halt at Cologne and refresh his memory of the Cathedral there, that perfect work of art which the genius of the past has bequeathed to us. An elaborate development of the obelisks and pyramids of Egypt whose forms were first suggested by the flames which ever thrust their pointed tongues towards the skies, it stands isolated and dominating—a complete embodiment of the fantastic genius of the Gothic, as the Pyramid of Cheops of the simplicity and conventionality of the Egyptian Age.

Far from Cologne the train rushes over the almost desolate plains of Holstein with their vast and sombre horizons, and plunges at last into the bustling commercial city of Hamburg, where, however, many picturesque streets and houses may still be found by the seeker who is really in earnest.

One cannot say much for the steamers which ply between Kiel and Korsör, but the railway to Copenhagen is admirable.

The stranger's first impression on reaching Denmark would I think be of the extreme fairness of the inhabitants, their delicate complexions, yellow hair and blue eyes—"the blue-eyed Danes," as Kipling characterises them. At first on leaving Korsör the country is uninteresting, but the train soon pursues its leisurely way through the heart of one of the characteristic forests of Seeland. In winter these forests are as lovely as in summer, though the charm is different: in front of a sombre mass of firs the naked branches of the beech trees stretch like protecting arms, a few red leaves still trembling on their stems, under the cool grey clouds which blur the tree-tops rather than relieve them. Here and there lie tiny lakelets like gigantic acquamarines half embedded in the earth; their intense blue under cold skies is one of the peculiarities of Denmark.

Hoardings are erected beside the line in exposed places to prevent the snowdrifts which would otherwise impede traffic. In passing we catch a glimpse of the two pointed towers of Roskilde, and half an hour afterwards the train reaches Copenhagen—a city of spires and red roofs built on land snatched from the surrounding sea.

CHAPTER III

COPENHAGEN

IT is said with truth that England is London and Paris France; but with still greater truth Copenhagen is Denmark, for it is the only large city in the kingdom. It has passed through many vicissitudes. First mentioned in history in 1027, it was then attacked by the Swedes and Norwegians, and was at that time only a fishing village called Haven. In the middle of the twelfth century Valdemar I. presented a portion of the land on which it is situated to the war-like Absalon, Bishop of Roskilde, then the capital; this prelate built himself a palace where Christiansborg now stands. Owing to its situation it became a resort of merchants, which gained for it its present name Kjöbenhavn — Merchants' Haven. In 1443 the transference of the capital from the see of Roskilde was effected. From 1658 to 1660 it was besieged by Charles Gustavus of Sweden, in 1700 bombarded by the combined fleets of England, Holland and Sweden, nearly destroyed by conflagrations in 1728 and 1795, and again bombarded by the English in 1807.

In appearance Copenhagen resembles that which

was presented by an English country town about fifty years ago, before sumptuous town halls, public baths and libraries destroyed their old-world look. If it is not precisely a beautiful city it is not wanting in a certain picturesqueness; its chief charm, however, lies in the numerous public gardens and parks with which it is lavishly supplied. The stranger feels at home at once in the friendly little town, and travellers who have seen the finest capitals of the world invariably like Copenhagen.

The city is built partly on the eastern coast of Seeland and partly on the little island of Amager; the channel which thus bisects it affords admirable facilities for shipping. The fortifications and ramparts with which it was formerly surrounded have now entirely disappeared.

Of the enormous progress made by Copenhagen in recent years, some idea may be gained by comparing the following figures. The population in 1868 numbered 180,000, in 1881, 250,000, and in 1893, 312,000 individuals, or 376,000 including the suburbs, an increase comparable only to that of the towns of some of our colonies, or of our own overgrown Babylon, London. In 1880 the value of its exports was £10,030,000, in 1898 it amounted to £18,131,000. Of this total Great Britain has by far the largest share, amounting to 37 per cent. of the actual total weight. These figures speak volumes for the prosperity of the little kingdom, and are probably as many as the reader will care to be troubled with.

Though Copenhagen can boast of no great architectural beauty, the irregularity of the houses, the picturesqueness of their roofs and gables, the frequent canals covered with boats, the spaces adorned with flowers, trees, and bronze statues, and the rich colour of the old brick walls, make up an *ensemble* which has a peculiar attraction of its own.

Bredgade is the finest, but Ostergade, with its continuations Amagergade, Nygade, and Frederiksgade, is the most frequented street in Copenhagen. Here are the best shops, and here the Danes delight to promenade in that leisurely manner which is characteristic of the nation, the girls two by two, their seniors arm-in-arm as was the fashion of our grandfathers and grandmothers, the men continually raising their hats to salute their apparently innumerable acquaintances. The streets are fast losing their old-world aspect; the ancient houses, with their windows without mouldings, and red tile roofs, are being rebuilt on an extensive scale, but fortunately not all in the French fashion, which it is too much the custom to imitate whenever an old city desires to adorn itself with newer charms, like a country girl aping the costume and manners of her town-bred sister.

At one end of Ostergade is Kongens Nytorv (the King's New Market) the old centre of the city; at the other is a huge open space which is the centre of the train and tramway service, and where rises the new Raadhus (Town Hall). It is characteristic of the pleasure-loving Danes, that here in the very heart of their city many acres are given up to their favourite place of amusement—Tivoli.

Norrevoldgate, Farimagsgade, and Vestre Boulevard, represent the efforts of Danish architects towards imitations of the French, and are really fine thoroughfares.

The finest and most interesting church in Copenhagen is undoubtedly Vor Frue Kirke (Our Lady's); the exterior is in the form of a Roman basilica, with which however the Doric porch is not in harmony. Like most buildings in Copenhagen, the present edifice only dates from after 1807, the time of the English bombardment, when there existed on this site a much more imposing and splendid structure, which itself replaced a church erected in the twelfth century. The bronze statues on either side of the portico are by Bissen and Jerichau.

The church derives its principal interest from the colossal figures it contains of Christ and the Apostles by Thorvaldsen, the former of which is placed over the altar, while the latter stand in solemn procession on each side of the nave. The grand but somewhat agitated figures of the Apostles contrast vividly with the superb calm of the immortal Christ, who in the semi-obscurity resembles the god of a temple, and stretching out His arms, to express by His action the words written at his feet, "Kommer til mig," "Come unto me." In simplicity, in sentiment, and in reverence, this figure nearly approaches the divine conception of Leonardo da Vinci at Milan; these two representations are the noblest embodiments of the great Teacher with which I am acquainted. From Thorvaldsen's statue a calm and benign influence seems to radiate as it stands speechless, immovable, eternal, over the simple altar of the undecorated church. Before Him kneels the same sculptor's well-known "Baptismal Angel." In completeness, in grandeur, in unity of design, few artists have ever executed a more satisfactory monument to themselves and to their country than this of Thorvaldsen.

Once, as often, wishing again to enter into the feeling inspired by the almost divine figure, I opened the three large doors which lead from the portal, and gazed in reverie through the bars of the last gate. Two women were dusting the church, and one of them seeing I was a stranger, asked if I would like to enter. "Yes," I said. It is characteristic of the Danes that in reply she warned me, "It will cost you a crown to do so." I at once realised I was not in Italy.

Very interesting from a historical point of view is Holmen's Church, built originally as a chapel for mariners, but raised to the dignity of a parish church by Christian IV. in 1635. The interior with its broad galleries and three-decker pulpit is rather gloomy; the long mortuary chapel which runs out behind beside the canal is its most remarkable feature. In it are long rows of oak coffins lined with zinc and covered with wreaths of flowers; these are the resting-places of people sufficiently rich to pay for the privilege of mouldering above ground. At one end is the tomb in which Niels Juel has rested from his wild sea-fights for over 203 years; at the other the black marble sarcophagus which contains the remains of Denmark's greatest hero, Peder Vessel, called Tordenskjold (Thunder-shield), who from being a simple cabin boy raised himself to the rank of Admiral, and whose name to this day is a terror to all naughty little Danish boys and girls. Silver wreaths lie on the lid of the coffin, and on the side is his simple epitaph the names of his greatest victories, "Dynekilen" "Marstrand" and "Elfsborg." The great composer Gade is also buried in this interesting chapel.

In Ostergade is the fine old red church Helligaandskirken (Church of the Holy Spirit). The Marble Church, of which the Danes are so fond of talking, would not awaken admiration in any other town. Vor Frelser's Kirke (Our Saviour's Church) is remarkable for the curious outside gallery which runs round the spire, whence a fine view extending to the coasts of Sweden may be obtained.

The island of Amager, joined by bridges to the city, still maintains its old-world appearance, though the kitchen gardens, to cultivate which and to teach the Danes horticulture Christian II. imported a colony of Dutch, have long since disappeared. The ancient houses are still to be seen, and the descendants of the old gardeners

THE MARBLE CHURCH, COPENHAGEN

still retain traces of their origin, while the fishing population has a picturesque character of its own. Amager, with its unpaved streets and curious houses, offers us a picture of what Copenhagen once was.

The National Theatre, where the works have been produced which have influenced so remarkably the development of Danish thought and culture, stands at one corner of Kongens Nytorv. Two fine bronze sitting statues, one of Holberg the other of the great Oehlenschläger, ornament the entrance. Near by is Holmen's Canal, where all the best hotels are situated.

In the centre of Copenhagen stand the trembling walls of the once magnificent palace of Christiansborg, entirely gutted by fire in 1884; the vast conflagration was visible so far as the Swedish coast. It is somewhat scandalous that the palace has never been rebuilt. The Right or Government party occasionally introduces a bill to authorise the expenditure of the necessary funds, which is as often thrown out by the Left or Democratic party, on the grounds that the king is sufficiently well housed in his little palace Amalieborg. In front of the ruined entrance stands a fine equestrian bronze statue of Frederick VII., a fine example of the great sculptor, Bissen.

One of the curiosities of Copenhagen is the round tower built for an observatory after the design of Longomontanus, the Danish astronomer, which now forms part of Trinity

Church. It consists of two hollow cylinders between which an incline plane leads to the top. The ascent is so easy that when Catherine of Russia visited Copenhagen with her husband, Peter the Great, she drove up it in a coach and four preceded by the Czar on horseback. From the top a fine panoramic view of the city, with the red roofs and tall spires which make it so picturesque, especially when seen from the sea, is to be had. The church itself is an inferior specimen of pointed Gothic, and was built for the convenience of the students of the University by Christian IV. Near by is a very insignificant monument to the poets Ewald and Wessel.

Langelinie is a beautiful walk along the shores of the Sound, here covered with the shipping of all nations. To the north are the slopes of Seeland, to the south the harbours, and in the dim distance the shores of Sweden may be seen.

Behind Langelinie is Kastelgraven, the property of a skating club where the king and royal family were in the habit of enjoying this amusement. On one occasion, it is said, the ice was particularly slippery, and the ladies, whose loyalty caused them to indulge in deep obeisances to the king, fell, one here, one there, like so many ninepins. The king, true gentleman that he is, ran to assist every lady who lay sprawling on the ice, but so many were the disasters, that His Majesty became extremely fatigued and at last

VIEW ON THE LANGELINIE, COPENHAGEN

said that "in spite of the pleasure it gave him to help the ladies, he begged them not to courtesy to him any more, as it was completely out of his power to pick them up any longer."

In the beautiful park of Frederiksberg is the castle where the Princess Caroline Matilda dwelt when she first came to Denmark at the age of nineteen, and where she spent her last days before exile. The castle remains unaltered and a secret door is shown which tradition says led from Struensee's apartments to those of the queen. From the terrace one of the best views of Copenhagen may be had. Here too the citizens of Copenhagen used to assemble to watch their good bourgeois king, Frederick VI., and his family, smiling and bowing affably, pass in a small boat over the canals by which the park is intersected.

Oersted Park, containing among others a statue of the great scientist after whom it is named, and Chapu's expressive kneeling figure of Joan of Arc, gifts of the munificent Jacobsen, with its artificial mounds and lake, is the most elaborate in Copenhagen, but to my mind the wildness of Frederiksberg and Solemarken, with their magnificent trees and the old-world air of Rosenborg, are far more congenial. In all, the city possesses five parks.

The English Church of St Alban's, built mainly through the instrumentality of Queen Alexandra, is a beautiful little Gothic edifice standing at the commencement of the Langelinie.

Hospitals in Copenhagen are numerous, well-arranged, and well-endowed, and are often visited by strangers for purposes of study. The city has one University, to which since 1875 women have had access on equal terms with men to all branches of the curriculum excepting theology, in which the degree carries with it a licence to preach. The library of the University, which consists of about 260,000 volumes, contains many valuable Scandinavian specimens, though the eleven oldest and most precious Icelandic books are in the Royal Library. Here may be seen Icelandic MSS., black with use and the smoke of the fires of the long winter nights when they were read and re-read; Norwegian MSS., which were kept in cloisters and so are still clean and well preserved; one of the rare Runic books (runes are generally written on stone), and an Icelandic translation of the Bible containing quaint illustrations—a very rare example. It is interesting to observe that the period during which Icelandic books were produced only lasted from the year 1200 to the year 1500.

The interior of the Exchange offers nothing of interest if we except the fine hall, at one end of which stands a bronze statue of Christian IV. by Thorvaldsen.

Nyboder consists of a number of little cottages built by Christian IV. for the accommodation of sailors, which remain unchanged to this day. Officers as well inhabit these tiny abodes, near which a bronze statue of that king, by a son of the great Bissen has just been erected. Bissen is

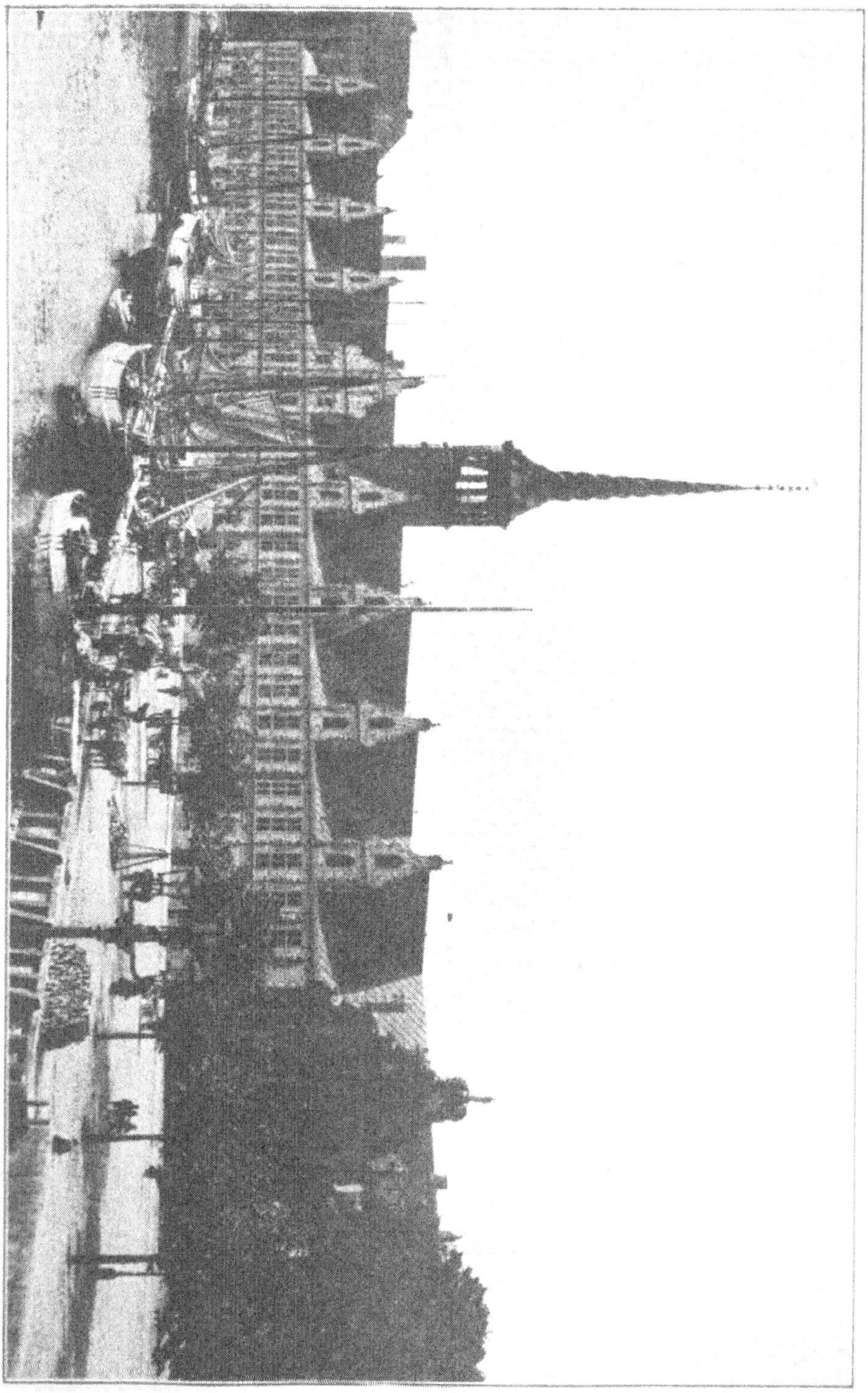

also the author of the group in face of the Raadhus which represents an event in the Slesvig-Holstein war, when a boy bugler, wounded and in a comrade's arms, continued to sound the call to advance—a deed which caused the Danes to score a victory.

Amalieborg is a small square on each side of which is a palace, originally built by a rich nobleman, two of which, connected by a corridor, are inhabited by the king. Here in a small house, into the windows of which the passer-by may look, with the salt sea almost at its gates, appropriately resides this ruler of a country rising as it were from the waves; the cries of the sailors must be ever in his ears, and the market people pass unhindered to and fro before his doors. Two soldiers, in hats somewhat resembling those of our Guards, pace tranquilly before the gates, holding doubtless what is profitable conversation with each other.

When the long winter has passed and the genial months of spring begin, the Dane hails with joy the happy change, and young and old pour forth in their thousands to view the flowering earth and swelling buds. Then let the cyclist look to his wheel, the pedestrian bestir himself, and the traveller by rail take advantage of his opportunity, and hie to the lordly forests and pleasant shores which are found within a very short distance of Copenhagen. At this season there are no more pleasant excursions than those to Klampenborg and Charlottenlund.

A short half-hour by rail brings the visitor to Klampenborg station, where the gates of the Dyrehaven lie before him. So early as May even the forest is enchanting; the dead red leaves of autumn lie thickly on the ground, and amidst them spring masses of the white flowers of the anemone resembling patches of snow left by the winter, still lying on the ground. From amid rise the tall trunks of the lordly beech trees, green with moss near their roots, silver-grey stained with dark brown or bright yellow lichen higher up, every twig adorned with pointed buds as yet unfolded, which shine like gold in the brilliant sunbeams. The dead leaves chase one another with a rustling sound along the ground and sometimes seem to pursue the traveller himself, amid whispers and songs, which are the voice of the wind among the tree-tops where the bullfinch joins his shrill chirp to the long trill of the lark. Dark pines fit for the tall masts of Viking ships, chestnuts with their young leaves hanging like green tassels from the branches, and slender birches with black and white stems, stand with their roots among the fresh green mosses, while herds of stags, white and brown, repose in the trembling shadows or rush in hundreds over the verdant plain. On one hand is the deep blue Sound bounded by the Swedish coast; the little island of Hveen crowned with the ruins of the old astronomer's tower lies in the midst, while ships of all nations pass to and fro upon the heaving waters.

The Hermitage, once a royal hunting pavilion, now a restaurant, is situated on the highest point of the Dyrehaven, and from thence the views in every direction are extremely fine. The Derby of the North, "a small Derby in a small country," is run here. Turning back along the Strandvei lined with curious little villas, and passing the fishing village Skovhoved, the park of Charlottenlund is reached, and here is the country residence of the Crown Prince, an ugly whitewashed building. This park is also beautiful, and on Sundays and *fête* days thousands fill its walks and glades and dancing and music go on till late at night.

The streets of Copenhagen are not very pleasant for ladies alone in the evening, and it is not advisable to walk alone in some of the faubourgs either by day or by night. All this is improving, but when I add that it has been found necessary to arm policemen with pistols in some of the outlying districts, it will be seen that a little caution is necessary in penetrating far into the lower parts of the town. However, the roughs and boys stand greatly in awe of the myrmidons of the law, while the country people absolutely detest them, and the stranger may be sure of protection by merely threatening to call the police.

Copenhagen is well supplied with newspapers and magazines. The *Berlingske Tidende* is the organ of the Government and corresponds to our *Times* in its coldness, correctness and impartiality. The *National Tidende* is the journal of the Right or Government party, as is also the

Dannebrog, which latter paper is distinguished by its vigorous onslaughts on the *Politiken*, the advocate of the principles of the Left or opposite party on which the more advanced journalists of the day are employed, and which has the (for Denmark) large circulation of 20,000 copies daily. The Socialists have an organ to themselves, the *Social-demokraten*, and woman's cause is voiced by the *Kvinderne's Blad*, and the *Damerne's Blad*. A weekly illustrated paper, the *Illustreret Tidende*, also appears, and is a not unworthy representative of our *Graphic, Illustrated News*, etc. Besides these there is a number of inferior journalistic publications, but they are low in tone and their production vulgar. An English penny paper costs fourpence in Copenhagen.

The currency of Denmark is based on the decimal system. The *krone* (1/1½d.) contains 100 öre. The Danish foot is a trifle longer than the English, and a mile rather more than four and a half of ours. Inland postage is eight öre, within the town limits of Copenhagen four öre, and foreign postage costs twenty öre.

A sketch of the beautiful environs of Copenhagen would be far from complete without a description of the Furresö and the chain of lakes connected therewith which are the favourite haunts of the inhabitants of Copenhagen — fortunate people who have at their disposition forest, sea and lake within a few minutes' journey of the capital. Let the traveller take train to Lyngby and there embark for the trip on the smart little steamer which, during the summer months, makes the tour of the lakes. He will then see Frederiksdal almost ideal in its charms, and passing through scenes of various beauty reach Holde; thence he can go back by train to Copenhagen. I do not know of any country which possesses so charming a chain of lakes, connected as they are in some places by canals, or a journey more easy and more beautiful than this over the Danes' own beloved Furresö and its sister lakes. There are no wonderful escarped rocks and mountains covered with everlasting snow as in Switzerland, no vineyards running down to the water's edge amid castellated villas as in Italy, yet there are as beautiful if less striking scenes; forests which touch the returning waves, fields of corn which are mirrored in the waters, happy homes and peaceful farms—such are the features of the Furresö. And when, as the setting sun lends its golden glory to the water, or the cold white moon streams athwart the gentle waves, as the reeds bend and bow, and the forests and cornfields lose themselves in the darkening distance the spirit of poesy and romance awakes, no scene on earth is more enchanting. Add to this the cheapness of living, the conveniences, the kindness and politeness of the people, and I do not know what more is to be desired to make a journey or a sojourn healthful and agreeable. I may remark also that in every direction round the Furresö charming forest walks may be enjoyed, and at every point of interest good hotels may be found at which to stay. The little towns or villages one thus visits are happy in that they have no history; in this village churchyard lies a native who from blacksmith became a painter; in that cottage lives a man, who being too poor to buy books, copied those he wished to have; or there one who is a hermit and only admits such persons as he prefers to visit his lovely garden which he has not left for twenty-five years; such and no more are the chronicles debated at evening under the wide-spreading village tree, where the elders and the children love to congregate. If it were not too trite I would say "*Nimium fortunatos!*" you know the rest. It is sufficient for me if I have given an idea of peace and mediocrity—that is of happiness—and such is the life of the Danes.

CHAPTER IV

INTRODUCTION TO NOTES ON TRAVEL

MOST tourists who visit Denmark return to their own homes carrying back as impressions of the little country and its Lilliputian capital a recollection of Thorvaldsen's Museum, Christ and the Apostles at the Frue Kirche, and as the *clou* of the affair, the Langelinie; also in admired disorder they have an idea of a multitude of lamps of all sizes and colours, of illuminated trees and flowers, and of sparkling lights and fireworks, the whole enlivened by music on every side like a pot-pourri more original than beautiful, which to them represents Tivoli—the Dane's pride and delight. As to the country itself, their knowledge of it is confined to a space of blue water covered with white sails large and small—the Sound; to a line of white, green and yellow villas all equally vulgar and ugly—the Strandvej; and to a mass of beech trees under which are stags and fawns—Dyrehaven. Some courageous travellers get as far as Skodsborg to see the "Bötlemose," a kind of morass; others, who are endowed with a very pronounced taste for adventure, go as far as Frederiksborg and spend two hours of their precious time in admiring the Castle; while those who are indefatigable explorers indeed, risk both time and money to render homage to the creations of their great compatriot, Hamlet and Ophelia, and in so doing cast a glance by the way at Kronborg.

But there is very much more than this to be seen in Denmark, tiny as it is, as I hope to show in the following pages, though unfortunately my description includes but a small portion of so much that is novel and interesting.

Murray assures us that travelling is expensive in Denmark. I, on the contrary, consider it extremely cheap, for though, as he says, a crown answers to our shilling and the French franc, there is a great difference in the number of these coins it is necessary to expend. Railway fares are extremely low and have latterly been again reduced, while for three and four crowns a day one can stay at the best hotels in the provinces, and for five or six at those in the capital.

I have tried in these my notes of travel in Denmark to retain the true perfume of the soil on which they were written, telling "the truth without modification," in the hope that some of my luxurious fellow-countrymen may be induced to investigate the beautiful scenes, hardy race, and simple customs of which they themselves are the outcome.

CHAPTER V

ROSKILDE

THE trains travel slowly over the plains* of Denmark with their vast horizon, plains which seem not to be overwhelmed by the sea simply because it has forgotten them though they lie so low, but which, some day remembering, he may reclaim. Here and there among the slight undulations which resemble the last heavings of the ocean after a storm, rises a little red-roofed village with its quaint white church and perhaps a mill or a gabled farmhouse built round a yard, otherwise for miles there is nothing but hedgeless fields surcharged with corn in one or another stage of development, or lush pastures on which the sleek, fat, tethered cattle graze. Occasionally however the railway passes through magnificent forests of beech trees which are the glory of Denmark, and which flourish nowhere else so well —giants which spread protecting arms as if to guard the soil which nourishes them. A somewhat melancholy country, but full of poetry for

* Nowhere is Denmark more than six hundred feet above the level of the sea.

those who love Nature and turn to her for that repose and peace which life in cities denies.

Such was the scenery through which I travelled when I went to Roskilde, the ancient capital of Denmark, in order to examine its celebrated Cathedral. Murray erroneously informs his readers that it is necessary to pay two crowns to see this church; fifty öre (6½d.) entitle the traveller to admission and also to a little pamphlet written in quaint English which describes its various curiosities. Provided with the address of the custodian, I made my way to his residence, the old palace, and asked for the necessary permission; seeing I was English he called his daughter, who speaks English, to talk to me. I explained that I intended to write a book about her country. "You are going to write about Denmark? Then I must show you the church myself," she said kindly. Arming herself with huge bunches of keys, the charming *cicerone* led the way through a long passage leading from the palace to the church, once used by the great Archbishop Absalon, and now by the members of the royal family and their guests when some State function requires their presence there; which is not seldom, for at Roskilde all deceased Danish royalties have been interred from the tenth down to the present century.

Roskilde was the royal residence till the fifteenth century, when the seat of Government was transferred to Copenhagen, and on this site Harold Blaatand, the son of Gorm the Old, the first

Christian Danish king and the conqueror of England, erected a wooden church in honour of the Trinity so early as the tenth century; this was replaced in 1060 by a stone building erected by Svend Estridsen. It has been many times burnt, and when the Lutheran belief superseded the Catholic, underwent great alterations; it was thoroughly restored in 1859-1881. In 1774 Frederick V. erected the ugly and incongruous chapel which has since been the burial-place of the members of the house of Oldenburg, the present reigning dynasty.

The Cathedral is the most important ecclesiastical building in the country; it is of brick, but behind the altar are some granite columns of unknown age; the mixture of round and pointed arches is remarkable, so also is the spacious clerestory continued from the gallery round the choir. The nave dates from the thirteenth century, and the view of the interior from the west door is imposing though the gloom and mystery which distinguish Gothic cathedrals are altogether wanting. The floor is covered with tombstones carved with recumbent effigies; among them, just in front of the west door, is the grave of a blacksmith who for a large sum bought it in perpetuity, and where his descendants have still the right to be interred. The building is not large, being in fact only two hundred and seventy-six feet long and eighty-seven broad, but its proportions are excellent. The exterior, of time-mellowed brick, is very quaint and original;

its two sharply-pointed spires are conspicuous objects for miles round.

The guide-book gives the list of sights in the Cathedral—I shall only record the impressions I received from some of them during a more than usually favourable inspection.

The royal pews, heavily gilt and surcharged with ornament, are opposite the organ, which is the finest in Scandinavia; the personages therein would have to open the quaint little windows when they wished to hear the service, and could close them if the sermon did not suit their views. A whole day might be devoted to the examination of the wood-carvings of the *miserere* seats which remain perfect and untouched from the beginning of the fifteenth century. Here some quaint old Gothic artist has recorded his ideas concerning the creation of the world, the history of Eve, of Cain and Abel, and all the old familiar Bible stories, clothing his personages with the costume of his day, and trying his best to give expression to that which he himself believed concerning them. What though Eve issues awkwardly from the side of Adam, who places his hand near the spot as if he felt a sudden pain there? what though Elijah goes to heaven in a hay-cart with the clumsiest of wheels? what though the torsos of his figures are like the blocks whereon the dressmaker arranges her "creations"? we feel the faith of the artist behind what he wrought in wood, as the thought of a child lies unexpressed beneath its few and stumbling words.

ROSKILDE CATHEDRAL
(From an old engraving)

The world will never again produce such sincere, as it will never again produce such unpolished, work.

The altar-piece, dating from the thirteenth century and in twenty-one compartments, is of carved wood coloured and gilt. It is said to be unique of its kind, and represents the chief events of the New Testament. A tradition states that a Dutch skipper intended to smuggle it through the Sound but was detained. He then declared its value at so low a sum that the king, taking advantage of the opportunity, bought it. Here we have again a representation of scriptural events which would be grotesque were it not for the simple faith which animates the quaint little figures in their curious attire.

It was a droll idea to immure the bones of Harold Blaatand, Estrid the sister of Canute the Great, King Svend Estridsen and Bishop William in the pillars of the choir, still more droll to read the inscription, "Haraldus rex Danie *Anglie* et Norvegie." It is a far cry from those days to these! In the choir is the tomb of the great Queen Margaret of Scandinavia. "According to tradition, the noted whetstone was buried with her, which she received from her kinsman and rival, Albert of Machlinburg, with the insulting message that she would do well 'to sharpen her needles, and leave swords to men,' a taunt which she repaid in kind, when the fortunes of war threw Albert into her power, by ordering that he should be brought into her presence clad in a woman's gown, and wearing a fool's cap three ells long, 'since he had not known how to fight in men's attire.'"* So much for my sex! Here also are the tombs of Duke Christopher, King Frederick IV., Queen Louisa, his wife, and Christian V. and his wife, which though historically interesting, have no value as works of art.

The hammered iron railings of King Christian IV.'s chapel by Caspar Finke (1690) are the finest of their kind in the north—it seems as if the iron foliage were really growing and ran riot over the supporting bars. The lateral walls of this chapel are covered with two huge paintings by Marstrand representing subjects in Danish history; they are black and cold but somewhat grandiose in style. All but one of the coffins are covered with black velvet ornamented with silver; the fine bronze statue of Christian IV. is by Thorvaldsen.

The finest of all the chapels is that of the Three Kings dedicated in 1404 by Christian I. The vaulted roof is supported by a much older granite column, in which are marks indicating the height of certain kings and princes. Peter the Great, the tallest, measures nearly seven feet; after him come, among others, the Czar Alexander III., King Christian VIII., King George of Greece, and King Christian IX. But Czar Peter himself was outtopped by an Irishman still remembered in Roskilde, who, if the measurement can be trusted, was at least eight feet in height. He is the only subject measured on the column.

* Otté.

The tombs of Christian III. and Frederick II. on either side are vile productions of the Flemish school; the effigies are of alabaster; King Frederick's favourite hound has not been forgotten, and on a pillar of the canopy of his master's tomb is inscribed: "Trew ist Wildpret"—Wildpret being the dog's name. There are some pathetic old frescoes in this chapel, pathetic because they are so sincere and naïve; how much may be forgiven to archaic work if it be only simple! and after all they are much superior to modern work of the kind in other parts of the church. On one of the old kings' tombs lies a heavy sword, the sheath of which was stolen by some relic-hunter with a blunted conscience, who, I regret to say, was an Englishman.

The attention of the traveller will naturally be drawn towards the chapel of King Frederick V.—that florid excrescence on the pure simplicity of the old church, because there in later days all dead Danish royalties have been placed—not buried—for they are nearly every one in sumptuous coffins above ground. The last to rest here was Queen Louisa, the wife of the present King. With all her love of simplicity, and her wish to escape anything like sumptuous obsequies, she could not avoid being placed here with a hundred gold and silver wreaths and emblems, which hang above her still in useless show. Fortunately those who knew her best and revered her love of benevolence, were able to appropriate much of the money subscribed for tributes of the kind to hospitals and homes for suffering children. Her coffin is covered with a mass of artificial flowers, among them, of course, many wreaths from members of our own royal family.

We penetrated also to the vaults and saw the mouldering coffins of many a long-dead count and baron, their rusted swords still lying on the tarnished velvet. Some were centuries old; one I remember revealed its ghastly contents—ah, far better the clean cool earth, or fiery purifying bath, or, as my daughter of the Vikings said, "the open sea."

Saxo Grammaticus and Tycho Brahe are both buried in Roskilde Cathedral.

One of the curiosities of the church is a clock belonging to the thirteenth century with two curious little wooden figures, one of which strikes the quarters and the other the hours. Beside them is St George on a grey horse encountering the dragon, and when the figures strike the bell, the horse tramples on the dragon, which thereupon gives vent to a hoarse shriek.

There is nothing else to detain the traveller in picturesque old Roskilde, though I may mention I saw in a modiste's window the English fashions for 1893; so I employed my leisure hours in watching the sun set over the Isefjord, on a branch of which the town is situated. My feet were in snow and ice through which the snowdrops essayed in vain to push their heads, and the shadows of the hoary cathedral were blue and cold, but the clouds became a blaze of gold and fire piled in tumultuous masses over the west. Soon the waters reflected the tint of the heavens, the still fjord lay like molten metal beneath a volcano's blaze, and in the distance the shores and islands which once were blue took on hues of purple and vermilion. This continued for some time as I thought of the courage and daring of the old Vikings who had won so much renown for their country. But the glory of heavens and fjord faded slowly away, and soon was dead and gone like Harold Blaatand and his followers; there only remained a grey extent of sky and water and still greyer shores. The cold was intense as I turned towards the station for a three and a half hours' wait for the train; even the cows turned out to graze had still their winter clothes on.

CHAPTER VI

FREDERIKSBORG

COLD and distrustful is the Danish peasant till you know him, but simple and confiding if you give him your confidence, when he quickly takes quite a kindly interest in you and your affairs. At least such was my experience when I went to Hilleröd, the little village near which the fine old Castle of Frederiksborg is situated and where I put up at the Hotel Kjöbenhavn, an inn such as artists love, kept by people of this kind. The large rambling rooms, corridors, and staircases are uncarpeted, the bed coverings are feather beds, but the food is possible for an Englishman and the welcome hearty; the garden runs down to the lake with, on the farther side, the old castle rising proudly from its couch of trees. The fact that I was a painter aroused the hostess's friendliest feelings; she confided to me that Frederiksborg being one of the very few places in Denmark visited by tourists, hotel-keepers were in the habit, to put it mildly, of making the most they could out of them, and that English people, and above all Germans, whom they detest, were their favourite victims. This

GATEWAY OF FREDERIKSBORG CASTLE

is meant as a hint to intending visitors to other hotels, and casts no reflection on the Danes' usual honesty.

It takes an hour to go from Copenhagen to Frederiksborg, once the noblest of the residences of the Danish kings, now the most interesting and complete museum of national treasures in Denmark. The original building was begun by Frederick II., but Christian IV. demolished his father's work and built, in the year 1602, a castle in all respects resembling that which exists to-day. In 1859 the interior was utterly destroyed by a terrific fire which spared only the external walls and part of the chapel, and in which a great mass of valuable historical relics were lost. Thanks to the generosity of the King, the Government, the public, and above all, to that of Mr Jacobsen, the castle has been rebuilt from ancient drawings and plans, and as we see it now is a perfect restoration of the favourite residence of Frederick VII. Built on three little islands joined by bridges in the middle of the lake of Hilleröd, with massive towers, pointed turrets, dormered roofs and florid ornamentation, Frederiksborg is one of the most perfect existing specimens of the Dutch renaissance architecture of the seventeenth century.

Evening is the best time to get an impression of Frederiksborg. Then a pleasant sentiment of melancholy pervades the old castle, whose time-stained brick walls are mirrored in the surrounding lake, which is so clear that the sky seems to lie at the bottom instead of above it —the tall spires pierce the clouds and often seem to mingle with them. There is a fine park adjoining full of beech trees, and a garden where the severely-trimmed box hedges and square beds are kept up exactly as they were at the period when the castle was built.

Naturally the fiery tints of autumn render the woods of Denmark magnificent at that season, but spring has a charm all its own which I almost prefer. Then the graceful beech trees, clothed in their robes of tenderest green, spring from a soil hidden in white anemones, giving rise to a sentiment of purity and virginity as touching as it is charming. The tender tones of yellow and green play at hide-and-seek on the quivering branches, the air is filled with the songs of amorous birds which sing lightly amid the fast-unclosing buds. The little waves of the lake lap upon the shore, and gently rock the sleeping swans cradled upon its bosom, while the sweet-toned bells of the castle seem to chant their lullaby. Evening approaches, the sun descends and his fiery hues suffuse the responsive lake; he sinks, blue and silver replace red and gold amid the silence of expectant eve; the clear long northern night, in which is no shadow of blackness, spreads its calm over the sleeping earth, and the moon rises bright as a diamond floating in unsullied light. All details are suppressed, all confusion and noise cease, leaving undisturbed the sentiment of beauty and peace which then constrains the soul, as a mother constrains her infant and presses it to her breast.

To enter the castle the visitor crosses a bridge and enters a courtyard; he crosses another bridge and sees another courtyard, the centre of which is adorned with a celebrated fountain. The first is not remarkable for any architectural beauty; in the second both the faults and merits of this singular style are sufficiently disclosed. Crossing this courtyard and opening a door (a closed door must never discourage the traveller in Denmark) the castle itself is entered. Happily, there is for once an excellent catalogue in French, the rooms are numbered, and the whole is so well arranged that no one can mistake his way.

Here the visitor may wander long amid rooms filled with curiosities of all kinds relating to the history of the country, and with portraits of its kings, statesmen, warriors, artists and authors, for Frederiksborg is a picture gallery as well as a museum. The collection of huge chests richly carved and gilt is also of great interest. The visitor should not fail to look from the windows at the various views over lake and forest which he will thus enjoy.

In the fifteenth room is a fine statue of Archbishop Absalon wearing a cuirass over his robes and brandishing a sword, by Bissen. Among the finest of the chests is that which once belonged to the Rosenkrantz; another good one is in room number twenty-five, and still another in room twenty-nine. A huge picture of the Danish royal family by Tuxen will interest many; the same artist has also painted some of the ceilings, which are very fine. A picture of the death of the Chancellor Niel Kaas by Bloch is fine, only the painter has forgotten to leave a space for the dying man's body and legs. The Hall of Knights (Riddersal) is a fine room but overcharged with colour and ornamentation even for the style; in it are several full-length portraits of modern kings, looking mean and weak in their uniforms and decorations as usual, compared with the grim, unadorned grandeur of the monarchs of former days. In the portraits of N. C. Lund, General Olaf By, and Dalgas, the Danish artist Jerndorff has shown the rare gift of blending portraiture with poetry; the picture of the old general returning from the battle-field with the shadow on his face from which the light of battle has fled and only the thought of its horror remains, with the setting sun behind him, is a masterpiece. Much cruder but equally forcible are Professor Otto Bache's pictures; his "Return of the Soldiers of 1849" is distinguished by its sentiment and truth.

Leaving the castle and re-crossing the courtyard, while wondering at the royalties who were content to rumble over such an atrocious stone pavement, one enters the highly-decorated chapel.

The inlaid wood of the pews is remarkable for its fineness and beauty of execution; the altar and pulpit saved from the fire, are of ebony and solid silver. The Bedekammer, or royal closet, is ornamented with pictures of New Testament subjects by Carl Bloch, which are much admired, but which, though full of feeling, I find hard and too pretty. Round the walls of the chapel are the coats-of-arms of the Knights of the Elephant, and the Grand Cross of the Dannebrog.

If the traveller will take my advice, he will not attempt to *do* the castle in one day, but will stay at the little inn I have mentioned. Let him go back there and rest and ponder over Frederiksborg and return to it again; he will find that at the smallest possible outlay, both of exertion and money, he has accumulated a stock of pleasurable impressions and a store of reminiscences that will serve him well in the long dark evenings of our English winter, and the still darker days of weakness and old age.

CHAPTER VII

FREDENSBORG

A VERY stony courtyard surrounded by long, low, whitewashed buildings, those on the further side surmounted by a copper-roofed cupola and entered by a flight of steps, in the centre a commonplace fountain with a statue, the whole shaded by stately trees — such is Fredensborg, the summer residence of the kings of Denmark. The simple gates of the domain open immediately on a picturesque little village with its pond, its shops and its villas. Called Fredensborg (Castle of Peace) because here was concluded a treaty which put an end to eleven years' war between Denmark and Sweden in 1720, it lives up to its name; nothing can be imagined more reposeful than the simple white house, the long alleys of tall trees ending in the enchanting blue of the lake of Esrom, the quaint statues, and the solitude of the park. It is not to be wondered at that the monarchs of certain nations, so many of whom are related to the Danish royal family as to have caused the late Queen to be aptly called "the grandmother of Europe," delight here to seek the repose their

FREDENSBORG CASTLE

own countries deny them, and to find in the utter simplicity of its retreat relief from the luxury and ceremony of their own palaces.

Mounting a few steps guarded by two insignificant stone lions, the visitor enters a very plain square hall painted white, containing a cabinet or so, from which three other doors open, that in front to the dining-room, that on the left to the apartments of the King, and that on the right to those of the Queen.

The King's ante-chamber is a model of frugal furnishing, his audience-chamber measures about sixteen by twenty feet. In one of his rooms is a screen worked by the unhappy Queen Leonora Uhlfeldt, and everywhere are little family memorials such as might be found in any English home if the proprietor had not grown too rich or too fashionable to despise them. Not grandeur, not comfort, not beauty render Fredensborg interesting, but these little evidences of home life common to all humanity which do such infinite credit to the goodness of heart of its possessors. The King's smoking-room has the ugliest of blue walls; in the next, among other pictures chiefly Danish (for, unlike ourselves in regard to works of art, the Danes are extremely national), is a portrait of Rembrandt by himself. From the King's plain working room is a good view of the Marble Garden, so called because of its statues, which is the only really private out-of-door retreat the royal family possesses. I omit a description in detail of the chairs and sofas, which are of ordinary damask with gilt frames: also of the stoves, which in every room are of black polished iron such as may be seen in any Danish home. A couple of little round tables in the King's apartments are ornamented with flowers very well painted by the late Queen.

The small dining-room is used when the family are alone or the weather is too cold to warm the large one—at other times it serves for members of the Court; it contains a round table, some red-covered chairs, a few pictures and little else. Naturally, when the inhabitants are there, the curtains hung, the little family ornaments in their places, these apartments have an air of comfort, but they can never be anything but simple and plain, nay, even commonplace.

The late Queen's working-room is panelled and painted white, in each panel is a little portrait of a member of the Oldenburg family; a fire-screen made of quaint little figures cut out and stuck on glass by her children stands before the round polished iron stove; in a corner is a table painted by herself. In another apartment is a magnificent head by Rembrandt (how he towers above all other artists, except, perhaps, Velasquez!) and a crucifixion by Vandyke—the only objects of luxury in the whole castle. The Queen's rooms contain besides one of those curious old cabinets which are also a piano, and the marble bust for which Queen Alexandra had the good luck to sit to Gibson in Rome just before the sculptor's death. Unfortunately, however, this bust fails to render the grace and elegance of the young Princess, though it is still like her in her undying youth.

In the centre of one room is a low square settee called "the settee of the Czar," because, seated on it, the late Emperor of Russia was wont to play for hours with the children he loved so well. From the Garden Room is a fine view over the park and down three long alleys of trees, at the end of each of which the lake of Esrom glimmers like a sapphire. In the breakfast-room is a very old Chinese cabinet — a present from the Asiatic Company to Frederick V.

We now come to the apartments of our own Queen, which, so restricted is the accommodation in the palace, are used as guest-chambers when she is not there. There are but three of these simple little rooms; the first is a bedroom, the whole furniture of which consists of two plain mahogany bedsteads side by side, a round table, an ordinary sofa, a few chairs and a dressing-table; of course curtains and ornaments were wanting when I saw the place, but no young girl in our days could be more simply lodged than is this royal lady when in her father's house. A small dressing-room is attached, and the third is a bedroom for the lady's-maid, in which is the plainest of iron bedsteads and just enough other accessories with which to pass the night.

The large dining-room is the only really fine saloon in the castle, and is situated immediately under the cupola. Built in 1760, it is eighty-eight feet in height and forty-four feet square; the floor is of black and white marble, and the panels are painted with scenes from the Trojan War. Around it runs a gallery to which so late as eighteen or twenty years ago the public was admitted to see the family at dinner; a proof of the intimacy of the Danish monarchs with the people, and of their simple habits, which still permit Christian IX. to walk the streets of Copenhagen with his dogs at his heels like any other gentleman. The royal table is in the form of a horse-shoe, and here, when the whole family is united at Fredensborg, the seventy or eighty personages of which it consists dine together.

Up a staircase painted white leading from the gallery, are three small rooms, consisting of a bedroom, a sitting-room, and a room for an attendant, furnished as plainly as any of the others. These are the apartments of the Czar of all the Russias when he joins, as he loves to do, the family circle at Fredensborg. Then indeed there is much ado in its quiet precincts; officers as well as soldiers are called upon to keep watch and ward in the park, and the King himself never sleeps at night till he has made the round of the guards. The beautiful little Russian pavilion in the grounds was built by the late Czar as a place for those gymnastic exercises of which he was fond; he also built the tiny villa which stands above the little pond shaded by trees at the gates of the palace.

I now come to what are perhaps the most interesting details about Fredensborg. Several of the windows, which are double, are rendered historic by inscriptions written on them by members of the royal family — inscriptions tender, pathetic, and of interest because not intended for public gaze, and dictated only by the private feelings of the writers. Some of these inscriptions run as follows and explain themselves:—

"Que Dieu veille sur le Famille Royale et la protège. Alexandra, 1867."

"En souvenir de ma sejour ici. 1867. Alexandre de Russie."

"Meneskenes Börn skitles ad, Guds Börn skitles aldrig ad" (The children of men part, the children of God never part).

The King of Greece inscribed his name thus, "Willy." Olga, the Queen of Greece, has written, "Danmark, Danmark, elskede Hjem" (Denmark, Denmark, beloved home), and the late Czar, "Farvel kjære gamle Fredensborg" (Farewell dear old Fredensborg), "23rd Juni, 5 Juli, 1876." In a single line are written the names, "Albert Edward-Alexandra, 1864," and lower down on the same window, "Nicola-Dagmar, le 11/29 Octobre 1864." Still another of these royal inscriptions reads, "Farvel, mit elskede Fredensborg" (Farewell my beloved Fredensborg). "Alexandra, September 1868." Then follows on these historic panes the names of "Valdemar-Marie, 1885," and "Christian-Louise, 1864"—those of the present King and late Queen.

The rooms of the King of Greece, like the others, contain only bare necessaries; all the bedrooms in the castle have plain wooden bedsteads with green silk screens standing at the foot to keep away the light, and black stoves.

So restricted is the space in this unique palace, that when other members of the royal family except the Czar, the Queen of England, and the King of Greece visit it, they have their apartments amid those of the Court, in the low white buildings which surround the courtyard.

The crowning glory of Fredensborg is the magnificent park which runs from its doors down to the blue lake of Esrom. Who could fail to love these sylvan scenes and tranquil glades, especially if attached to them by reminiscences of childhood and affection? I happened to see it in its happiest season, the spring, when the young leaves of the beeches were bursting yellow and tender from their pinky sheaths. Avenues of the same magnificent trees, with interlaced branches, led down to spaces bluer than the sky, which were the lake; others with long arms swept the ground and guarded like memories the frail, dead leaves of last year; the lake opened far and wide, and into its glassy waters green fringes of trees drooped and were reflected there as clear as the reality; on its farther shores lay mighty forests growing bluer and bluer, till they hid themselves at last in the mystery of the horizon. Tall dark pines suggested masts for Viking ships and made a sombre background which relieved young trees clothed in the tenderest hues of spring; anemones and violets mingled their blossoms on the soil and nestled in their couch of green. Through these peaceful scenes and tranquil glades the visitor may wander for hours without meeting a living soul, though the park is always open to the public, even when the King is in residence.

One of the avenues is called the Alley of Sighs. Here the Russian Emperor was accustomed to walk, and after he had bought one or two pictures of Fredensborg, was, it is said, one day astonished at the number of painters seated hard at work under their white umbrellas on both sides of his path. They *sighed* that he might buy their productions, said the comic papers of Copenhagen, hence the name.

In a little valley called Normandsdal about sixty rough stone figures representing Norwegian peasants in their national costumes are placed. Very rude are these figures but yet not wanting in a certain simplicity which contrasts favourably with some other works of sculpture in the garden.

In this park Caroline Matilda of England, to this day the darling of the sympathetic Danes, indulged without restraint in her favourite amusement of hunting, which was counted against her as levity by the Danish women who were not familiar with the art of riding. One can still imagine the robust young queen with the graceful and gifted Struensee by her side, her idiot husband for a while forgotten, bursting through the shady coverts, and pity if not excuse the faults as yet unproved which led to her untimely fall. I conclude with the words of the Queen who loves it so much :—

"Farvel, mit elskede Fredensborg."

CHAPTER VIII

HELSINGÖR

"Welcome to Elsinore."
SHAKESPEARE.

HELSINGÖR is a commercial town which, owing to its fine harbour and favourable situation at the mouth of the Sound, has doubled its population in the last ten years. Hundreds of vessels of all nations pass by it every day, the Swedish coast is only a rifle-shot off, and the grim old fortress of Kronborg keeps watch over the gleaming water. Its streets are narrow and the houses crowded together; many of them are picturesque. The coast is not considered dangerous, but a pilot confided to me that he had seen so many as six wrecks in one night.

The hotel I stayed in appropriately resembled a stranded ship; there were long wooden passages with steps up to this room and down to that, the bedsteads were what a sailor would call "standing bed-places," the dining-room was furnished like a cabin with lockers, mariners were constantly occupied in looking out of the small windows with telescopes, the happy but scarcely practical idea of locking the doors and hanging the keys on a nail beside them was the one un-nautical thing about the place. It was very much in keeping with the seaside character of the town which in England goes by the classic name of Elsinore.

The Sound dues claimed from the earliest historic times by Danish kings were levied here, but in 1857 Denmark was compelled by the other maritime nations to accept thirty million ridsdaler in compensation of this burdensome tax on trading vessels, since which Helsingör has lost much of its prosperity, now, however, apparently slowly returning.

Helsingör is Kronborg Castle much as Windsor is Windsor Castle. Built by Frederick II. between 1574 and 1585 for the purpose of enforcing the Sound dues, Kronborg is the most perfect specimen of Renaissance castellated architecture remaining in Scandinavia. Rising directly from the sea on the extreme point of land between the Kattegat and the Sound, it presents a very imposing appearance whether from the water or from the land. Its massive walls, fosses and escarpments are maintained in a perfect state of preservation, and being built of stone and in a simpler style than the Castle of Frederiksborg, it has an imposing solidity wanting in a building made of brick and ornamented in a more florid manner. To look at the castle you would not give it its age; the edges of the carvings are still sharp, the stones look freshly cut, and the copper-sheathed towers

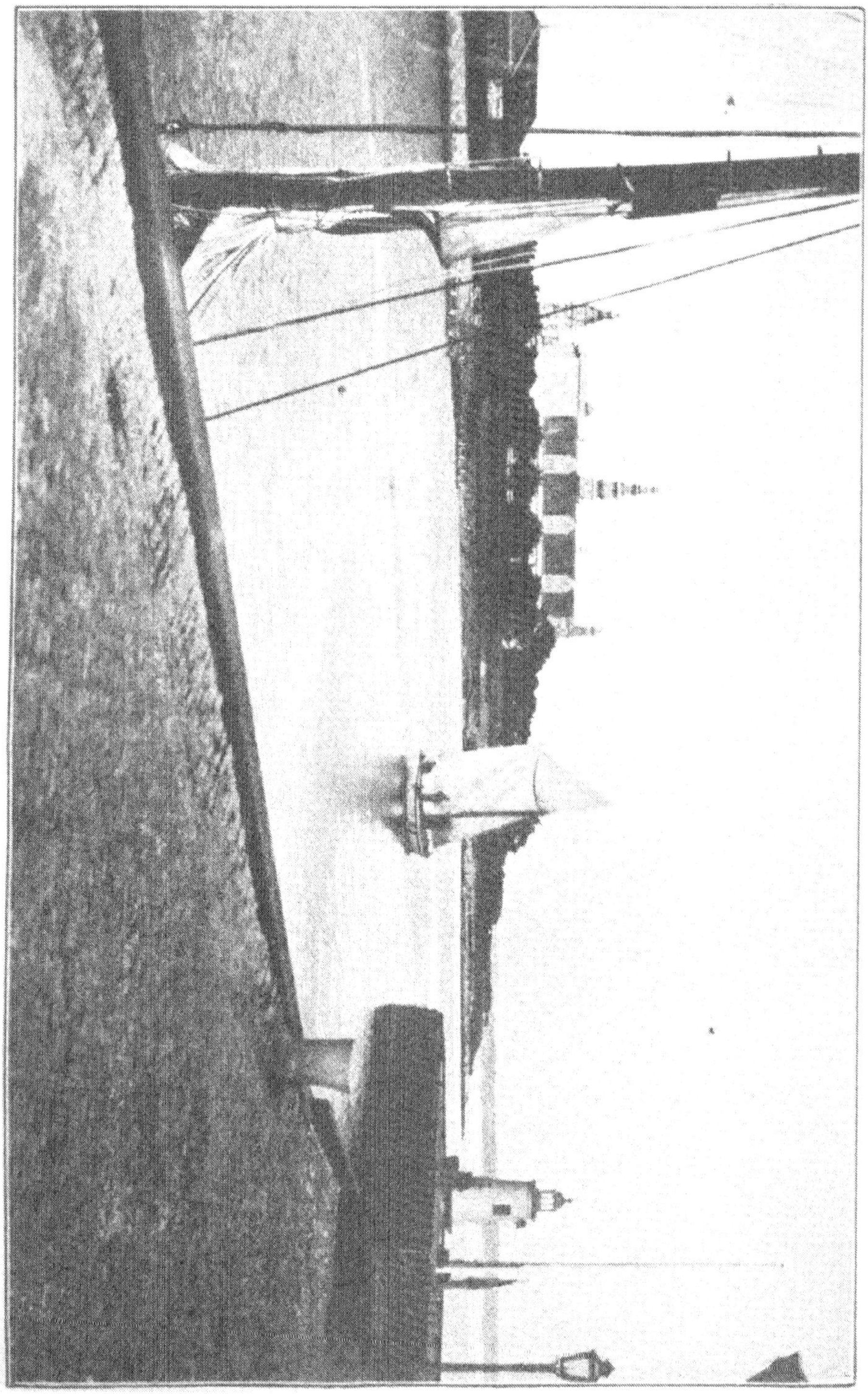

rise uninjured towards the heavens; it seems to regard grimly the Swedish coast it has watched so long, and the shipping which passes unceasingly to and fro below it.

The picture gallery is, as Murray remarks, not worth seeing, though the paintings may perhaps be historically interesting to the Danes. I am disposed to say that those pictures, which are not bad Danish, are copies; but there is a portrait of Cromwell among them which, even if a copy, is a most excellent work, and in which the character of the great Protector is admirably delineated. The marble chimney-pieces in all the rooms, of the same epoch as the castle, are worthy of remark. Some of them are placed in corners, and look as if, when fires were lighted in them, they really would make the place quite habitable.

The effect of the architecture of the chapel would have been beautiful if it could only have been left as the architect designed it, but everything is painted and gilt in atrocious taste, especially the wood carving of the pews. The representation of the Crucifixion in gilded marble over the altar is not bad, however, and a small copy of Thorvaldsen's Christ ornaments the holy table.

The ascent of the tower is fatiguing but ought to be made if possible. From the platform at the top is a magnificent view over sea and land, with below, serried ranges of such cannon as modern methods of war have rendered useless.

There they stand like decayed veterans who, their years of service past, have nothing now to do but to observe, listen to the tales of the heroic youth which has superseded them, and patiently wait for death. Let us look farther afield. The Swedish coast is so near that the windows of the houses may be seen; on the Danish side rises forest after forest varied with the white houses of tiny villages nestling in their embrace, but the ever-changing effects of sky and sea in all their vastness are the greatest charm of that far-extending view. The ghost of Hamlet's father, if he parade this platform, is to be envied his chance of studying effects—effects which are the opportunity of the poet and the despair of the artist. In this fortress Queen Caroline Matilda was confined after her downfall and that of Struensee, to await the squadron which her brother George III. sent to convey her to Germany—one wonders why he did not bring her to England. Who can realise the sufferings of her who at one single blow lost all—home, honour, and love itself? No wonder that no other members of the royal family have ever cared to occupy her apartments.

Commentators on Shakespeare have been surprised that he should have been so well acquainted with the details of the scenery described in "Hamlet," whom he represents as living at Elsinore in Seeland, when, as a matter of fact, he was born and lived in Jutland, without having visited the country. Light has been thrown

COURTYARD OF KRONBORG CASTLE

on this subject by the discovery amid the archives of Helsingör, of a curious and instructive document which shows that in 1585 a wooden theatre in which a troupe of English comedians had been performing, was burnt down. The names of the artists are given, and almost all of them belonged to Shakespeare's company.

To the very blue-eyed maiden who had so far accompanied me in this ramble I expressed a wish to see Holger Danske, the national hero, who, wrapped in slumber, is supposed to be in the vaults below awaiting the hour when his country shall stand in need of him; so long has he waited that his beard is said to have grown into the stone table at which he sits. She replied that I must ring at a certain door in order to find him. Thereupon appeared a youth with face burnt by the sun many shades darker than his flaxen locks, from which his light blue eyes gleamed abruptly, who led me through innumerable long, dark passages and turnings which seemed to run under the entire castle, and through apparently impenetrable casemates, which we traversed by the aid of a lamp, bending low in our efforts to do so, till we came to two fragments of stone, one of which he told me was a piece of Holger's table, the other his pillow. "Where then is Holger Danske?" I said. Solemnly the boy turned round towards me and, as if in pity of my ignorance and stupidity, said sadly, in English, "He lives no more." So even from the peasant mind the old tradition has vanished before the light of facts. Here is another enlightenment, another disenchantment, and life goes on like the exit from the grim old fortress of Kronborg into the noise and bustle of a shipbuilder's yard, romance and picturesqueness behind us, utility and ugliness before.

Of Marienlyst, a pretty and fashionable watering place close to Helsingör, it is not necessary to write, neither shall I waste time over those supreme deceptions which the curiosity and ignorance of travellers have rendered possible— the grave of Hamlet and the spring of Ophelia. Better dwell on the genius of the immortal English dramatist who has peopled Helsingör with beings whom we know; who has galvanised the past into life, and rendered this little corner of obscure Denmark forever interesting wherever the English language is spoken or translated, and that is—the whole world.

> "And I knew that where I was standing
>   In old days long gone by,
> Hamlet had heard at midnight
>   The ominous spectre cry.
>
> And the art of Shakspere was added
>   To the great glad splendour there,
> Fulfilling the physical beauty
>   And glory of light and air."
>   EDMUND W. GOSSE.

CHAPTER IX

ODENSE

THE island of Fyen lies between Seeland and Jutland. A couple of hours takes the traveller from Copenhagen to Korsör, where part of the train itself is shipped, and the boat crosses the Great Belt in an hour and a half, landing its passengers at Nyborg. To Odense, the next largest town in Denmark after Copenhagen, the city of St Knud and H. C. Andersen, the run is made in an hour and a half, or, as the guard of whom I inquired said, "It ought to be about that."

Odense is one of the oldest towns in Denmark, though you would not think so to look at its asphalted and well-paved streets and electric lights; it takes its name, Odins Ey (island of Odin), from the fact that here Odin had one of his chief temples. His worship was very promptly replaced by Christianity; the altars of the pagan deity were scarcely broken down when those of the new faith arose; and when Hans Tausen, a native of Odense, preached the reformed religion, it was also here that it first took root. The earliest Danish book was written here in 1109, and here too in 1482 was issued the first book printed in Scandinavia—a Latin history of the siege of Rhodes.

Odense with its 33,000 inhabitants is one of the cleanest and prettiest of towns; enough of its old houses remain to render it picturesque as well. Its principal attractions are the Cathedral of St Knud, the national saint of Denmark, and the house where Andersen was born.

St Knud (Canute) was a nephew of Canute the Great who intended to dispute the conquest of England with William of Normandy. But, owing it is said to foreign machinations, his army became insubordinate, and his subjects, on whom he inflicted severe punishments, rebelled; an insurrection broke out and he was killed while kneeling before the altar of the Church of St Albanus. His brother Benedict and seventeen faithful followers were slain at the same time, which fact is recorded in the crypt of St Knud; to use the words of the inscription, "As they suffered death with their king and master, so their memory ought to be held in remembrance with his." Knud was canonised in 1101 and buried the next year in the church which he himself had begun to build.

The Cathedral is a fine specimen of Early Pointed Gothic, possibly one of the best things of which brick is capable; even the slender mullions of the windows are of brick; the little colouring which relieves the interior is delicate and appropriate, and it is purer and simpler in style than that of Roskilde.

Two chapels exist like excrescences on either side. One is that of Count Vitinghof, who lies in his faded coffin on the pavement with his wife and children around him. At their feet is the coroneted coffin of Christina Munk, the morganatic wife of Christian IV. This coffin was originally open, but was closed by order of Frederick VII. to please his also morganatic wife, the notorious Countess Danner, who professed to be shocked at the sight of the remains of her predecessor in the title—a sense of delicacy sufficiently curious in a woman whose presence even was an insult to the ladies of Denmark. It is related of this woman that once, when driving with the king near Frederiksborg, a quarrel sprang up between the pair, which ended in his ordering the coachman to stop and set her down in the road, saying, "Formerly you were well able to walk, so you can do so now." The Countess accordingly commenced to return to the castle on foot, but was encountered by a gentleman of the Court, who conveyed her there in his own carriage. "Ah!" cried the king to the gentleman on seeing them arrive, "I thought you had more respect for yourself than to pick up the dirt I left in the road."

The other chapel contains the very remarkable metal sarcophagi of Count Ahlfeldt and his family, a couple of mourning standards, and a suit of armour worn at the siege of Copenhagen.

In the semi-crypt is a slab of Swedish marble bearing the rude effigies of King John II. and his wife, dated 1513, removed from the Church of Greyfriars; also slabs covering the remains of other ancient royalties. The shrine of St Knud is a fine example of Romanesque wood-work; the gold plaques with which it was ornamented were stolen by the Swedes. A few bones of the saint are yet visible beneath the singularly well-preserved shroud lined with silk, which was woven by his queen; the same pattern is still in use in Denmark. Besides the saint's remains lie, in another shrine, the bones of his faithful brother Benedict.

Over the high altar is a very extraordinary triptych of carved oak, painted and gilt, containing more than three hundred figures, the work of Claus Berg, a famous artist of Lubeck toward the close of the fifteenth century; it is said to have occupied the labour of twelve men for eight years. In the centre is the coronation of the Virgin, the Crucifixion, and other subjects; on the wings various scenes from the life of Christ; and the predella represents Queen Christina, the donor, and other royal personages adoring the risen Saviour.

On one side of the altar is a slab with the coloured effigy of Dame Margrete Skofgaard. Tradition relates that she *was danced to death* at Koldinghus, but whether that was a form of punishment in those days, or only means that she caught cold at a ball and died, I have not been able to ascertain. The amusing part about this lady is that when erecting her own monument she had the somewhat sumptuous dress covered with gilt, but Christian IV., some say because he thought the gold too gay for a church, and others because she refused to lend him some money he wanted, had it painted black, and so it now remains. On the other side is the tomb of a general, the principal event of whose life seems to have been that he had a dream resembling that related in Ezekiel, chapter xxxvii., which is represented in a picture behind the kneeling figure of the soldier himself. On either side of him are inscribed "Labor-Quies." Truly rest only comes after death to most of us.

Vor Frue Kirke is the oldest church in Odense but carries it age too well to be interesting; it is, however, a fine building of red brick and dates from the twelfth century.

Odense also contains a very perfect little museum. On the ground floor are curious old domestic utensils, among them a glass rolling-pin inscribed in English, "Love and be true," old chests, corner cupboards, weapons, some remarkably large pre-historic flint implements and boats hewn out of trees; on the second some exceedingly well-stuffed birds, geological specimens, and an interesting collection of coins, while on the third is a small but good collection of Danish paintings. A number of casts of ancient and modern sculptures occupy the central hall.

The town boasts two theatres, at one of which I saw a far from despicable representation of an operetta by Offenbach.

The little house in which H. C. Andersen was born lies not far from the Cathedral. It is a two-storied unpicturesque-looking building, now a furniture shop. How I wished it was worth sketching!

I should like to call the attention of those who would travel economically in Denmark to the Mission Hotels, one of which may be found in most towns of any importance. They are clean and cheap, a room may be had for two crowns a day, and the food, even for an Englishman, is more than tolerable.

CHAPTER X

VEILE

EVERY Dane will tell you that you do not know Denmark if you do not know Jutland (Jylland), which they call the "continent," so there I went accordingly.

After leaving Odense the country becomes characteristically Danish, that is to say it consists of a continuation of soft, low hills which resemble the heavings of a sleeping woman's breast. When I passed in June these hills were green with corn, amid which gentle winds were at play; here and there white thatched cottages, nestling amid hawthorn, lilac, and laburnum in full blossom, varied their somewhat monotonous outline. This part is noted for what the Danes call "living hedges," which are nothing but hedges such as are commonly seen in England; indeed, much here resembles England, and the Englishman may recognise everywhere the wild flowers of his native land.

At Strib there is a powerful steam ferry which takes part of the train on board and crosses the Little Belt in a quarter of an hour to Fredericia, the scene of a brilliant episode in the Slesvig-

Holstein campaign of 1849, when the Danes, after a two months' siege, made a sortie and took thirty field pieces and upwards of three thousand small arms from the besiegers, who were forced to retire. Bissen's celebrated monument, "den Danske Landsoldat," is a worthy memorial to those who fell on this occasion. Half an hour after leaving Fredericia, Veile, a small town whose history goes back to ages preceding Gorm the Old, and which is renowned for its charming environs, is reached.

Situated at the end of a beautiful fjord, Veile is one of the few places in Denmark which may justly be called hilly, and to this it owes much of its charm; a little river bordered with houses runs through its midst. As in other Danish towns, one is struck by the entire absence of public-houses, which are so unpleasantly obtrusive in our cities. I do not know if the Danes really drink more than English people; if they do, it is certainly not done so publicly or so ostentatiously as with us.

Apropos of drinking, once asking the person in whose house I lodged where I could find her husband, she replied that I could not see him that day "as he had the carpenter in his attic." "But I have just been there and seen no one." Bursting into laughter she enlightened me, saying, that to have "carpenters in the attic" was the Danish method of describing that sort of "head" which follows a period during which one has drunk deeply but not too well.

I cannot imagine a lovelier spot at which to spend the months of summer than at Veile, where the charms of sea and forest are combined. A beautiful excursion is that by steamer along the fjord, or by train, to Munkebjærg, a height covered with the richest and most varied vegetation. Another is to Griesdal, one of the most enchanting valleys in Europe, and I who say this have seen many of them. Of course, as there is the choice, it is better to drive down it than to go by train. The road is shaded by an avenue of trees, and so level that, as in many other parts of this country, the cyclist does not need a brake. On both sides are wooded heights, a little stream runs down the middle, and tiny pink cottages are dotted here and there. In these woods the traveller may wander for hours in solitude at his own free will, beneath the indescribably tender green of beeches, the heavy plumes of firs, and lighter foliage of oaks, with, under his feet, a carpet of fern and flowers.

This is really Denmark, not epic but lyric, not war-like but pastoral, not grandiose but charming, not like a tragedy queen or woman of fashion, but like a simple cottage maid whom some might perhaps prefer.

From the valley an ascent of 281 feet proudly recorded, leads to Skraedder-bakken. The view hence, down its whole length of four Danish or eighteen English miles, with Veile in the distance, is remarkably fine. In the book at the little restaurant there, in which I wrote my name, an

Englishman had previously recorded his opinion that more English people ought to come to Griesdal, and I most heartily endorse his sentiment, for a more romantic, healthful, and to those to whom it is a consideration, more economical spot, it would be difficult to find.

A small train goes at a walking pace from Veile to Jellinge, a village lying on a plain covered with wind-tossed rye-fields. Here are two Kongehoj, large flat-topped mounds covered with grass, beneath which Harold Blaatand buried his father, Gorm the Old, and his mother Thyra, surnamed the "Danes' Pride." These tumuli are the largest of the kind in the north; when they were opened in 1861 the sepulchral chambers were found to have been lined with painted wooden plates over which hangings had been suspended; the few objects discovered are now in the Museum of Northern Antiquities at Copenhagen. In the churchyard which lies between the mounds are two runic stones, one of which was erected by Gorm in honour of his queen, while the other was set up by Harold in memory of his parents.

Everywhere I found the peasants, once their natural distrust overcome, kind and friendly, but it was always necessary to make the first advances. Education has made such progress among them that it is not at all uncommon to hear them discussing literary and scientific matters, the history of their country, and other kindred subjects. Of course there are exceptions whom education has not reached, and these are rough indeed. The bourgeois are less estimable, and not free from the ignorance and pride of purse which distinguish the same class in our own country.

The language of Jutland more nearly resembles English than that of Seeland; it is not very difficult to make one's self understood there, owing to the fact that the conquerors who brought the Danish tongue into England came from Jutland.

CHAPTER XI

SKAGEN

Between Veile and Frederikshavn the country is flat but fertile; at Skanderborg lake and forest again commence. As the traveller draws nearer the north the scenery grows gradually more and more desolate till he comes to the wild heaths of Jutland, in the endeavour to reclaim which so much money and labour has been spent. Evening approached, the moon rose red and round in the clear green sky, and soon the wind-blown little town of Frederikshavn was reached.

There is nothing attractive about Frederikshavn, which from a little fishing village, once sold for the sum of £440, has developed into a town of no inconsiderable importance. All the winds under heaven seem to assemble there in stormiest conclave; the houses have only two storeys, and the streets are paved with rough stones which barely maintain their precarious hold in the sandy soil. But it has a fine harbour where hundreds of vessels take refuge in the winter when navigation in the Kattegat is extremely dangerous. The best oysters in Denmark are found at Frederikshavn.

The Government system of railways ends at Frederikshavn, and to reach Skagen it is necessary to go by a tiny private line which creeps due north over a peninsula five miles wide at its widest part and only two at Skagen. The scene around is desolation itself, and consists of low sand-hills covered sometimes with sombre heath, at others with the scanty rye-crops of the poor farmers; here and there are plantations of firs which, broken and blasted, endeavour to maintain a precarious existence in the shifting soil. Lonely huts, half buried in the ever-shifting sand, are the only objects which rise above the vast horizon; mile after mile the savage landscape stretches, bounded only by the blue of the sea whose breakers wash the shore in a constant endeavour to swallow more and more of the unresisting land. The only living things which cross the sand-hills are huge hares and a few birds. Over all, a joyless grey sky, darkened here and there with masses of clouds which scud before the driving wind.

There is probably not a wilder or more desolate spot on earth than this slender peninsula lashed by the storms of two northern seas, whose menacing roar falls ever on the ear. The monotony of the journey is broken by the train stopping at the little wooden stations; a few peasants, hard-featured and serious, get in or out, the women wearing handkerchiefs on their heads, the men in sabots and caps tightly tied down; no one sings, no one whistles, no one even talks more than is absolutely necessary, so serious are they by reason of the sad conditions of their lives. I dwell on this subject for the sake of those who love solitude and desolation; they can find them here within two hours of the idyllic beauty and luxuriant vegetation of the more southern portions of Jutland.

It is not to be wondered at that the character of the natives of this wild and sombre district differs considerably from that of their fellow-countrymen in the milder and more verdant parts of Denmark. Wrestling always with the cruel sea and barren land where Nature has placed them for the bare means of a joyless subsistence, they are serious, gloomy, and suspicious. Laughter seldom rises to their lips, smiles seldom lighten the expression of their eyes. They look upon dancing and all amusements with displeasure. Life offering them so few attractions, their thoughts naturally tend towards another existence from which they expect a better fate; they are therefore religious above all things. Shipwrecks are frequent on their coast, their very homes are sometimes swallowed by the devouring sea, and their harbours silted up with sand; thus they are familiar with death.

Skagen is a fishing village built among sand-hills which cover what once was corn-fields and the site of a town long ago buried beneath them. Trees cannot flourish there, and the scanty vegetation is wrested with much care and labour from billows of sand, which are often blown away just as the crop looks most promising. Its history is "a history of gales, and sand-drifts, and shipwrecks."

It was discovered by some Danish artists in search of subjects who stayed there to paint, living in the fishermen's cottages; naturally a hotel sprang up, then another, and then another; visitors came and houses were built. At the present time, the fashionable world, which unfortunately delights to follow in the footsteps of artists and ape their ways, resorts to Skagen as it does to Capri and to Barbizon; in fact, it is almost spoiled for its first patrons. At one hotel, the favourite resort of artists now rebuilt and refurnished, the walls of the dining-room are covered with pictures by those who have stayed there; among them is a fine collection of portraits of artists by Kröyer and by Michael Anker, who live at Skagen. Here one may take one's ease and comfort also, for there is no need to rough it, at Brondum's Hotel.

The few monuments which exist at Skagen tell only of shipwreck and disaster. In the little lonely cemetery on the heath is a memorial to fifteen German sailors whose torpedo boat was wrecked on this coast; the remains of their vessel are picturesquely piled at the base of the stone. A granite obelisk in the town records the loss of the Swedish boat *Daphne* on the 27th December 1862, when the whole crew perished as well as that of the life-boat which was launched to their assistance.

Skagen boasts its hero, whose life has

formed the subject of one of Holger Drachmann's finest poems. Lars Andersen Kruse was a fisherman whose noble record it is to have saved no fewer than (it is said) two hundred lives on this stormy coast. It is sad to say that he perished in the same terrible sea from whose devouring grasp he had snatched so many of his fellow-creatures; his boat was capsized in 1894 in comparatively calm weather, and he and part of his crew were lost. His monument, inscribed with some lines by Drachmann, may also be seen in the solitary graveyard on the wide wild heath. There are those who say that Kruse owes his celebrity entirely to Drachmann, that other fishermen have equalled him in courage and daring but have not been fortunate enough to find a poet to record their deeds; this, no doubt, is jealousy—a virago who never sleeps.

There were some amusing people in the hotel when I was there. A Norwegian gentleman, whose home is at some distance more or less removed from the North Pole, related that when he went to London to see the Exhibition of 1862 he incautiously ventured too near Hyde Park, and was in consequence garrotted and robbed. He vows he will never trust himself in London again for nothing is good there, not even the salt; the milk is chalk and the meat impossible. I also learnt from him that when English people see any behaviour at table they dislike, they immediately rise and leave it, with many other interesting little particulars as to our national peculiarities.

The Skagenese will impressively enjoin the stranger to visit what they call the "Plantation," a number of wind-blighted and partially leafless trees wrung with great labour from the unwilling soil, which is the only representation of a wood they possess.

The walk or drive to the uttermost point of Denmark is singularly romantic, of course across a desert of sand and heath; the strand consists of acre after acre of solid sand whereon whole armies might manœuvre. The "rimmer" or sand-ridges, which divide the heath-covered plains from the sea, do not rise to more than ten feet in height, leaving everywhere the horizon unbroken; the waters of the Skagerak and Kattegat wash the opposing shores. The sentiment of romance and desolation which this scene inspires is scarcely broken by the lighthouse, which is the last thing the Danes see on leaving their beloved country and the first they look for on their return. There is also a new hotel, which does not a little to disturb the romance of the place; however, the traveller may easily exclude it from his range of vision and enjoy Nature in all her solitude, immense, illimitable, undefiled.

During the month of June the sun seems to be so amused with what he sees on earth that he never intends to take repose; however, he finally decides to disappear shortly before ten o'clock, only to rise again between two and three. The skies then are bright and clear, eclipsing the light of the stars, a soft pale green softening to blue above. Even then there is no escaping the huge feather beds which are piled on every bed, a national custom by which Danes and Norwegians may always be recognised even when they settle abroad.

The natives are of course pietists, solemn and serious in the extreme; however, a trace of humour may sometimes be found among them. A tale by Holger Drachmann aptly illustrates their characteristics. He says:—"A fisherman, who recovered consciousness after being nearly drowned, was asked by a priest what was his first thought on coming to his senses. 'I wondered,' he said, 'where the devil the boat had got to which ought to have picked me up.'" They live almost solely on fish and by fish, for which former reason perhaps they are not a very robust race. They are punctilious, too, after their fashion. Communication between them is carried on thus: "What!" says the interlocutor on seeing his friend. "What!" replies the person addressed, and without this prelude it is not considered polite to enter into conversation. Life is so primitive that ordinary laws are not understood or are unavailable; the burgomaster therefore administers justice at his own discretion and as occasion seems to require. The train may be stopped by any traveller who wishes to enter it *en route*, as indeed I have seen done in Spain. A very cruel custom obtains here; if a man cannot pay his taxes, a functionary goes the round of the houses beating a drum and proclaims the fact; he also announces sales, losses, and other information in the same way.

About half a mile from Skagen, amid a scene of complete desolation, the tower of an old Gothic church rises from the sands which have devoured the rest of it. This tower is the sole remains of a whole village, and suggests the mysterious traditions of some half-forgotten creed, the whole of which it is not worth while to disinter—a creed once instinct with life as the church was once filled with worshippers. No human being exists in those wastes, near them is no sound save the song of viewless larks, no vegetation save the poor clinging weeds on the sand-hills to chase away the gloomy and sad impressions to which this poor remnant of a buried church and its surroundings give rise; one can but sorrow over the ruined house of prayer of a destroyed village as one sorrows for a lost belief which can return no more.

There is near Skagen a whole Danish mile—more than four miles English—which consists of nothing but white glistening sand, impassable by human foot. Sand is the same everywhere, and there is much here to remind the traveller of the African deserts—the same bareness and aridity, hopelessness and cruelty, the same sentiment of helplessness and death; only the camel is replaced by a few meagre sheep, the Arab in his flowing robe by the fisherman in his jersey and high boots. Richard Jefferies found Nature cruel even in the soft southern counties of England; he would have thought her unspeakably so in this remote, unfertile part of the peninsula of Jutland.

CHAPTER XII

AALBORG

AGAIN over the wild sands of the north, again over the rich pastures of Jutland, two strongly-marked regions divided by the Limfjord, which converts the former into what is really an island. Aalborg is a very old town, which to a great extent preserves its former appearance; it is rich in picturesque old houses, the most remarkable of which is "Jens Bang's Stenhus," built in 1624, and now, on account of its being a chemist's shop and having two swans over the door, known as the "Svane Apothek." Built of brick with three large gables, a curious little tower in front, and adorned with Renaissance ornamentation, it is one of the finest specimens in Denmark of seventeenth century domestic architecture. Many framework houses of the days of Frederick II. and Christian IV., reminding one of the old houses of north German towns, also still stand.

Aalborg is far from a flat town; it rises considerably above the Limfjord, its little winding streets with old houses, and new ones which nearly always manage to turn a picturesque gable towards the street, its nooks and corners and old pieces of ornament, are amusing. It still retains an air of past prosperity when it coined its own money, and had wealth and importance enough to draw upon itself every storm of war that broke over the land. It has two noteworthy churches, St Badolf's with a fine pierced tower, and the Frue Kirke, erected so early as 1100, only four hundred years after the real history of Denmark begins; the curious old granite Norman portico still serves as an entrance to the carefully-restored building. Aalborg, like all the small towns I have seen in Denmark, is clean and well kept; there seems to be a spirit of emulation among them which stimulates each to do its best. Like the other towns, too, it is roughly paved, a cause of great discomfort to those who do not wear sabots —sabots and cobble-stones should go together.

Living in a Danish town is like living in a village; everybody knows everybody and everybody's business, and the same interests unite the whole community. Then all towns seem so complete in themselves, each has its schools, its baths, its park or garden, and often a theatre—all, in fact, that renders life possible and even agreeable without need to have recourse to the capital city. For this reason perhaps the Danes are less corrupted than those nations where it is the custom to flock to great centres, vicious, luxurious, and unhealthy.

There is, however, another side to this question. For lack of amusement young men frequently assemble in the evening with no other object than to drink, I might even say to get drunk; on these occasions the quantity of beer consumed is enormous, as, after their potations of brandy, each man manages to put away seven or eight bottles of beer. There are some who can drink over twenty bottles a day of this favourite beverage.

CHAPTER XIII

VIBORG

THE country between Aalborg and Viborg is both interesting and diversified. Nature is kind to Denmark and shows herself there in all her many and varied moods, except the most savage and angry. She resembles a sweet and gentle mother whose humour, though changeable, never rises to angry bursts of passions, but who knows well how to become stern and sombre when occasion requires. In these parts, fir forests both natural and artificial are interchanged with beech woods, but the trees in the latter have not the imposing grandeur and luxuriant foliage of those in Seeland; a tiny river meanders peaceably beside the railway track, storks seek their living in the newly-turned earth, and fat cattle graze tethered in the lush pastures. Höbro is passed, a red-brick town on a blue fjord backed by low and verdant hills. At length the scenery is sterner, the river is lost, cultivated fields become rarer and rarer, and the black heaths arise amid which Viborg is situated.

Viborg is a clean and picturesque old town; it seems as if it was always Sunday there. It is so quiet, so peaceful, and its inhabitants so unconscious of the passing of time and so full of repose, you would think they were only taking a gentle walk as they go down the streets amid the quaint old houses to pursue their ordinary avocations. But it was not always so. In Odinic times the priest-kings of Jutland were elected here; Icelanders traded here so early as the tenth century and were converted and baptised at the same opportunity; here under Canute the Great the first Danish money was coined, and here also the great annual fair, the "Snapthing," was held. It is one of the oldest of towns, and under its ancient name Vebjærg (Sacred Hill) was the principal seat of national worship. It is also intimately connected with the history of the Middle Ages, but its population has greatly diminished since then, and though it has a larger area than that of any of the towns of Denmark except Copenhagen and Fredericia, its inhabitants barely number 9000. As a proof of its smallness, on first entering the house where I was to lodge, I was quickly informed, though I came unexpectedly, that there were letters at the Poste Restante for me, which were immediately delivered; no doubt the advent of an English person is a rare occurrence in Viborg.

The chief glory of Viborg is its Cathedral, "one of the finest specimens of Gothic architecture in the North."* It was founded in the eleventh century but rebuilt between 1130 and 1170, and con-

* Murray.

sists of a nave and aisles, transepts, and a circular apse with an exterior open gallery; the chancel is raised, and under it is a crypt untouched since it was built. Unlike most of the churches of Denmark, the material is granite; its severe and simple style, round arches, and strong square pillars and towers are in harmony with a northern climate, yet on entering one is reminded by the decorations and frescoes of some old Italian churches.

To realise fully the great beauty of this Cathedral the visitor should go round the outside, examine the charming outer gallery of the apse, the windows and doors: from east, south and north, the noble and simple proportions are better seen than from direct west.

The elegant but plain stone pulpit is supported by pillars which rest on couchant lions; in front of the steps leading to the chancel is a seven-branched brass candlestick, nine feet high, made in Lübeck in 1497, which serves also as a reading-desk; the gilt reredos is ornamented with figures of Christ and the Apostles in no mean style of art; from the chancel a little chapel opens, where in a glass case are the bones of the murdered King Eirik Glipping, his armour, and some very curious old metal coffins; the massive crypt contains only an old stone coffin with a hole cut out for the head; the frescoes which adorn the fine old wooden ceiling, the apse, and walls are chiefly remarkable for the northern type of feature with which the Biblical personages are endowed. The popular type of Christ may be found more often in the North than in the South.

In the vaults are many coffins placed above ground, as the Dane apparently prefers to take his last rest; a similar arrangement may be seen in the chapel of the Krags, which is closed by a fine iron gate dated 1665. In the triforium is a collection of quaint wooden figures removed there during the restoration of 1873; against the square pillars of the church are placed portraits of the priests who have officiated.

Among its curiosities I remarked a very old relief giving an almost ludicrous representation of the Last Judgment. Christ of course sits in the centre, below Him a couple of fat cherubs blow trumpets; on His right, below, the sturdy righteous, much astonished at their position, are received by angels, while on the left the devil, represented as a huge goat, enchains the wicked in hell, who are furthermore pushed down into the flames, as a pudding is pushed down into a pot, by another goat-like figure with a pitch-fork.

The only other church in Viborg has one of the finest brick towers I have seen in Denmark.

On the highest point of many of the houses friendly storks have established themselves, building their nests of sticks on little platforms erected by the inhabitants, to whom they are supposed to bring good luck. It is said that when they depart for their annual peregrinations they leave either an egg or a young bird in return for the hospitality they have received. If one of the young, when taught by his parents to fly, is too weak to take what they consider a proper amount of exercise, it is killed. It is also said that the stork is faithful to one mate, whom in case of infidelity he punishes with death. There is nothing more quaint than the stork on his elevated position relieved against the calm evening sky, as, standing on one leg, he watches the partner of his affections engaged in her domestic duty of hatching eggs. Evidently he loves the vast horizons of his native land, and the broad expanse of the changeful sky. His note is not musical; it resembles the noise of two boards beaten together more than anything else.

Hans Tausen, who was to the Danes what Luther was to the Germans, lived in Viborg and his house is still shown. "Was that Hans Tausen's house?" said I to a native. "Oh, no, it is Carl Jensen's," was the sapient reply.

The public garden is exquisite; the broad lake stretches beyond, on one side rises the pyramidal red town with the noble Cathedral as an apex; on the other, almost smothered by trees, the white remains of some old cloisters now transformed into a comfortable dwelling-place.

The environs of Viborg are very lovely—forests of pines, shady groves of beeches, lake and hill in endless variety, surround the little town and minister to the pleasure and health of its inhabitants.

Six miles from Viborg is the Lake of Hald,

one of the most beautiful spots in Jutland. Wooded down to its very rim, yet with here and there clear spaces which afford excellent views over its clear and shining waters, the lake lies as it were on a couch of green and fertile earth, but is close to the wildest and most weird scenery, creating a sentiment which adds a charm to the sylvan scene, as the thought of possible danger does to a soldier's life.

The ruins of the Castle of Hald, around which cling so many traditions, are, to say the least of it, not imposing. One of the Valdemars once besieged this castle and endeavoured to reduce his rebellious subjects, who had taken refuge there, to submission by starvation. At last only one cow was left to the besieged, and this they caused to be paraded many times before the eyes of the king, each time with a different covering on. "Oh," said the king, "if they have so many cattle it is useless to attempt to starve them out!" and raised the siege. There are also to be seen the ruins of a tower built by Bishop Friis as a prison for Protestants in the days of Hans Tausen, but who, the people say, chanced himself to be the first prisoner there as the reformed religion gained ground. Near the lake stands the fine old manor house, Althovedgaard, with its numerous and picturesque outbuildings, one of the best specimens of its kind in the country.

North Jutland is remarkable for its apparently interminable tract of waste land called Ahlhede

(All Heath). It consists of perpetual undulations, or vast unbroken plains stretching from horizon to horizon, covered only with a thick carpet of dark heath; the traveller there seems to stand in the middle of an enormous circle of which the sky is the unbroken circumference. A few rude cabins, each having a minute barley field or a few trees around it, here and there a little lake which looks white in the surrounding blackness, give only at times variety to the scene. Here the winds howl their worst and the sun gives its least heat. All is so vast, so melancholy, so poetical, that one sees almost with regret the success of the strenuous efforts being made in some places to redeem Ahlhede, the plantations of firs, the fields of meagre rye wrested with so much labour from the desert waste.

Comparatively few years ago these heaths were haunted by a strange race of beings called "Natmaend," who ostensibly gained a precarious living by tinkering and juggling, but really by robbery, smuggling, and kidnapping. It was considered prudent by the peasants to keep them in a friendly disposition, and they allowed them sometimes to sleep in their barns and gave them what they could spare of their scanty provisions. It is not to be doubted that they were of gipsy origin, as is proved by their other appellation, that of Zigeuner or Bohemians.

The heaths have their poet, Steen Blicher, who was born and lived in a little village there; and

Ingemann's novel, *Erik Menved*, records the murder of Erik Glipping by Marsk Stig at Finderup, which is also the subject of Heise's most magnificent opera. For more than four centuries afterwards a special service, called "Vaadesangen" (The Song of Woe), was performed daily in the crypt of Viborg Cathedral.

The efforts now being strenuously and successfully made to reclaim this pastureless and cornless tract of country originated with Lieutenant-Colonel Dalgas, who hoped in that way to repair the loss of territory sustained by Denmark in the Slesvig-Holstein war; he therefore advocated the making of extensive plantations of fir trees. To carry that idea out two societies were formed, the "Plantningsselskab Steen Blicher," or "Steen Blicher Society for Planting," and the "Jyske Myremalm Selskab," or "Jutland Bog-iron Ore Company," both of which now make use of the labour lying hitherto unproductive in the prisons of the State, thus at once endeavouring to ameliorate the condition of condemned criminals and to carry out their initial purpose.

Punishment for the crime of murder by decapitation is the law of Denmark, but the law is rarely carried out, and the reason is this. On one occasion the executioner was so *maladroit* as to fail to kill the unhappy victim with less than three attempts; this atrocious fact coming to the knowledge of the king, he declared he would never again sign an order for the execution of a criminal. And for fifty years he has maintained his resolution, except in the case of a man who specially desired to be killed, and committed crime after crime till the necessity of doing so was forced upon him. The punishment for murder has therefore resolved itself into imprisonment for life, which, in point of fact, becomes reduced to twenty years of incarceration, or less if the criminal behave himself well. Under these circumstances it became more than ever a question as to how to rehabilitate convicts when they were suddenly let loose from prison, and how best to accustom them again to the life of free men.

Urged by these philanthropic motives, the societies named above applied to the State for permission to employ convict labour in their efforts to reclaim, by planting, drainage and other works, the hitherto unproductive heaths of Jutland, which again led to the formation of the establishment I am about to describe. It is hoped a double end may be attained—the reclamation of the heaths and the reformation of the most debased criminals. It is believed by treating them well, and trusting them, together with a life of remunerative labour in the open air, they may be gradually led into an honest way of existence. It is yet too soon to form any exact idea as to the probable results, for it is only two years since the first batch of convicts was set to work upon the heath. I am told all Europe is interested in the result of the experiment.

Permission to visit the Gedhus (Goat house),

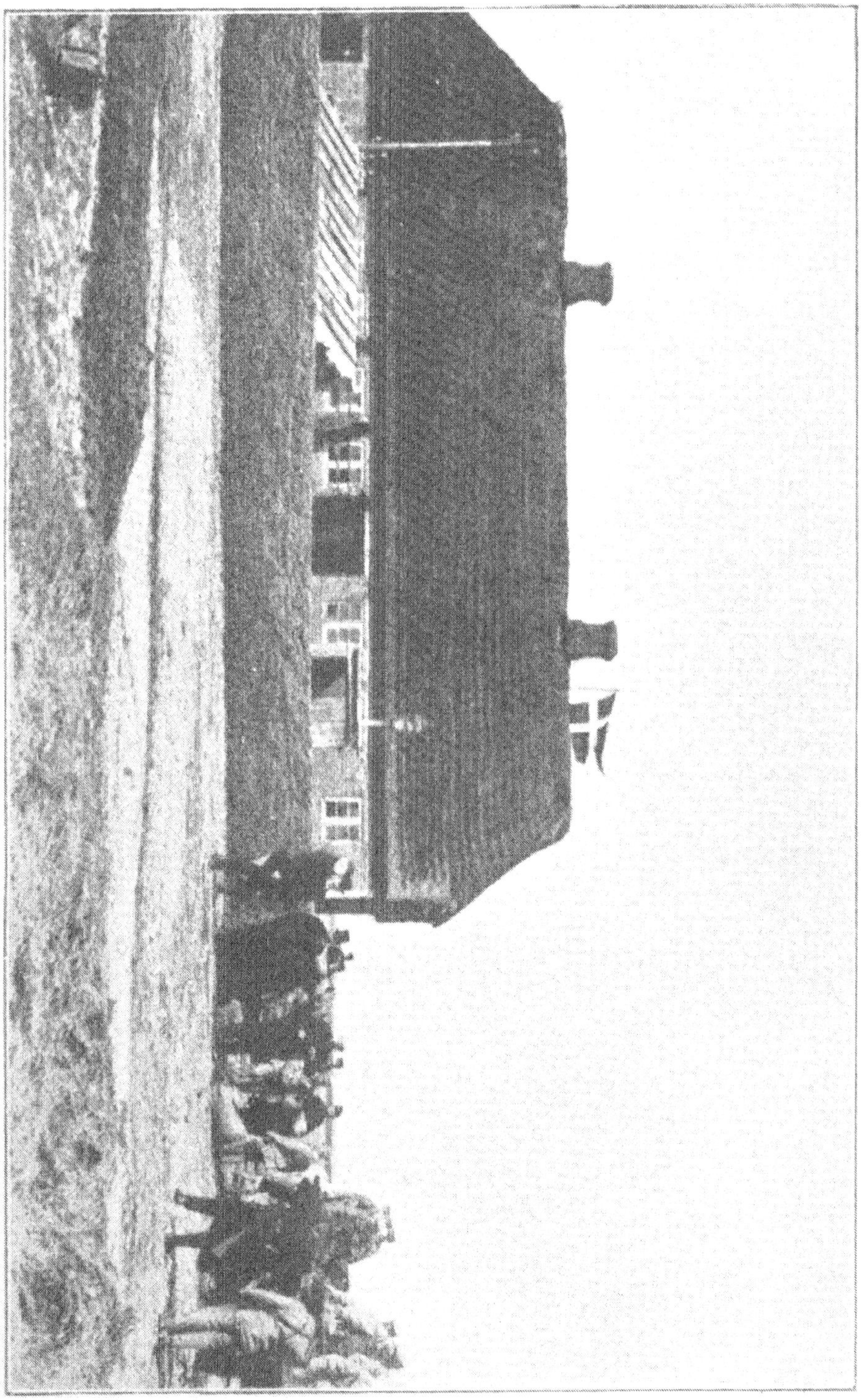

a farm which has been taken for the accommodation of the prisoners and the staff, is given very rarely indeed, but thanks to the good offices of the British Ambassador with the Danish Minister of the Interior, I was enabled to obtain it, and I am told that I and the friend who accompanied me are the only women who have ever had that privilege.

We started by carriage from Viborg, for there is no railway anywhere near, and the mail-cart goes no further than to Karup, a village consisting of four or five houses between three and four miles from the Gedhus.

The contrast is sharp between the smiling environs of Viborg and the straight, shelterless road which leads across the dark and wind-swept heath. At the period I write it is of a greyish red colour near, in the distance mingled with a little blue as the atmosphere smooths away every inequality and renders it soft as velvet. An infinite variety of wild flowers nod beside the road, a plover rises now and then and pursues its solitary way, larks sing unceasingly, nestled in the short strong tufts of heather, or poised invisible in the greyness of the sky. A few houses are reached which are those of some Germans who first endeavoured to do what the slower Danes had left undone—namely, extract some advantage from the stubborn land by planting it with the usual first crop of virgin soil, potatoes, which they sold in the neighbouring towns and thus gained the name of "Potato-Germans."

Their descendants dwell in the same old farms, and have their own little church, but have now become completely Danish.

Just after leaving Karup a few solitary cabins are seen, each having its little field of poor thin rye beside it; then succeeds a vast level plain consisting of petrified sand in which the sturdy heath plant can alone take root and flourish. For the last few miles no habitation whatever is seen. The Gedhus is situated in the midst of this desolate scene, and here we were received by the polite officials and afforded every opportunity for inspection. The inspector himself was most courteous and kind, and had prepared for us such refreshments as the rough conditions of his life could afford.

The house consists of seven rooms, two sleeping-rooms, with peep-holes in the doors for the convicts, the warders' room, the inspector's room, dining-room, office, and kitchen, all of the simplest and most primitive construction and furnishing. There were at the time of our visit twenty prisoners who were under the charge of only four unarmed officials. We asked one of these men if he had no fear in thus being at the mercy of some of the most atrocious criminals, who outnumbered their warders so considerably. With quiet courage he replied, "No, I don't think there is any danger; we have indeed one revolver but the prisoners don't know of it." There are no walls, no chains, no locks, no restraint whatever is put upon the criminals; they must observe the rules and do their work—that is all. Absorbed in their own interests, they are profoundly ignorant of the affairs of the world, do not know even that President M'Kinley has been assassinated or that Lord Roberts has entered Pretoria. They sleep on rough beds on the floor, and of course wear prison dress; their rations, which are good and ample, are served out to them every evening; the cook himself is a convict.

These prisoners are selected from the others on account of their good behaviour while in prison; they are divided into six classes, from the lowest of which they may rise by degrees, the highest giving them the right to certain deductions in the term of their detention, and also to a small payment for their labour. Their task is to dig two hundred holes a day for the planting of young trees; if they do more they are encouraged by a reward; one is so skilful that he has succeeded in digging four hundred in that time. They go out on the heath to work at six o'clock in the morning, in charge of two unarmed warders only, return to dinner at twelve, and at one go back, taking their evening meal with them; they go to bed at half-past eight. This is no hardship, for the Danish peasants are accustomed at the end of winter to extinguish fires and lights for the whole summer. The convicts may play a game of skittles, read during their leisure books sent to them from the prison library at Horsens, and have permission to smoke one hour a day and half of Sunday. They live and work on the heath from April 20th to June 21st, after which they are sent back to their various places of confinement. The men who thus live, who lead the life of an ordinary working man, with the only difference that his living is less assured than theirs, are guilty of the greatest crimes some of which are nameless, and all have undergone various terms of imprisonment.

The sentiment which has inspired this experiment is sublime—namely, to accustom the criminal deranged by prison life again to resume a proper mode of existence, and to take his place by degrees among his fellow-men. It is well known that the most well-disposed convict, on issuing from the prison he has occupied for many years, has almost insurmountable difficulty in rehabilitating himself and in getting employment. This the institution I have described seeks to remedy by affording him a comparatively free life in the open air, by inculcating the practice of self-reliance, self-respect and industry, and by the opportunity of earning a little money with which to begin the world afresh. As I have said, the experiment is still in its infancy, the result as yet uncertain. Some go so far as to call the Gedhus only a country-house for criminals; and criminals themselves have said, as has also been said in England, that they prefer the prison to the workhouse as being more comfortable, and as affording the chance of an agreeable relief from prison life. But however that may be, the idea does honour to Denmark, also the first country to emancipate slaves; its success is to be devoutly hoped, and afterwards its extension to all countries where the extreme rigour of the law has failed to extirpate crime. The man who after seven or eight terms of imprisonment is given this chance and does not take advantage of it does not thereafter deserve much from his fellow-men.*

We afterwards saw the prisoners at work on the heath; there were of course some most decidedly criminal types among them, but they seemed to work willingly and to be content. The inspector, who had followed us in his carriage, presented several (we were warned not to go within fifty feet), among them a musician, to whom some kind person had given a violin, and who taught his fellows to sing.

We drove back to Viborg in the semi-darkness of the northern summer night. Huge clouds rolled over the broad space of the sky, in the distance thunder muttered, but the sun went down like a red ball over the blackening heath, and later his resting-place was marked by ruddy clouds which gleamed brightly athwart the rugged trunks of oaks. One solitary deer lingered outside the forest; even the noise of the carriage wheels did not disturb him at his evening meal.

* These prisoners were sent back to prison the day after I saw them. Their conduct, like that of the previous gang, had been excellent, and the success of the undertaking seems to be assured. They had planted 120,000 fir trees and dug one hundred and twenty tons of land, and there was not a single case of misconduct. —June 1900.

(A ton of land = 14,000 ells; an ell = a little more than two English feet.)

At the scattered farms near the town the inhabitants were looking to see if the postman had left any letters in the little boxes on posts put outside their gates for the purpose, and dogs rushed viciously barking from the holes in the barns made for them.

Of all the peasants in the world I think those of Jutland would easily take the palm for slowness and dunderheadedness, to which is added, however, a certain amount of rustic irony. Like those of Ireland, they never give a direct answer if by any means imaginable they can avoid doing so. For example. Let us imagine a traveller who wishes to know how far it is to Karup and inquires of one of them. He ought properly to commence with the long drawn out wh-a-t which is demanded by the rural etiquette of Jutland, for no conversation is considered polite there without a preliminary wh-a-t? from both parties. The peasant of whom the question is asked slowly suspends his labour and remains open-mouthed for a good half minute before he drawls,—

"Wh-a-t, Karup?" with an intonation which expresses at once his supreme contempt for a person who does not know that village and his appreciation of his own superior wisdom.

"Yes, Karup," continues the traveller.

"Are you going to Karup?" he asks.

"Yes, is it far?"

"Wh-a-t? Ye-s."

"Is it very far?"

"Ye-s—"

"How far? Half a mile?"
"Half a mile? Ye-s."
"Is it further? Three quarters of a mile?"
"Three quarters? Ye-s."
"Is it more than a mile then?"
"Wh-a-t?"
"Is it more than a mile?"
"More than a mile? N-o."
"Only a mile, then?"
"Yes."

This last "yes" is uttered more quickly than the others, and a kind of grin slowly passes over the peasant's face, for light has at last broken in upon him, and he feels a sense of satisfaction that the questioner has found words to express his own thought.

If you are imprudent enough to risk a question as to the road, the whole ceremony must be gone through again; and if you inquire for a certain house in a village, he will describe every other house there, and inform you it is not that, before you can get out of him which it really is. The English language can give no equivalent for the long-drawn-out "j—a j—o, n—a n—ei" of a Danish peasant.

The peasants have a pronounced sense of the ridiculous, and a gift of irony, as is proved by some of their sayings: "'Ladies must have ladies' manners,' said madam, as she trailed her skirts through the gutter." "'There must be someone to do disagreeable things,' said the boy when he was made to go to church." "'I should like to see

G

that,' as the boy said when his mother exclaimed 'May the devil take me!'" "'Cleanliness is a blessed thing,' as the woman said when she turned her chemise on New Year's Eve." "'One misfortune always comes to drive out another,' said the woman; 'yesterday my husband died, to-day I have lost my needle!'" "'Everyone to his taste,' said Karsten, the vintner, as he drank the leavings while the guests were fighting." "'Keep your foot to yourself,' said the cock to the horse." "'Peter,' said the goose, 'I am driving!' as the fox carried her into the wood."

In these popular sayings the character of the peasantry is perfectly shown, their heaviness, their want of enthusiasm, and their good-humoured sense of the ridiculous, so different from the piquant and malicious satire of the Latin races. Difficult to arouse, they hold themselves aloof from all that does not immediately concern them; events in which the French and Italian lower classes become bitter partisans, such as the Transvaal and Chinese wars, are to them matters of complete indifference; like the vintner occupied in drinking the dregs, they are content to pursue the even tenor of their way, leaving it to others to dispute. The trait of the woman who trailed her skirts in the gutter to prove she was a lady, and of the goose which, carried off by the fox, made believe she was driving, illustrate the good-humoured irony with which they regard the pretentious and the snobbish. The woman who placed her husband and her needle in the same category is an example of that stolidity which is so marked a characteristic among them. The following popular saying describes the difference in the characters of the natives of the three Scandinavian nations:—" A Dane, when he strikes a match to light his pipe, offers the light first to his companion and then uses the match himself; a Norwegian lights his own pipe first and afterwards offers the match to another; a Swede lights his own pipe and throws the match away."

Coffee is their favourite drink; tea they seem to think has not taste enough, so add all kind of spices to give it a flavour! Cinnamon, ginger and cloves are preferred.

CHAPTER XIV

AARHUS

The country between Viborg and Aarhus consists principally of half-reclaimed heath; on the way the traveller catches a glimpse of the old manor house of Ulstrup, once seized by the Government in default of payment of taxes, and sold to its present peasant proprietor. These fine old buildings, surrounded by their picturesque outhouses, are the Danish representatives of our noblemen's seats.

Aarhus is one of the first towns mentioned in the history of Denmark; it is next in size to Copenhagen, its harbour is never blocked with ice, and it is an important railway centre. Hence its air of general prosperity.

Having unearthed the man whose duty it is to show the Cathedral for a crown, I was astonished that, contrary to the usual practice of Danes, he remained mute as a fish when he had unlocked the door. After many efforts I extracted from him the information that a description of its contents would cost another crown; he was rather discomfited when I showed him the description and history together, with much other interesting information, in a pamphlet which cost seventy-five öre.

Bishop Peter Vagnsen, a member of the Hvid family and a nephew of Bishop Absalon, obtained in 1194 letters from Pope Celestine III. granting forty days' indulgence to whomsoever should contribute to the expense of the Cathedral of St Clement, and in 1201 he laid the foundations. The Bishop devoted his fortune to the work, and King Valdemar Seyr remitted all taxes on the church's property. At that time Roman was the fundamental style of ecclesiastical architecture, and traces of it are still to be found in the present church. In 1642 the spire, which is said to have been six hundred and eighty feet in height, was destroyed by lightning, and that which replaced it by a storm. The present spire is two hundred and eighty-six feet in height.

The Cathedral is built of brick, and owing to the beauty of its architecture, size, and simplicity, has a most imposing appearance; the massive tower, pointed gables, elongated windows, and slender turrets of the east end are very characteristic. The effect of the interior, with its remarkably long nave, tall pillars without capitals, and delicate colorisation, is far from solemn, yet it is religious in the extreme.

On entering the west door, the first chapel to the right is noticeable as containing the most expensive monument ever erected in, it is said, Denmark. It is that of a certain Baroness Rodsten - Constantin; the sculptor, Quillinus, a

Dutchman, has represented her as magnificently attired, with her two husbands, in the costume of Roman Emperors, wearing enormous flowing wigs, on either side of her. Her obsequies are said to have lasted six hours.

The nave is two hundred and ninety-two feet long and seventy feet high, the pulpit is of carved oak boiled in oil; round the nave and aisles are various tasteless monuments to persons well-known in Danish history. In front of the choir is a huge brass candlestick, dated 1515, with seven branches, each of course representing one of the seven churches. In the centre is a curious old bronze font covered with a brass dish. The very fine flat tomb of Knud Gyldenstjerne, the last Catholic Bishop of Odense, who died in 1568, and his wife, occupies the middle of the choir; the two figures are remarkable for their elegance. On one side is the tomb of a nobleman named Skeel who is represented at prayer while his two wives opposite seem to gaze at him with undisguised admiration. Under an altar tomb with a black marble top lie the remains of the founder, which were discovered wrapt in silver brocade in a leaden coffin in 1830. The altar-piece is remarkable. Of wood, painted and gilt, it is said to be the best specimen of fifteenth-century work in Denmark. In the centre are life-sized figures of St Anne, the Virgin and Christ, with, on either side, St Clement with his anchor, and St John the Baptist; these again are flanked by the apostles and twenty-four saints much smaller in size; on the wings are oil-paintings which remind one of early Flemish work.

In the ambulatory many old tombstones have been placed upright; among them are two dated 1519, remarkable for the excellent carving of the ornaments and lettering. A fresco representing St George killing the Dragon, a princess with her crown on praying for his success, and a king and queen looking on from their window, is more amusing than beautiful. Above it hangs a large model of a ship which Peter the Great had made at Dunkirk and intended sending to Russia. The vessel which carried it was however wrecked at Skagen, and two citizens of Aarhus bought and presented it to the Cathedral.

Among the tombs is that of Manderup Parsberg, who cut off Tycho Brahe's nose in a duel, which it is said the astronomer replaced with one of silver or gold. The gravestone of Fröken Lasson is surrounded with a faded wreath; she left a sum of money in order that her tomb might always be decorated with leaves and flowers —a feeble immortality. A well-worn effigy of a young woman holding a prayer-book in one hand, and with a bullet in a wound in her side, is that of a girl who, having deceived her lover, was shot by him just as she was about to enter the church door.

We are all interested in the prolongation of life, and I am happy here to be able to contribute a small amount of information derived from the

Cathedral of Aarhus, on the subject, with results that will astonish doctors, temperance societies, and anti-tobacco-smoking advocates.

On an upright tombstone the following epitaph is inscribed:—

"Here lies Christian Jacobsen, who was born in 1626 and died in 1772 and therefore lived to the age of one hundred and forty-six years." The guide-book account adds: "Two Englishmen are the only people who have lived to be older. He was of a changeable disposition and dainty in his food, but always preferred simple dishes, and at the ripe age of one hundred and eleven married a widow of sixty. He drank beer, brandy, and mead, but always in moderation and preferably at other people's expense, and used a great deal of tobacco. He was never confined to his bed but after a good fight, and had himself bled regularly four times a year at the waxing of the moon. He made use of various simple domestic remedies, as for example, when he suffered from constipation he swallowed a bullet."

The simplicity and purity of the architecture of the old churches of Denmark contrast rather violently with the florid Dutch Renaissance style which here is called by the name of Christian IV. and in which so many of the later public edifices are built.

CHAPTER XV

SILKEBORG AND THE HIMMELBJÆRG

BETWEEN Skanderborg and Silkeborg lie the highest chain of hills, the finest forests, the most beautiful lakes of Jutland, in fact, the scenery about these towns is a panorama of lake and forest, forest and lake, each more beautiful than the last.

Silkeborg was a manor belonging to the bishops of Aarhus. One of them, highly delighted with the beauty of the scenery, vowed he would build a house wherever his silk cap, which the wind had carried away, should remain; hence the manor was called Silkeborg. It is a very scattered town without the least pretensions to beauty, but its situation and surroundings are so ideal that it has become one of the most fashionable of country resorts. It possesses several ferruginous springs which rise in the midst of vast fir forests, and here bathing establishments have been erected for the treatment of various diseases. Silkeborg owes its present prosperity to the enterprise of the brothers Drewson, who have established there flourishing paper mills.

I have already "enthused" considerably over the grand virgin forests of Denmark; those near Silkeborg exceed any I have seen in beauty, variety and extent. In some parts are masses of one kind of tree only, fir forests, beech forests, oak forests; in others the whole variety of sylvan monarchs which the climate produces are mingled in unimaginable beauty. Everywhere one has glimpses between the branches of gleaming water; far-stretching valleys clothed with the illimitable forest disclose themselves, and chains of lakes now narrowing, now widening in inexhaustible variety. But a few tame adjectives fail to describe this scenery; one should see it for one's self.

The chain of lakes connected together by brooks and canals known as Brassö, Borresö, Julsö, and Birkesö are navigated by small steamboats, and from their decks the traveller has the best view of what is really the only hilly scenery in Jutland, and of the Himmelbjærg, said to be the highest elevation in Denmark, which however only rises about five hundred feet above the sea level. The hills are clothed with woods which as it were dip their feet in the edge of the murmuring water; in the distance the serried tree-tops resemble velvet shot with blue and gold. On the few plains which come down to the lake amid reeds which bow to each returning wave, and water lilies ruffled by the wind like girls whose dresses are blown about, lie fields of corn and little picturesque thatched cottages.

Though the æsthetic sense is so conspicuously wanting in the Dane, he nevertheless knows well how to select the prettiest spot for his parties of pleasure and that open-air amusement of which he is so fond. On such a spot there is generally a small "kro" or inn, and thither he drives his family or comes on his bicycle, bringing with him a good supply of eatables, to spend his Sunday or his holiday. Such a place is Laven. There families become acquainted and old friends meet, the strong and healthy-looking youth of both sexes mingle together and much harmony and good feeling prevail. It is one of the characteristics of the peasants that the sexes keep much apart; groups of men and groups of women amuse themselves separately. At all these resorts —indeed, in all my country travels in Denmark—I have never met an Englishman, a Frenchman, or a German. Denmark is for the Danes with a vengeance.

The Danish peasant is very careful of his cattle, and on these occasions his first care is to stable his well-fed horse. A peasant was reproached for not having called in a doctor to his dying wife, and replied that he could not afford it. "But I have often seen you get the veterinary surgeon for your cows and horses when they were ill."

"Yes, they are dear and hard to get, but a wife costs nothing and I can easily get another," was the reply.

He has also a shrewd eye to the main chance.

"Will you marry me to So-and-so?" asked a peasant of a priest.

"Why, how so?" said the priest. "Your wife is not dead."

"No," was the answer, "but she is very ill and must die soon, and *we* think it best to make sure of So-and-so in case someone else should get her as she has some money."

Another peasant story is difficult to give in English, however, I will try. To die is sometimes called to "bite the grass"—as we say in the romantic style, to "bite the dust." An old peasant with an abscess in the throat was given up by the doctor, who had exhausted all his prescriptions, with the words, "There is nothing for him now but to bite the grass." Hardly had the medico departed when, with the aid of his wife, the poor man crawled out of bed and, extended on the ground, endeavoured to take some mouthfuls of the plant which was to cure him. The effort caused the abscess to break, and when the doctor called the next day to give the attestation of death, he was much astonished to find his patient comparatively well. "Ah, doctor," said the man, "your last prescription was the best. Why did you not give it me before?"

A peasant was sent some leeches to apply. He told the doctor afterwards that "he could not manage more than one or two raw, so he hoped it made no difference that he had *cooked* the rest a little before eating them."

THE ASCENT OF HIMMELBJÆRG.

When the adventurous Dane wishes to go mountaineering in his own country, he betakes himself to some village on the borders of the lake and thence takes boat or steamer to the foot of the Himmelbjærg—the spot nearest the sky in all the kingdom of Denmark. Arming himself with a huge basket of provisions, numerous bottles of beer, and a long alpenstock duly engraved, he commences the gentle sylvan walk which leads to the ascent. He goes on, but beer is heavy to carry, and after all, alpenstocks do not greatly avail, so he reposes and refreshes himself many times. After Vesuvius, the Pyramids and certain mountains in Switzerland and Palestine, I thought but little of the twenty minutes' ascent, but when I looked round for my so thoroughly-equipped fellow-traveller, I saw him at some distance below extended on the ground, refreshing himself as usual. At the top, or Kol, is a brick tower erected by Frederick VII., and there, when at last he arrived, he inscribed his name with the proud sense of having accomplished something, and proceeded to repose on his laurels beside his empty bottles.

The view from the Himmelbjærg over hill and forest, lake and fields, is such as Turner would have loved to render in all its atmospheric beauty and charm of light and shade, but which baffles the ordinary painter. Lake succeeds lake, forest succeeds forest; Silkeborg and a few little red villages lie in their nests of trees; here and there dark mounds covered with heath relieve the lighter foliage of the trees and the sparkling of the water—all is peaceful, pastoral and Danish. But the vastness of the unbroken horizon is that which most strikes the dweller in a mountainous country or in a city.

CHAPTER XVI

FARUM

To know Denmark thoroughly it is not precisely necessary to be acquainted even with the existence of Farum, a primitive and remote little village about twelve miles from Copenhagen, where I stayed for some weeks for the purpose of painting. Its characteristics are those of most other Danish villages—a quaint tree-shaded church surrounded by humble graves on a hill, and whitewashed thatched cottages turned at every possible angle towards the street, with its large tree in the centre, under which the village gossips have for centuries grouped themselves to smoke their pipes and discourse of the weather and the crops. However, it excels many in the beauty of its surroundings, its lake embosomed in woods and cornfields, its stretches of noble forest unmutilated by the axe of the wood-cutter. The railway has left it on one side as too insignificant to be worth stopping at, the post comes and goes but once a day, echoes merely from the outer world are heard there, and even the loudest and most astonishing of these fail to arouse for more than an instant, even if it arouse them at all, the slumbering interests of its inhabitants. If South Africa be Boer or British, if China be divided among the clamouring Powers or left in the sullen integrity of its thousands of years, if the noble Umberto of Italy lie dead with the assassin's bullet in his breast—all is one to the villagers of

Farum, wrapped in a calm far more profound than that of the old lotus-eaters, sunk in oblivion deeper than that of the opium-drugged Chinaman on the dingy couch of his den. Nature at Farum is fair and vigorous, man is simply her keeper and servant, but he is happy and seems to desire no better lot.

In considering the peasantry of all such villages it must never be forgotten that only fifty years ago they were serfs, bound absolutely to the soil on which they were born, and that they are now even what they are is astonishing, and due solely to the excellent system of education which Denmark places within the reach of all her sons.

On the subject of serfdom in Denmark, a Dane writes to me, " May I be permitted to point out that the lesson which modern Denmark can chiefly give to England is, how the farming classes in the course of a century from being, not serfs, as often wrongly asserted by English writers—serfdom as in Russia never existed in Denmark—but under the power of landlords and masters who blocked the way to progress, from being devoid of education, a despised and miserable class, have now become the leading force in the State, having some of their own representatives in the ministry. This is entirely due to their own efforts, and forms a unique record in the history of the world."

Their slowness, stolidity, and shyness arise from this cause, and also many of their still existing customs, including, perhaps, their curious habit of separating the sexes at their social gatherings. At these entertainments the guests stand in a row at one end of the room till they are invited by the serviceable *vær saa göd* of the hostess to seat themselves around a table covered with a white cloth and partake of sweet biscuits, and chocolate which is passed round in a huge ewer; the men then retire to talk over their own concerns, while the women take out their knitting and occupy themselves in gossiping about theirs. Hour after hour is spent in this way, the men enjoying pipes and spirits, the women regaled with coffee. How the young people manage their courting it is difficult for a stranger to understand, yet "as it was in the beginning, is now, etc." I purposely ventured once into the apartment where the men were sitting; utterly astonished at my want of etiquette they asked "if I wanted anything?"

A rich peasant's funeral took place during my stay at Farum. The road leading to the church, and the narrow little aisle of the church itself, were strewn with branches of yew and box; the altar at which the priest stood was a blaze of candles, little branches of yew were stuck at the end of every seat, the coffin was completely smothered with flowers, and the entire number of the inhabitants turned out in their best, carrying most of them immense wreaths, which they either deposited in the porch or hung in their pews during the service. The grave itself was lined with yew. On these occasions people come from far and near and "make a day of it," often, after the rites due to the dead are paid, finishing up with drinking, fighting, and even dancing. Only a few years ago it was the custom to keep the corpse uncovered and dressed in its best for eight days, in a room draped entirely in white, where candles were burning, and during all the time festivities were going on; friends brought their own provisions, the women were accommodated in the house, the men at the inn.

The lake at Farum is one of the most beautiful in Seeland; separated by a narrow strip of land from the more celebrated Furresö, it was once possible to make the tour of these lakes without leaving the boat, which was drawn across on rails. In the midst lies a tiny island about which it is related that it was bestowed by King Valdemar on his jester, who asked him for a small kingdom. The jester was discontented with the gift, and invited the king to a banquet; when the guest arrived and demanded where was the feast, he replied that "the lake was the soup and the king might catch the fish himself, for they represented a banquet as well as the island did a kingdom."

For an artist the atmospheric effects in Denmark are all and more than he could desire. One August evening rowing round this island I was especially struck with the intensity and variety of the colouring. The forests were a deep velvety black, above them floated purple clouds in a yellow and violet sky, while in the west, huge crimson masses of cumuli floated, each of which was faithfully reflected in the mirror-smooth water. Here and there a fleck of crimson pierced the thinner foliage, while swans coasted along the silent reeds, and from the church above came the triple sounds of the evening bell mingling with the thud of the oars in the row-locks and the splash of water as they were lifted rhythmically.

PART II

INSTITUTIONS, LITERATURE AND HISTORY

"There is not another of the minor countries of Europe that can point to names so universally illustrious in their different spheres as Oersted, Thorvaldsen, Oehlenschläger, Madvig, and H. C. Andersen."

E. W. GOSSE.

"Der er et Land det Sted er hoit mod Norden
  Og Polens Bjerge svamme naer det Havn;
Men skjönt som det er ingensteds paa Jorden
  Og Danmark naevner man det gamle Navn.
I sölv-blaa Vesterhav en deilig Have
  Med Bagehegn, hvor Nattergale bo;
Og Hver en Deel gav Himmelen sin Gave
  Paa hver en Plet Velsignelserne gro."

(*Danish Song.*)

CHAPTER XVII

THE DANISH PEOPLE

THE fundamental characteristics of the Danes are irresolution, phlegm, confidence and saneness—saneness of mind and saneness of body. The decadents of Denmark are young men who, desiring, as youth ever desires, to attract attention to themselves, if not by their genius at least by their eccentricity, have exercised great influence on the art and literature of the present day. But, as his natural good-nature reasserts itself in riper years, the decadent gradually recovers, ranges himself as a husband, and becomes the honest father of a family. The rage for money-making and luxury not having yet seized upon the greater part of the people, the average Dane usually follows the path his fathers have traced for him, lives happily where he was born, and has abundant leisure for study and the amusements which he loves. As Denmark has no exaggeratedly wealthy inhabitants, so she has no submerged tenth; life flows on calmly and happily, rarely disturbed by throes of ambition or by gusts of passion. Thus there is little fear of revolution there; the last attempt of the kind was easily subdued by the simple means of the fire-hose.

Though the Danes are thus heavy and bourgeois in character, there is not wanting a certain youthful set in Copenhagen, corrupted and vitiated probably by the influence of foreign literature, which is only prevented by want of means from living on the same scale of luxury and extravagance as others of their class among richer nations. For, as I have said, though there is but little abject poverty in Denmark, so there is also a conspicuous absence of that abnormal product of our civilisation—the millionaire. The richest man is a manufacturer of margarine with an income of 800,000 crowns per annum; next in wealth is a nobleman who boasts 300,000 crowns a year, and after him come about ten men, each possessing 200,000 yearly. All other incomes are far below these sums. It speaks well for the morality of the people that, when a certain variety actress became too much the mode and there was some danger that she would cause the ruin of a set of young men who were her professed admirers, the Government thought right to interfere, and prohibited her from ever again following her profession in Copenhagen. Hence it would seem that the corruption and vice of the upper classes, about which there can be no doubt, has not yet penetrated very deeply or irretrievably ruined the whole of society.

Of their simplicity of life the habits of the royal family are a proof. The King walks in the streets of Copenhagen accompanied only by his aide-de-camp and his dogs; to avoid giving both him and the people the trouble of continual salutations, it is the fashion to pretend not to recognise him. He has even been seen to ring himself at the door of the British Embassy. The Prince Royal often walks through Ostergade with his two daughters, while the Princess Marie is an enthusiastic member of the Fire Brigade and does not fail to attend every considerable conflagration. Naturally she is adored by the members of the brigade, who can boast of possessing her photograph taken in their uniform, which she has obtained permission to wear. A fireman, whose wounded hand she bound up with her own handkerchief, still retains it as a memento of the kind action.

Once, walking alone in the precincts of Fredensborg, the Crown Prince was accosted by a stranger who did not know him, and who inquired of him his way. "I am going in that direction and will show you," said the prince. Arrived at their destination the stranger asked him to drink a bottle of beer as a reward for his trouble, and when the prince refused this refreshment, offered him ten öre instead. This the prince laughingly accepted, saying it was "the first money he had ever earned by his own work."

The excellence of the education of the present royal family is shown by the following anecdote. Like the boy he was, Prince Valdemar once amused himself by running through the rooms of the palace and leaving all the doors open after him, till the patience of the footman whose duty it was to close them was completely exhausted. The King seeing this, said to the prince, "Now, Valdemar, the footman shall go in front and you behind to shut the doors after him, and so you will learn not to give people unnecessary trouble."

So far as my personal experience goes, I have been much struck with the air of uniform moderate prosperity among these people, and I have never once seen a beggar or been asked for alms.

Nearly exactly a century ago, that very clever Englishwoman, Mary Wollstonecraft, the mother of Shelley's wife, visited Denmark, and she has left in a series of delightful letters her impressions of the country. Copenhagen had just then been devastated by a terrible fire, and many poor families driven out of their habitations were encamped in the fields around, while she herself was in a most melancholy state of mind, all of which may probably account for the severity of her judgment on Denmark and the Danes. Of Copenhagen she says: "The streets are open and many of the houses large; but I saw nothing to rouse the idea of elegance or grandeur, if I except the circus where the King and Prince Royal reside." On the inhabitants she is still more severe. "A kind of indolence respecting what does not immediately concern them seems to characterise the Danes. The men of business are domestic tyrants, coldly immersed in their own affairs, and so ignorant of the state of other countries that they dogmatically assert that Denmark is the happiest country in the world. As for the women, they are simply notable housewives, without accomplishments or any of the charms that adorn more advanced social life. This ignorance may enable them to save something in their kitchens; but it is far from rendering them better parents." Again she continues: "The Danes in general seem extremely averse to innovation, and if happiness only consists in opinion, they are the happiest people in the world, for I never saw any so well satisfied with their own situation."

If by this she means to say that the Danes are extremely patriotic and warmly attached to their country and its institutions, she is right; but if she means they do not wish to introduce into it the latest improvements and most modern ideas, she is far from having given expression to the truth. However, in all she says there is a certain foundation in fact, but our clever author's judgment must be taken with caution, as, acute observer as she was, she did not remain long enough in Copenhagen to form a very reliable opinion. It is interesting enough to compare her criticisms on the Danes with the description which Malte Brun has left of his countrymen—it will then be seen that the most striking traits remain essentially the same—which is also confirmed by my own observations. The only passage in the latter author's criticism I entirely disagree with is the statement that the Danes are cool and ceremonious towards foreigners; I on the contrary, have ever found them friendly and kind, and almost too confident in the good faith and sincerity of strangers.

MALTE BRUN'S DESCRIPTION OF THE DANES

"It may be that the humidity of the air and the quantity of flesh and fish they consume has contributed to make this nation heavy, patient, and difficult to move. In former times insatiable conquerors, they are now brave but peaceable; little enterprising but plodding and persevering; modest and proud, hospitable, but not over assiduous. They are cheerful and frank among compatriots, but somewhat cool and ceremonious towards foreigners; loving ease before luxury; rather sparing than industrious. Imitators of other nations, we also find them discriminating observers; deep, but a little slow, and minute thinkers endowed with more energy than fertility of imagination. Constant, romantic and careful of their cherished aims, they are capable of a rush of enthusiasm, but rarely of flashes of inspiration, that suppleness of thought which commands success or admiration. Bound are they by strong ties to their native soil and to the interests of the fatherland, but not jealous enough of the national glory, and though accustomed to the calm of a monarchy, enemies of servitude and despotism. This is the portrait of the Danes."

It is but natural that among a people, especially a peasantry so far removed from the reach of modern influence, so credulous and so simple by nature, all kinds of superstitions and beliefs should arise and take long to disappear. Barely twenty years ago, and so far as I have been able to ascertain even now in the remoter districts of Jutland, every house was supposed to possess its *nesser*, a sprite who was not really evilly disposed, but whom it was the interest of the inhabitants to conciliate lest he should play them some nasty trick, which he never did if well used. Therefore on every festive occasion, especially on Christmas Eve, it was the custom to leave outside for him a plate of rice gruel seasoned with cinnamon and sugar, and on the top a lump of butter, with a good bottle of ale beside it. These naturally disappeared during the night and the nesser was supposed to have devoured them. A man once by accident put the butter underneath instead of on top of the rice, and when the nesser came to partake of his meal, thinking this ingredient was left out, he, in a rage, twisted round the tail of a favourite cow. However he began to eat, but finding the butter underneath he repented of what he had done, and placed a sum of money beside the cow to atone for the injury. Nessers will also, if slighted, blunt tools, hinder cows from giving their milk, make dirty the dairy utensils, and do many another vicious trick out of spite. If a servant goes to sleep and leaves her candle burning, she avers she has put it out, but that the nesser has relighted it, to avenge some slight she has put upon him, and so it has burnt out. Sometimes, for a like purpose, he will turn people round in their beds, quickly run to the other side and turn them back again till they are completely shaken. A nesser who had been teased by a boy threw him over the roof, but not wishing to do him great injury, ran round the house and caught him before he fell on the other side. A troll is a more wicked little being who lives under the hills and whom it is not well to see at night.

Gnomes dwell in the mountains and are distinguished for their skill in working metals. Loke once wickedly cut off the beautiful hair of Sif and strewed it over the valley of Guldbrand in Norway, whence corn sprang up; for which reason also the girls of the country have such glorious piles of golden hair. Thor, the husband of Sif, was not unnaturally enraged, and called on his friends the gnomes to help his wife in her difficulty; and they, searching amid their stores for the finest gold, made Sif another head of hair. The gnomes made Thor's hammer, and the reason the handle is so short is that Loke, turning himself into a wasp, stung the hand of the gnome who was making it and so hindered him from finishing; they also made for

Freya the golden-haired boar she was accustomed to ride.

These supernatural beings are common to the whole of Scandinavia, but the Elvepiger or fairies are more specifically Danish. They inhabit forests and morasses, about which they move with long floating veils, which undoubtedly represent the vapours often hovering in these places. The imprudence of sleeping out in these mists is no doubt indicated in the belief that if a young man slumbers at night on the Elverhoi or Fairy-hill he is sure to die slowly afterwards; the refrain of one of the Kjœmperviser says:—

> "Young man, if you go to Elverhoi,
> Go not there to sleep."

This graceful fancy forms the subject of one of the most popular ballets, "Folkesang," where the movements of the fairies' robes are so managed as to give exactly the impression of thick, floating mists penetrated by the moonlight of a summer night.

The Hellheste is a three-legged horse, to see which is a certain presage of death.

I once stayed at an old house in Yorkshire down the corridors of which a lady was supposed to walk with her head under her arm; and I have found the same legend in Denmark, which has also its haunted houses, ghosts of all shapes and sorts, and witches for whose convenience in their excursions up and down chimneys on broomsticks, fires and candles are still lighted on Midsummer Eve. Nightmare is supposed to be caused by a black cat sitting on the chest, and I have myself known a peasant whose belief in this superstition it was impossible to shake, as he averred he had seen the animal himself on the bed of a friend in whose room he was sleeping.

Popular education has reached a higher level in Denmark than in any other European state. The numerous public schools are maintained by communal rates, and are partly paying, partly free; in addition to these there are United Church schools, which, besides instruction, provide students, when they leave, with clothes and some small pecuniary help.* There is, I believe, no country in which so much assistance is given to those in need of it, and, to the honour of Denmark be it said, nowhere more liberal institutions, nowhere more opportunities of obtaining assistance in study, help in poverty, and succour in illness.

I have failed to give a correct idea of the Danes if the reader has not already gathered that they are a stolid people, unesthetic, unambitious, and very much concentred in themselves, but honest, hospitable, brave and worthy, and

* High schools for the sons and daughters of peasant farmers, the courses arranged so as to interfere as little as possible with farm work, have been established in Denmark, "the aim being to open the mind and eyes to intellectual values—that there are more things in heaven and earth than manure, crops, money, and what may be bought for money."—PROFESSOR DYMOND.

possessing powers of reflection and a sentiment of poetry which have resulted in some of the finest productions of modern literature.

Nevertheless, Denmark sleeps, tired, perhaps, after the mighty sea-fights of her Vikings and the glorious battles of her Valdemars. Will she ever awaken from her long-contented slumber? Or, is it to be wished for her?

CHAPTER XVIII

MANNERS AND CUSTOMS

ON the following subjects I desire to write in general terms and to describe that middle class which forms so large a majority in Denmark; if the reader has here a picture resembling an interior by Teniers rather than a romantic production of classic art, or a little pastoral poem rather than an epic, the fault lies in the subject itself. However, I console myself; a good Teniers is better than a bad Claude and may please as many connoisseurs, and some people would rather skim the pastoral poem than pore over the twelve or twenty books which go to make an epic.

Most of the inhabitants of Copenhagen reside in flats; the ground-floors are occupied by shops, to get into which you sometimes have to go down several steps and open a door, perhaps two. The flats are approached by a *porte cochère*, beyond which is a courtyard, and perhaps a garden planted with trees, common to all the inmates. To the right and left inside the door are wooden staircases, generally clean and sanded, which lead to the upper storeys. Each flat is, as we say in England, self-contained, and usually has two entrances, one to a small hall the other to the kitchen.

There are generally a sitting-room, a dining-room, two or three bedrooms, and a kitchen; the good-natured servant, who is often a Swede, and who considers herself well paid at fifteen crowns a month, often has but a small room partitioned off the kitchen to sleep in. The furnishing is a model of simplicity and frugality; the dining-room contains a sideboard covered with domestic utensils in polished brass, which are the inheritance and pride of the Danish housewife, a table and a few chairs; in the sitting-room are chairs, sofa, and perhaps a piano, while in the centre stands the time-honoured round table with the best books and a Bible on it, as in our own country life of years ago; the curtains are white, the windows filled with plants in pots, and in the corner of each room is one of the tall iron or terra-cotta stoves which are such a boon in northern climates.

Simplicity and frugality rule the simple household; where the Englishman seeks some superfluous luxury on which to lay out his abundant cash, the poorer Dane has to make his income go as far as it will for mere necessaries. This, however, is not so very important to a man who can put on his door "Captain and Wine-seller."

We find here the good old family life of our bourgeoisie of fifty years ago; in the evening the members gather round the table with its white cloth under the lamp, the children learn their lessons, the housewife does her simple embroidery (I cannot imagine what becomes of all the embroidery the Danish ladies are always occupied in producing), and the master of the house smokes a huge pipe holding half an ounce of tobacco, while perhaps a splendid hound snores peaceably by the glowing stove. Such scenes are rare in our England now, but I believe the Dane to be a happier man than the Englishman of the same class.

Birthdays and all possible anniversaries are strictly observed, presents are exchanged and simple amusements freely indulged in, chocolate, tea, and cakes generally forming the refreshment at these entertainments. If it is only a flower or a little tree growing in a pot, the Dane cannot resist the pleasure of giving, and making every festival as happy as possible in a simple way. Christmas, when young and old, rich and poor, gather round the inevitable tree laden with gifts and all sing and dance together, is rigorously observed; Queen Alexandra has done much towards introducing this charming custom into England. It was the old fashion on Christmas Eve to eat gruel made with milk, and beer sauce, goose stuffed with prunes or chestnuts, and apple beignets called "aebleskiver." The aebleskiver are purposely made as hard as possible by the peasants; the mistress of the house distributes them to her family and servants, who keep them in drawers or in their pockets, using them as counters at cards, etc., until the birthday of the king. They are always offered to visitors during this period, and if not otherwise trying, are so to the teeth. The peasants also once had a custom of throwing the remains of each day's soup into a large wooden trencher kept for the purpose; the contents were eaten on Saturday and called "Bænkevalling" or soup made in a bench.

Holy Thursday, being the anniversary of the institution of the Lord's Supper, is very strictly observed, and at Easter, Good Friday, Saturday, Sunday and the following Monday are kept, offices and shops are closed and all business is at a stand-still. On Good Friday, as a Dane who prided himself on his English, remarked, "We eat sheep." At Easter, too, very good music is to be heard in the churches. The religious festivals formerly held on other days of the year are now abandoned, and the whole commuted for one day, called the "Great Day of Prayer," which is kept on the fourth Friday after Easter.

The fifth of June is kept as a public holiday to commemorate the granting of the Grundlov, or Universal Suffrage, by Frederick VII. Undoubtedly the suffrage was granted prematurely to a people only in the former reign released from serfdom, and whom it would have been better first to have educated; the result was that a number of ill-prepared deputies entered the Folkething, whose principle it is to refuse consistently supplies for objects they cannot appreciate, such as science, art, etc., of which fact the unbuilt palace of Christiansborg is a salient example. To remedy this state of things, the Minister of the Interior, Estrup, who enjoyed the complete confidence of Frederick VII., succeeded in passing, with the aid of twelve members for life whom the king has the right of electing, certain provisionary laws, which brought him into such unpopularity that his life was attempted and he finally resigned office. From this it will easily be understood that the festival of the fifth of June is celebrated with great enthusiasm by the Left or Opposition party; all business is suspended, shops and offices closed, streets decorated, bands play, processions defile, and the statue of Frederick VII. adorned with wreaths of flowers.

In their food and their manner of partaking of it one finds some of the innumerable shades of difference which exists between ourselves and this people, a people who in so many ways remind us of what the English were in the days of our mothers and grandmothers, and from whom, in our present stage of development, we differ so curiously. Their hours for taking their food seem marvellously well adapted to wasting the best portions of the day. A cup of tea made with one spoonful for the pot and none for the drinkers is served in bed, *frokost* or breakfast at twelve, dinner at four, and supper at or near seven in the evening. For breakfast, on the perfectly spotless cloth (the Danes are a very clean people), little plates of various cold viands are placed; for instance, slices of cold meat, fish raw and cooked, plates of butter, trays containing thin slices of the rye bread in which the Danes delight but which it takes a good deal of hunger to render palatable to us, and white bread, which they call French bread, are placed. A bottle of beer is put beside each plate, and tea is also served. Your true Dane takes a piece of bread, plasters it with butter, then searches about with his fork for the slice of meat or fish he prefers and puts it on the bread and butter; he eats this holding it in his hand. This is called "smörrebröd" and is the national dish. The meal finished, the mistress of the house rises, saying " Velbekomme," which is also repeated by each guest on entering and leaving the room There was formerly a more elaborate ceremony on this occasion, when it was considered necessary for each guest on rising to shake hands with the hostess and say " Tak for Mad" ("Thanks for the meal"). This however is now quite obsolete.

At dinner soup, sweet, O so sweet! is served; it may be made of the juice of fruit, of milk flavoured with cinnamon, of sago or rice made with milk and eggs, of a kind of gruel with vegetables, but even worse is a soup made of beer with crusts of rye bread floating in it; when wanted especially elegant, whipped cream is added to the incongruous mixture. If the object of these concoctions be to take the edge off the appetite, they are admirably well adapted to the purpose. A dish of hot meat is then placed before the mistress of the house, who carves it and hands on a plate the pieces cut off to the nearest guest, who having taken his portion passes the rest on: or the whole joint is cut up and sent round on its native dish. When such a thing first came into my hands, I confess I was puzzled to know what to do with it. With hot meat and fish, preserves and stewed fruits are eaten; the Danish method is to cut up the meat, rest the knife on the plate and eat with the fork only. The plates are generally cold. Game is eaten fresh and carefully washed, cleaned, and soaked in milk. I once saw a joint of fresh boiled meat and some sauce in a boat and wildly hoped for mutton and caper sauce, but another illusion was destroyed! The meat proved to be fresh beef, and the sauce a decoction of horse-radish and currants. Raw ham is another ordinary dinner dish. The national röd-gröd is a kind of jelly flavoured with the juice of different fruits and eaten cold, as the Danes usually prefer to have their food.

Röd-gröd, fruit, and tea and coffee follow the meat, seldom what we call sweets, such as tarts and puddings, but on extra occasions a little very sweet pastry is obtained from the confectioner. Sauces and pickles, if we except salted cucumber, are seldom seen at Danish tables. Beer of course is the beverage taken, and the meal ends with the same ceremony as breakfast. Like most continental nations, the Danes do not care for mutton and eat much more and much older veal than we do. Supper resembles breakfast, but I think the Danes almost always finish this meal with a very thin slice of cheese (to cut it thin enough is an art), a large piece of which is found on every table having in it an ivory nob for the thumb, eaten on bread and butter like the meat.

It will be noticed there is but little variety in a Danish *ménage*, and that it is somewhat difficult for an Englishman to get accustomed to the living. However, the Danes are an extremely hospitable people, and are never more pleased than when giving of their best to the " stranger within their gates."

The stoves in use in Denmark might with advantage, I should think, be introduced into our hardly less rigorous climate. They are from three to twelve or more feet in height and stand well into the room ; the ordinary ones are of iron, the more elegant of tiles. They burn coke, coal, and turf with equal facility. They are lighted in the bedrooms before you rise in winter time, and for something like threepence can be kept going the whole day, giving out enough heat to thoroughly warm the room they are in and the one adjoining. In fact, the houses, shops, railway carriages, etc., are heated to a degree almost disagreeable even in the very coldest weather. Another of their customs would be of use here in winter; they place a cushion or pillow upright at the end of their beds, by which all draughts are excluded from the feet.

The Danes have the same predilection for the lottery, which is a Government institution, as the southern nations of Europe, and will pledge their last pair of shoes to pay for a ticket. In every town there are offices for the sale of these tickets, and the Dane is rare who has not some interest in the drawing which takes place every month. The highest prize is 120,000 crowns.

The slowness of the Danes is something quite peculiar to themselves. I have already alluded to the sluggishness of the trains, but even this is surpassed by the slowness of the trams and omnibuses; anyone who is in a hurry walks rather than employ them. Let us suppose the tram standing at its starting-point in the centre of the town; the driver is beside it talking to his apparently innumerable friends, the conductor deeply engaged in conversation with some of the passengers, as if he were specially retained to amuse them during the delay. *En parenthèse* it may be remarked that the Danes are as a rule great talkers. Gradually the tram fills, and the last stout dames, who arrive panting, fail to find a place. But the tram does not start; all remain tranquilly in their places, the driver reads his newspaper, the conductor ceases not to entertain, the well-conditioned horses seem to sleep. This state of things lasts some five or ten minutes; more belated passengers arrive but the tram does not stir. After another interval a pleased expression, as if something were really about to happen, passes over the placid faces of all concerned, the conductor once more amiably surveys his passengers as if to ask

ROSENBORG CASTLE

if they wish any more remarks from him, and finally the driver seems to think something really ought to be done to relieve the tedium of the situation, so he swings his burly figure into his seat and looks at his horses contemplatively. Another wait, a still more satisfied expression on the part of the travellers, a bell rings, finally the tram begins to pursue its calm and cautious way amid the rest of the traffic of Copenhagen.

One day, painting the Castle of Rosenborg, I took up my position beside a youthful but spectacled soldier who was doing sentry duty there. He had evidently not had time enough to complete his toilet, so he employed his leisure in brushing down his coat, and amused himself arranging his belt and in playing with his rifle. He approached me, apparently very anxious to see my work, and said something in Danish. I replied that I did not understand him, being English. This seemed a sufficient explanation that my ignorance was a matter of course, so he said "All right," and with that his knowledge of our tongue came to an end. Such of his friends as could possibly manage it passed that way and held conversations with him to relieve his tedium, and passers-by asked questions to which he gave prolonged answers. With such diversions the time came for relieving guard. Two other military youths jauntily arrived, advanced, gave the sign and countersign, looking all the time at me in an amused fashion as if to say, "Yes, we know it is all very stupid, but it is not our fault," and then, polite as Danes always are, said "Good day, how are you?" to the retiring sentinel. He who replaced him commenced to walk about here and there, sometimes almost at a run and sometimes very slowly, as the fancy took him. It does not seem a very arduous task to do sentry-go in Denmark.

So slow are the Danes that it usually takes a quarter of an hour at least to find a cab in the streets of Copenhagen, which cab, after all, crawls imperturbably to its destination, whatever may be your hurry.

They are not a handsome race; they are rather short than tall and inclined to be stout; the women are usually very fair, and looking at those who pass in the streets one cannot compliment them on their taste in dress. Though not polished, they are excessively polite, and greetings and farewells, with much raising of hats, are frequent and ceremonious. They shame us in their thorough knowledge of and interest in their own traditions and history.

The people are exceedingly devoted to dancing, and lose no opportunity of enjoying this pastime. At all social gatherings, on market days and holidays, by day and by night, the Danes dance, the men sometimes in their hats, the young girls with their handkerchiefs tied round their waists, a salutary precaution when the cavaliers wear no gloves. On the slightest pretext, such as a birth, a festival, or a death, the houses are decorated with their beloved Dannebrog—the national flag.

Sunday is not kept as we understand keeping it; everyone does as he likes best, even the peasant tills his field if he be so disposed; the shops indeed are shut, but only to set their owners free to attend theatres and concerts, which on that occasion are in full fling.

The religion is the Evangelical form of Lutheran Protestantism, and the form of divine worship is extremely simple; the priest, who wears a black gown and a ruff round his neck, chants the service, remaining at the altar till he preaches his sermon; the congregation stands to pray and sits down to sing. The hymn-book of the Danes is a collection of exquisite poetry gathered from all sources; and the music to which the poems are set is appropriate and solemn. The following hymn by Oehlenschläger, which is sung at funerals, may give some idea of the attitude of the Danish mind towards the mysteries of religion—an attitude reverent, pure, and unsophisticated, proper to the character of a people who live closer to Nature than we do, and who do not spend their existence in large towns, ignorant of her teachings, and untouched by her influence:—

"Teach me, O forest free from grief,
To fade as fades the autumn leaf,
There comes a spring more vernal:
There green my tree towards the skies
Shall, deeply rooted, lordly rise
In summer days eternal.

> Teach me, thou little bird on high,
> Like thee undauntedly to fly
> Towards an unknown haven.
> When all is winter here and ice,
> Then shall an endless Paradise
> To me henceforth be open.
>
> Teach me, O thou light butterfly,
> To burst the case wherein I lie
> In slavery's dominions:
> I crawl on earth a worm so frail
> But soon shall float with gauzy veil
> The gold and purple pinions
>
> My Lord and Saviour Who dost smile
> Above the clouds, teach me the while
> To master grief with scorning;
> Hope's verdant flag to me display;
> Good Friday was a bitter day
> But glad was Easter morning."

The rite of confirmation is of much more importance in Danish life than in ours. It takes place between the ages of fourteen and sixteen years and marks the entrance of the boy into manhood and of the girl into society, or, as we say, "coming out." It is celebrated with much ceremony, giving and receiving of presents, etc. The lower classes are fond of concluding the festivities with a dance, but the upper classes and more serious persons greatly deprecate this habit.

Betrothal is also a solemn ceremony. The fact is publicly announced, the parties interchange wedding rings, which both wear on the third finger of the right hand both before and after marriage, and go out together in society and elsewhere. At the betrothal a reception is held, and presents given just as at the marriage ceremony; the breaking of this tie is a serious affair.

The Salvation Army has taken deep root in Denmark, and all with whom I have conversed are unanimous in extolling its beneficial influence.

Family surnames have not been in use among the lower classes for more than fifty years, and indeed are scarcely so now in the remoter districts. Peter, the son of Ole, was called Olsen, and the son of Peter, Pedersen, while his daughter would be Peder's Datter. Appellations such as "Shepherd," "Red-haired," "Shoemaker" and such like were added to help in distinguishing individuals. It was the custom of the nobles to use the name of the property belonging to the head of the family; in the case of the burghers who possessed no land, the greatest confusion as to names prevailed. Thus the edict of Christian V. requiring all Danes to assume and keep a family name was both useful and necessary.

The wives of doctors, professors, military and naval officers, and State officials take the title of their husbands, thus they have Professorinde, Majorinde, Etatsraadinde, etc., etc., etc.

In the little villages the inhabitants still retain the touching custom of ringing the church bells when the sun rises and sets so that each may on hearing it say a prayer at the beginning and close of day. At the end of the ringing three notes are struck three times with intervals between them—probably this custom has reference to the Trinity.

In most Danish villages the church is situated on the top of a hill and the flower-covered graves of the "forefathers of the village" cluster round the sacred walls. Of course, the lake which supplies the inhabitants with water lies below it, which has given rise to the ghastly saying, "The villagers drink their ancestors."

Our own old-fashioned epitaphs have their kindred inscriptions in Denmark, some of which have come under my notice. I transcribe two, perhaps not the most ridiculous:—

> "What a storm in a moment!
> The sea of life is like the world
> Storms follow calms;
> Hope itself declines in the channels of life
> And even the haven menaces shipwreck
> As the mortal remains prove which lie here
> Of her who was in life
> The most estimable and most honourable lady
>
> KIRSTINE LACHMANN
>
> Born the 22 Nov. 1736
> United in marriage
> The 23 Sept. 1757
> TO
> The most estimable and most honourable
>
> MICHAEL WILLIAM SUNDT
>
> Surveyor in chief of the Norwegian fortifications
> Of His Royal Majesty,
> And Captain of Infantry.
> She triumphed over death
> Fighting against it to give life
>
> To her first and only Son
> The 20 May 1758

> But fell outside the field of battle
> Twelve days after the victory
> Amid hope's triumphal song.
> Kindness and meekness
> Piety and love
> In a word
> All the virtues
> Sighed over this fall.
> Oh why did'st thou eat, Eve?"

The last line is sublime!

> Under this stone reposes
> HANS MATTHIAS SCHMINCKE
> Who in his journey to eternity
> Glanced at the world
> On the 19th day of July, 1761
> He was
> The first-born of his father
> The second son of his mother
> The joy of both
> But would you know for how long?
> Only five days!

Railway travelling in Denmark is cheap and comfortable—a second-class ticket available over all the lines, and lasting a fortnight, may be had for thirty-two crowns, or sixty crowns for a month. The trains go at a very tranquil pace: for example, it takes two hours to go from Copenhagen to Holbæk, a distance of about thirty-five miles; there are no tunnels, no cuttings, no viaducts to speak of, and even the third-class carriages are well warmed. One accident only has occurred since railways were first introduced, and that was a collision a few years ago at Gentofte, when about fifty people were killed and injured, a catastrophe which caused the greatest consternation throughout the country. Tickets are collected *en route* by the guard, who seems to remember every passenger who comes into or leaves the train; if his memory happen to fail him he inquires of the travellers with touching confidence, if a fresh occupant has entered; and one must wait patiently to mount or descend till he opens the doors, which he does at every station. The clocks at the railway stations are kept five minutes fast, so that the leisurely Dane may not miss his train. It is a lamentable fact that Danish travellers invariably keep the carriage windows closed both in winter and summer, and permit no fresh air to enter.

Denmark is remarkable for the races of dogs it produces; there is no finer animal than the Grand Danois, a hound which stands about two feet six inches high, and has small ears and short hair. Though the tax on dogs amounts to no less than twenty crowns a year in Copenhagen, but few Danes are without their faithful canine companion.

In wet weather goloshes are universally worn both by men and women, and left at the door on entering a house. The little children go to school carrying their books in a knapsack on their backs; peasants in sabots, servant girls with short sleeves, and old women with curious poke bonnets adorned with lace, are also characteristic figures.

In the fish shops live fish are kept swimming in huge tanks of salt water, so the Dane can always have his fish fresh. Stags are still found wild in

Denmark, and their carcasses may be seen in the season hanging at the doors of the game-sellers' shops, among other game I have never seen elsewhere.

In search of change of food I once hailed with joy a shop over which "delikatesser" was inscribed. Now I thought is my chance! To my dismay, on further investigation I found these "delicacies" to consist of dried herrings, cheese, and a little jam. But much may be excused the Dane on account of his politeness and kindness. If you buy a stamp, he will stick it on for you; if you want an address looked out, he will write it for you; train and omnibus conductors bid you "Good-day" as you enter, and "Farewell" as you depart; these little attentions render life in Denmark leisurely and pleasant.

Inferiors are obliging but never servile, independent, yet always willing to go out of their way to do a service for others, laborious and economical, yet ready to enjoy to the full the simple amusements and pleasures which fall to their share.

In my opinion the climate of Denmark is superior to that of England, for though the thermometer falls lower in winter, and reaches about the same altitude as with us in summer, the cold is not so penetrating or the heat so enervating. Snow does not necessarily mean cold; snow, rain and sunshine may diversify the same day, and in early spring, though the earth may be white, the soft breezes and clear air remind one of our finest days in May. Sea mists, which are rare, sometimes envelop the country, but pass away as the sun rises high, and there is nothing which reminds one of that infamous production we are accustomed to call fog.

"Moist blanket dripping misery down,
Loathed alike by land and town,"

As George Borrow says.

Oh, the beauty of the clear summer nights of the north in which there is no shadow of darkness! The sun sinks gently into the west in a haze of crimson light, and when he has gone leaves a trail of yellow radiance behind him. Above the yellow the pure clear sky takes a tint of faintest green, which in its turn melts to the tenderest blue; in it floats the moon and one or two pale twinkling stars. The frequent waters faithfully reflect all the tints of heaven, the winds seem to be silent with admiration, the forests become dark masses without a single detail, and the little white houses with their tall red roofs take on a tinge of blue. The south and east have their glory, but cannot match in tenderness and tranquillity the clear, calm heavens of the north.

One of the Danes' popular weather sayings resembles our own:—

"Monday's weather till mid-day is the week's weather till Friday.
Friday's weather is Sunday's weather.
Saturday has its own weather."

Summer bursts suddenly from the embrace of winter and advances by leaps and bounds. During the last few days of April and the first of May the trees are bare and still expectant of the coming change, the earth is flowerless. A few showers, a few hours of sunshine, and the flowers spring to life, the trees cover themselves with tender foliage, and you have the forest in all its pride of youthful beauty, exultant at its release from the long and trying winter. "Blinkeveir" ("Blinking weather") is the happy phrase by which the Danes distinguish showery days.

Strangers do not usually arrive till July and August, yet May and June are exquisite months. Already the frosts have disappeared, the tender green of beech trees enlivens the forest, the soil is covered with wild flowers, the fields are green with corn, and that out-of-door life of which the Danes are so fond commences. It may be added that it is, comparatively speaking, mild quite up to Christmas. The mean temperature recorded from May to September is $59\frac{1}{2}°$ to $62\frac{1}{2}°$ Fah., while in winter, the days on which the thermometer falls below zero (the ice days) are considerably more than in England.

Books are dear owing to the smallness of the population to which works in Danish appeal, but the few that appear are produced in a style as to printing and illustrations that leaves nothing to be desired.

I once had occasion to attend a sale by auction, a description of which may amuse, and which it is only fair to add took place in a provincial town. A long, low room, with a platform at the end was filled with country people; most of the men were occupied in smoking long pipes with bowls as big as coffee cups; those who were not seemed to wish they were, and had long pipe stems hanging out of one or another pocket; the women all had fair hair strained back from their foreheads, on which were perched hats far too small, and were otherwise dressed with that peculiar absence of elegance which distinguishes the natives of the north. The effects to be sold were arranged round the room; the auctioneer stood at a small desk with his bottles of beer beside him, and a soup plate, in which he put the money he received. In a stentorian voice he named the object to be sold, attaching to it the most exorbitant price his florid imagination could furnish. A stander-by mentioned a sum as ridiculously low, and amid jokes and *bon mots* from the auctioneer, and laughter and reciprocal jokes from the buyers, the object in question was finally knocked down to the highest bidder, paid for, and handed to him, when possible, over the heads of the crowd. Articles were sold in small parcels, or one by one, and the thrifty housewife who, for example, had secured a frying-pan or a perambulator, shouldered her way through the throng, took possession of her prize, and returned to her friends delighted with her bargain; or the youth who had become the happy possessor of a single book paid his money, tucked it under his arm and departed forthwith. Adjoining the auction-room was a bar where beer flowed copiously, the auctioneer and his clerk frequently retiring to partake of this refreshment.

Family legacies are an institution peculiar, I think, to Danish social life. Wealthy persons of both sexes will sometimes leave at their death sums of money, the interest of which they direct to be paid to some poor member of their family as an annuity; of course, widows and sick persons chiefly benefit by this liberality. On the death, or in case of flagrant bad conduct on the part of the recipient, another relative similarly situated may solicit the legacy, and should the family of the founder become extinct, the money is bestowed on others in need of help, and so on in perpetuity. Surely there is more of the Christian spirit in this manner of disposing of one's abundant means than in giving a large sum to a public institution patronised by royalty for the selfish satisfaction of being addressed as "Sir So-and-so," and of becoming an object of special interest to toadies and footmen — a bargain, however, which can be made in Copenhagen as well as in London.

The Danes are provisioned with a more complete scale of rewards for those monetary merits which we are obliged to recompense with a simple knighthood or baronetcy than we are— the grades of social position are more nicely defined, and rewards more proportionate, than with us. For in England we requite a victory or a lucky investment in beer, a poem or a patent medicine with our poor pretentious knighthood, and the donor of an immense sum to a bloated institution must throw in his lot with these heroes. But they " manage these things better in Denmark." The seller of soap and candles in a little shop in a courtyard, who has brains enough to manage his business more than usually successfully, and who bestows some of his spare cash on a public charity, is dubbed a " Kammerraad" (Councillor of the Chamber.) His affairs still prosper, he gives more money, and receives in exchange the high-sounding appellation " Justitsraad" (Councillor of Justice), in which, if you go deeply into the thing, there is perhaps some sense, as he can probably, after his mercantile experience, give sound advice as to how *injustice* may be practised. Our friend still flourishes, makes fresh donations of his superfluous riches, and the proud title of "Etatsraad" (Councillor of State) rewards his expenditure, for if he is capable of buying soap and candles at a low price and selling them at a high, he surely must be the man to guide affairs of State, even if his knowledge of the three R's be somewhat limited. There is still another title, "Konferensraad" (Councillor of Conference), but our soap-seller would have to part with a very considerable sum in order to reach its proud altitude. The wife of the soap-seller is excessively interested in the question of her husband's progress through these different stages, for, like the wives of knights, she shares in his advancing honours, as I have before stated.

There are more public institutions, artistic, literary, charitable and otherwise in Denmark than in any other country compared with the number of the inhabitants, which devote sums of money to the payment of annuities, either temporary or permanent, and to giving rewards for the encouragement of native talent.*

Lay convents are a peculiar institution of this country; among others, at Vallö is a richly-endowed establishment of this kind for unmarried ladies of the higher orders of nobility; and at Vemmetofte, which was endowed by Frederick IV., two hundred ladies, of whom the greater number are non-resident, receive different annual stipends.

At Gisselfeld is a lay convent for ladies which differs from those of Vallö and Vemmetofte in not being a residence for its members, who receive, instead, an annual income from the rents of the estate; its honorary lady superior and thirty visitors must be daughters of men belonging to one or other of the two highest grades of nobility.

The Danes precede every request with the phrase, "*vær saa göd*" (be so kind). A Frenchman once said he could go through Denmark with the help of this sentence only. When dinner is ready you are informed of it by the servant saying, "*vær saa göd*," your change is handed to you with the

* The Danish Mæcenas Jacobsen has just given almost the entire proceeds of his brewery, about 600,000 crowns per annum, for the encouragement of art in his own country.

same words, the conductor of an omnibus or train says them as he gives you your ticket, and the gentleman who wishes you to precede him repeats them. No expression is more frequently used, no phrase so indispensable.

The people have little aptitude for those out-of-door exercises, the love of which distinguishes the Englishman everywhere, but the taste for them is slowly coming in, and tennis, cricket, and football clubs are now formed. Everyone who can manage it seems to cycle, but a Danish lady a-wheel has neither the grace of the English nor the *chic* of the Frenchwoman; the much-debated question of an appropriate cycling costume has not yet disturbed the peace of mind of the hardy daughters of Scandinavia, still their strength and energy make good wheelwomen of them. The strongest wrestler in the world, Bech Olsen, is a Dane, of whom his countrymen are exceedingly proud.

It is not generally known that the national toast "Skaal," or "Skol," is a word formed by taking the first letters of four words, "Sundhed" (health), "Kœrlighed" (love), "og" (and) and "Lykke" (happiness).

A cattle fair in the country here is not unlike the fairs in England which are so gradually disappearing. The object is of course to exhibit and sell animals, but a spice of amusement is added to render it popular and draw a little money with which to defray expenses. I will endeavour to describe one I saw.

At early morning the Dannebrog, which is kept to hoist for these occasions, and for births, deaths, marriages and other celebrations in the large lofts of the houses, was protruded from the slanting roofs and windows, and the country people, who came in crowds, and the belles and beaux of the village, commenced the day by promenading up and down the principal street, the men together, the girls together; the former with their long pipes or cigars in their mouths, the latter dressed in their Sunday best. There is something to me touching about this Sunday best, so poor, so out of taste; about the valueless little trinkets bought with the savings of years, or the gift of some well-beloved; about the common gowns ill-fitting jackets and showy hats worn by their possessors with such an air of pride that it would be a thousand pities to undeceive them as to the effect they produce. At anyrate their robust forms, rosy cheeks and masses of golden hair are veritable treasures.

The entrance to the enclosure was an archway adorned with branches and flowers; the little booths, where tickets, which were little bits of blue and white ribbon with the name of the village and the date printed on them to be worn in the button-hole, were sold, were hidden in fragrant boughs. Inside there were many drinking tents, where men and women seemed continually occupied, the inevitable carousel with its tinsel and shrieking music, a swinging boat, an elk-deer with extra large horns, a shooting-gallery, and a band, every member of which wore a chimney-pot hat. There was also a contingent of horses, cattle and poultry; the horses were first-rate, so were the cows and poultry. The pigs were as big as large donkeys cut off at the knees, and stretched their hideous pink lengths lazily in the holes they scooped for themselves in the earth. Young men and boys amused themselves in trying their strength either by striking with a mallet a machine which recorded the weight of the blow by an automatical contrivance, or by hitting violently the nose of a stuffed cow which, if the blow was heavy enough, sank down on its knees and uttered a discordant groan. Some played at skittles, hurling a wooden ball along a plank at the end of which the pieces were placed. (I did not see how they could well avoid hitting them.) The ball was sent back in a trough such as we see our receipted bills and change come back to us in, in certain shops. Women sold sweetmeats which had a wonderfully distasteful appearance, honey cakes and pancakes. A man cut out likenesses in black paper in less than a minute with remarkable adroitness, and a pedlar sold popular songs, teaching the air at the same time to those who bought them, and who continued singing around him. He did a flourishing business with a profoundly moral ballad which related how a youth murdered a man with a spade in order to steal a bicycle, and another which contained the sapient line,

"The north wind blew and the clouds came up from the west!" Over all the blood-red Dannebrog; amid all beer booths and eating places.

At night the fun and frolic were at their height. The whole place was illuminated; in the clear spring heavens rose the crescent moon accompanied by one faithful star alone; the cattle, prize-winners and otherwise, went to sleep, and birds, tired of all the strident, human noises, went to rest. Then the bands redoubled their energy, and in a huge tent with well-boarded floor, young people assembled for that dancing which the Dane loves. The young men were all ready well primed with beer, which they drank from its native bottle without troubling themselves about glasses. They kept their hats on their heads and their cigars in their mouths; some of the young women also wore their hats and jackets, some had short sleeves, whence their red arms emerged, finished off, perhaps, with white cotton gloves, perhaps without. The dancers were packed so closely that there was not a hand's breadth between the couples, and there is no question about it—it was violent exercise, which caused cheeks to become inflamed and perspiration to stream from every pore. The favourite peasant dance is a so-called *Trippe-valse*, which consists in turning round and round with a little continual trot. Dancing was kept up nearly all night, and the entertainments concluded with a display of fireworks, which were reflected in a lake and gave intense excitement to the bucolic souls of those who saw it, and who expressed their feeling by the long and subdued "Oh——" proper to these occasions.

The sympathy of the Danes has been mostly with the Boers during the present war (1899-1901), and at several minor places of amusement where performances representing the Boers and English were given, the former were always applauded and the latter derided; this, however, must not be taken to mean any enmity on their part towards us, but rather as an expression of sympathy for a small nation engaged in a deadly struggle with a much larger one, as was their own case when Slesvig and Holstein were rudely taken from their grasp by the Prussians, and also as a far-off echo of their indignation at our having twice destroyed their fleet and once their city. The Danish papers write with fairness on this matter; some, as the *Politiken*, are even completely pro-English, and personally I have never suffered the slightest molestation on account of the war. Far different, however, was it in Belgium, where, as I passed in the streets, every urchin took occasion to shout in my ears, "*Vivent les Boers!*" "*A bas les Anglais!*"

CHAPTER XIX

COPENHAGEN—INSTITUTIONS

In this connection I will only mention such institutions as I have been enabled to examine personally.

Medical science has long been assiduously cultivated in Denmark, and Danish physicians take high rank amid their brethren of the profession. One of the most eminent of them lately died of a disease which he did not understand, and almost his last words were an expression of regret that he could not assist at his own autopsy!

One of the greatest medical discoveries of modern days is due to the genius of Professor Niels R Finsen, a Danish physician, whereby that horrible scourge of humanity, lupus, may be radically and completely cured—a discovery which ranks with those of Jenner, Koch, and Röntgen. It has now been tried for five years with the happiest results, eighty per cent. of the patients so treated being cured; if the wounds have not eaten away the flesh itself, no scar even is left to tell the sad tale of sorrow and suffering. When Dr Finsen looks, as I have done, on the cheek of a young girl where no trace remained of her horrible malady after his treatment, he must feel the highest and noblest sense of satisfaction it is given to humanity to know.

By his kindness I was permitted to inspect his institution in Gammelstoftgade for the cure of lupus—a series of wooden buildings erected and maintained partly by himself, partly by subscription and partly by Government aid. There are couches beneath the apparatus specially prepared for the purpose, on which lie the poor patients in various stages of the disease, which, cruelly, mostly attacks the face, each attended by a white-robed nurse. There are five hundred patients in this institution suffering from *lupus vulgaris* and thirty-five from another form of the same malady, who are in the charge of thirty attendants. The necessary treatment occupies on the average a year and a quarter, and an hour and a quarter must be devoted to it daily, but the hope, the almost certain hope, of being forever rid of a horrible disease which fastens on him like a ghoul, would naturally sustain the patient under far greater trials.

The treatment consists in concentrating on the wound certain properly-prepared rays of the sun, or, in default of the sun, of the electric light.* The red and yellow rays are completely eliminated, the blue and violet only retained, and these are made

* The recent discovery by a Dane, of the most powerful light yet known, will accelerate the cure.

to pass perpendicularly through lenses between which is contained a blue liquid, of which the chief ingredient is sulphate of copper; they then go down tubes like telescopes suspended from the apparatus for collecting the rays, at the end of which are lenses about an inch and a half in diameter. The rays thus prepared are received on two lenses between which water is put to cool them: these last are arranged so that they may be pressed by the nurse very tightly on the affected part, or firmly fixed by elastic bands in order to drive away the blood. The rays cover a spot on the wounds of only half an inch in diameter, which of course renders the cure longer than if a larger space could be operated on at once. There are now five of these apparatuses for collecting and diffusing the salutary rays; as patients flock here from all quarters of the globe, more will necessarily be added. Cancers and ulcers are also amenable to this treatment, and doubtless this wonderful discovery is capable of other and even greater developments.*

Professor Niels R. Finsen was born in the Faroe Islands, where his father was then governor, in 1860. He belongs to one of the noblest

---

* A very interesting department has been opened at the London Hospital for the treatment of lupus and some other diseases of the skin by Professor Finsen's method of phototherapy, or "light treatment." The introduction of this method of treatment at the London Hospital, the first in Great Britain to adopt it, is due to the Queen, who has taken the greatest interest in it since she first saw it carried out in Copenhagen. The treatment consists in the application of the chemical rays of light, either sunlight or electric light, by means of carefully-arranged appliances.—*The Times*, 29th June 1900.

Icelandic families, tracing his origin back to one of the discontented Norwegian chiefs, who, in 874, landed in Iceland, and he numbers many bishops and learned men among his ancestors. His education was commenced at the College of Rejkjavik, whence he proceeded to the University of Copenhagen. He has through life been an acute observer, and was a zealous sportsman before his health failed.

He has made several discoveries in medical science of great utility—such as a preparation of hæmatin albumen for anæmia, a method of treating small-pox patients by means of the colour red, with the result that the malady leaves the patient unscarred, now widely adopted in the East, in addition to his celebrated cure for lupus and other cognate diseases.

Early in 1901 Professor Finsen opened a sanatorium for the treatment of heart and liver diseases—a treatment of which his personal experience forms the basis. There patients with incurable maladies may learn how to prolong their lives with mitigated suffering. The establishment is already crowded. He and his collaborators are now deeply engaged in further experiments for the cure of disease by means of rays of light.

On the 12th August 1901 his new institution, for which the Government voted the necessary funds, was opened in Copenhagen, just five years after Finsen first commenced his cure of lupus by the application of chemical rays of light.

It is not astonishing to learn that the efficacy

PROFESSOR NIELS R. FINSEN
(From a photograph by Fred. Rüse)

of Professor Finsen's treatment has been called in question by certain of the medical profession. A Russian physician has asserted that the light treatment would be inefficacious if pyrogallic acid were not employed also; and a professor of Vienna has declared that lupus can never be cured without the use of the knife. With the object of combating these statements, Finsen, through the liberality of a fellow-citizen, sent twelve of his patients, cured without either acid or knife, who had been most severely attacked and whose cure had lasted at least twelve months, to the Medical Congress in Paris in 1900. The result was a complete triumph for him, and he was awarded a gold medal. It is now said that, as the violet rays destroy bacteria of all kinds, consumption and cancer may also be successfully combated by their means.

In the April of 1900 a most useful institution was inaugurated in Copenhagen, one which should prove a great attraction to English and American visitors. This is the Anglo-Danish Club (det Engelske Selskab), the object of which is "to spread the knowledge of the English language and institutions of Denmark, and to promote closer relations between the Danes and the English-speaking people, and to make Danish characteristics better known in England and America." Both ladies and gentlemen may become members on introduction by a previous member: the entrance fee is eighteen crowns, and the subscription the same sum per annum.

The rooms, situated in the most-frequented part of the town, at the corner of Ostergade and Amagertorv, are large and elegantly furnished; the Club boasts all the conveniences of an English one, such as a lift, electric light, dressing-rooms for ladies and gentlemen, billiard-table, restaurant, a library of English books, and the principle English and American newspapers and magazines. It is open from ten in the morning to twelve at night, and though so recently established, has already some six hundred members.

The movement for the advancement of women only dates from the last ten years; during this time it has made steady progress, and their position is now as good as that of the women of England. A most excellent Ladies' Morning Club is established at No. 9 Pilestrœde; the qualification for admission is that the applicant must be a lady; the subscription is four crowns a year. Members may invite their men friends, the best Danish papers are taken, and a restaurant is attached. The same rooms are shared by a kindred society, "Hegnet," the Hedge, or Woman's Protection Society, formed about four years ago for the benefit of women employed in shops, offices, etc. The Ladies' Club is only open till seven o'clock, then "Hegnet" takes possession; readings and lectures are arranged once a week, instruction is given in foreign languages, typewriting, etc., to such as desire it, and an agency is opened for obtaining employment for women, who may write their qualifications in a book accessible to those in search of assistants; a bicycle club and an office for insurance against illness also form part of this useful institution. The necessary qualification of members, of which there are now four hundred, is that the applicant shall have completed eighteen years and be really employed in business. A useful establishment also is the Woman's Kitchen (Kvindernes Kökken), where breakfast may be had at prices varying from twenty to fifty öre, dinner from forty-five öre, and other refreshments at the same rate. The meals are decently served, the characteristic paper serviette is never wanting, and the management seems excellent.

The Kvindelig Læseforening, or Women's Reading Society, is an institution something between a club and a library, to which we have no exact parallel. It consists of a lending library, reading-room, newspaper-room, and *salon de conversation*, where members may meet their friends and even partake of refreshments ordered from a neighbouring restaurant. The members meet once a year to decide upon what new books shall be ordered. Lectures are also given here occasionally. The library of about 30,000 volumes consists of the works of authors of all nations, and the choice is extremely liberal, ranging from the works of classic writers to the latest outpourings of Marie Corelli and Ouida. Candidates are elected by a majority of the members, and enjoy all the advantages of the institution on payment of ten crowns a year; strangers are also admitted to membership for three weeks on payment of one crown.

It is not uncommon for women to earn their living as carpenters and wood-carvers. They serve a regular apprenticeship; in one case I know of, a girl was purposely made to do the heaviest work of the shop, fetch beer for the men, carry heavy planks, etc., but I am glad to add she surmounted the jealousy of the other sex and now makes an excellent livelihood as a wood-carver and carpenter.

The theatre plays a much more important part in Danish popular life than similar institutions in any other country; the dramas of Ewald and Oehlenschläger have rendered it a veritable school of patriotism, to which foreign elements are entirely subservient; the motto of the National Theatre, "Ej blot til Lyst" (not only for pleasure), denotes its more extensive scope and elevated aim. The works of Holberg, Heiberg, and Hostrup have influenced Danish life and manners to a very remarkable extent, and elevated the stage from a mere place of amusement to the rank of a national institution.

At the Theatre Royal, the scene of the triumphs of the great native dramatists, operas alternate with comedies, and with that singular product of Danish imagination—the ballet, invented by Bournonville about fifty years ago, at which for three hours at a time, dancing and gesture engross public attention without a word being spoken. The great composers, Hartmann and Gade, have written music for these ballets. The subjects are chosen from the Odinic mythology or from the national history; trolls and dwarfs run riot underground, the youthful knight wandering in the forest is surrounded by Elvepiger or fairies, which represent the rising mists and gradually envelop him, and other poetical and innocent conceits are enacted, which an English audience would scarcely sit out, but which to the simpler Dane, animated with patriotism, are of vital interest, for he loves his country dearly, and all its associations and legends are for him sacred and inviolable.

Tickets are cheap, the hours are early, and evening dress unnecessary—a Danish lady's theatre toilette being simply a high dress with white collar and cuffs.

The Danes are essentially a pleasure-loving people, though to a stranger they seem to take their pleasure rather solemnly; one has only to see them as they pour forth in their thousands on Sunday to visit the various places of amusement, or gather wild flowers and green boughs from the newly-budded trees, or dash on their cycles along the smooth and sunny roads (all Denmark is a-wheel to-day), each in his or her Sunday best, good-humour beaming from their broad and honest countenances, to verify the fact. Naturally, therefore, Copenhagen boasts of many places of amusement not all of the highest class. At the Cirkus-Varieté and at the Scala are variety entertainments with very little variety; singing, dancing, performances of animals, gymnastic feats and conjuring go on while the crowd of people sit at little tables drinking their favourite national beverage and eating everlasting "smörrebröd" as sellers of flowers and newspapers pass to and fro. To beguile the intervals at the former place a curtain descends covered with advertisements which may be read at a distance; personally, I did not find it added to my enjoyment to learn the address of a cheap dentist, or the merits of the last patent medicine, as I listened to the strains of Lumbye's latest galop, and waited for the next *danseuse* to kick the back of her head, or the turn of the next wretched animal denaturalised for the amusement of his human torturers. On the whole these entertainments are only worthy of the lowest music-halls, and to those who know London and Paris scarcely worthy of a visit.

More curious, because to be taken less seriously, is Sommerlyst, chiefly patronised by artizans and small shopkeepers, where, indoors in winter and out of doors in summer, a variety of entertainments are always in full swing. Here I once saw three stout and lusty Danes, bursting, the lady as well as the gentlemen, out of little terra-cotta-coloured jackets and unmentionables, with tiny black caps worn very much on one side (supposed to be particularly characteristic of Italy), go through part of "Trovatore" to the deafening roar of a bad piano thumped by a stalwart and perspiring musician. If the reader can imagine Leonora sighing out her passion in the costume I have described, Manrico and the Conte di Luna roaring at each other in bad Italian, and the noise of the violent pianist mingled with the fumes of beer and tobacco, he will have some idea of the delights of Sommerlyst. Old men and women looked solemnly on at this entertainment, young men and maidens almost wept and seized each other by the hand, as it were involuntarily, at the pathetic parts; not a word interrupted the grotesque performance, and the whole audience seemed gratified as they gazed across their glasses or athwart the smoke. These performances are long, between thirty and thirty-five numbers being given. Time is not of much consequence to the leisurely Dane, and he will calmly and contentedly sit out the whole.

As summer advances the wealthier citizens of Copenhagen sensibly pour into the country, and the theatres are closed. But Tivoli, a place of amusement without parallel in any other country, is opened, and is the delight of every true son and daughter of the city, with whom it reckons as something national and indispensable. This is a large pleasure-garden situated in the middle of the town, and here the people crowd to listen to the music of bands, look at performing acrobats and jugglers, rope-dancers, animal-trainers, athletes and clowns, eat suppers and amuse themselves generally. The establishment possesses two large concert-rooms, in one of which excellent renderings of orchestral and vocal music are given; the other is devoted to music of a popular character. The open-air theatre, where pantomimes are performed, and Pierrot, Harlequin and Columbine run riot in harmless revelry, always attracts a large audience. The curtain is represented by a huge peacock, which shuts the spread feathers of its tail and sinks beneath the stage as the band commences the music accompanying the performance, which, like the ballets at the Royal Theatre, consists solely of mimicry. The theme generally touches the national superstitions; in one that I remember, "Cassander's Matrimonial Agency, or Harlequin as a Father," a stork brought a baby on its back, which is one of the supposed offices of that useful bird, and gnomes filled sacks with money to enable Harlequin to marry Columbine, naturally the lady of his choice. Pierrot is the darling of the public and never fails to awaken their liveliest sympathy and heartiest laughter. The place is seen to greatest advantage on Sundays and public holidays, when young and old, rich and poor, high and low, drawn thither by the same attractions, meet their friends, join in good-humoured gaiety, and fill the numerous restaurants. The doors open with a salute of cannon at four o'clock; from then to twelve the illuminated garden is a scene of healthful amusement and festivity; healthful because in fresh air under green trees, where the Dane loves best to take his pleasure when at all possible.

The Skydebane or Shooting Club, of which the King of England is a member, includes among other personages the King and late Queen, the Czar of Russia and Queen Alexandra. Thorvaldsen, Oehlenschläger, Oersted and other celebrities were members of this society, which has been in existence upwards of four hundred years. The large and fine rooms in Vesterbrogade are covered with 1400 shields painted with appropriate emblems and the names of the members; for instance, there is one which belonged to a certain tenor whose voice reached the upper B, and who is represented pointing proudly to that note written on the sky!

CHAPTER XX

COPENHAGEN — THORVALDSEN'S MUSEUM— SCULPTURE, PAINTING AND ARCHITECTURE

> "The Danes and English are wonderfully alike; neither people can pretend to art instincts as sensitive or subtle as those of the Italians or the French, but yet in recompense are granted honesty, truth, industry and the soundest common sense. On a basis thus solid it is possible to rear a national art, which, if not fraught with brilliant genius, may reflect nature faithfully and respond to the aspirations of the people."
>
> W. B. ATKINSON.

To write of Copenhagen without including Thorvaldsen would be more inapt than to write of Rome without mentioning Raphael, of Florence without Michael Angelo, of Siena without Sodoma. All these great men are completely and indissolubly identified with the scenes of their artistic careers, but not one of them is so intimately associated with his nation's fame, not one of them so absolutely the idol of his countrymen as Thorvaldsen the great Danish sculptor. There is not a Dane among them all who does not feel a thrill of pride at the mere mention of the artist's name, and as if his glory were not of his own.

That Denmark has produced excellent sculptors and but mediocre painters is a singular fact for which there seems no adequate explanation. Thorvaldsen, Bissen, Jerichau are three great names in the history of this refined art, and though the style of the first is too cold and classical to suit the taste of the day, and the two latter are not well-known out of their own country, it would be difficult to find three sculptors of equal merit anywhere but in the most highly cultivated and artistic nations. It might be urged that the sombre hues of the north attune the mind rather to the calm severity of sculpture than to the glowing tints of the painter's art, did we not remember that Rembrandt and the old Dutch masters were, with the single exception of the Venetians, the greatest colourists the world has ever seen. Another cause must therefore be sought.

Bertel Thorvaldsen was born in Copenhagen in 1770, and, like many another artist of the Scandinavian School, was of peasant origin. As he showed great promise when a student, a subscription was raised to enable him to continue his studies in Rome, then the art-centre of the world, and the Danish Academy, which does so much to assist native talent, awarded him a pension. In Rome he lived for twenty-three years without returning to his native country;

he was accustomed to say that he dated his birth from the first day he saw the Eternal City. Here he worked in the studio which had once been Flaxman's; Canova, then in the zenith of his fame, and the Englishmen, Gibson and Wyatt, were his contemporaries. Living as they did under the influence of the classical statues with which Rome is peopled, many of which were being unearthed day by day from the teeming soil, it was natural that these artists should draw their inspiration from their immortal charms, and believe that to create something which should resemble them was the highest aim of art. Canova, Gibson and Thorvaldsen, indeed, pushed their adulation of the antique to its extreme limits, the consequence being that their productions have but little interest for us who live in the days of that uneclectic and blatant realism which is due to French initiative. Yet there is a great deal which is beautiful and worthy of study in the works of these artists—works which will live when much of our popular art shall have perished. Thorvaldsen was sincere according to his light, though not sufficiently great to escape the tendency of his age; he was led captive where a more original genius would have been conqueror. He was accustomed to insist on the absolute perfection of Greek art, and, it is said, used to walk through the galleries of the Vatican as one lost in reverie.

Thorvaldsen last returned to Copenhagen two years before he died, and his native city outdid itself in efforts to do honour to its famous son. His journey was like the home-coming of some victorious general or beloved monarch, processions were organised, flags unfurled, poems written by the most renowned poets, and wreaths showered on the unappreciative sculptor; never in the annals of the world has an artist received such an ovation, which does equal credit to the Danish nation and to him who was deemed worthy of it.

His museum, which is one of the principal attractions of the city, was built partly by public subscription and partly by the community of Copenhagen. It was commenced in the artist's lifetime, and he bequeathed to it his models and art collections: it is the only example of a complete collection of the works of an artist in the midst of which is his tomb, and is, moreover, a wonderful example of how much may be produced in a single lifetime by continual labour. Like Omar Khayyam, Thorvaldsen used to say he wished to have roses growing over his grave, but his wish has not been gratified; the vault which contains his remains is covered with ivy instead.

The architecture of the building is borrowed from old Egyptian and Greek sepulchral buildings. The " Victory " in the chariot over the entrance was a present from Christian VIII., and the much-damaged paintings on the exterior represent Thorvaldsen's arrival at Copenhagen in 1838, when, after an absence of eighteen years, he returned in a vessel sent out to bring back a great part of the works destined for this museum.

In the vestibule are the models of a number of colossal monuments executed by the sculptor, among which those of Pius VII. for St Peter's, Rome, and of Maximilian I., Elector of Bavaria, are the most satisfactory. The corridors contain numerous busts and reliefs. Thorvaldsen's portraits are not excellent examples of that branch of art, but some of his reliefs are very fine, for example, the "Triumph of Alexander," executed for the palace of Christiansborg, and the well-known "Night," a flying angel bending over two sleeping babes which she carries in her arms—a most tender and poetical rendering of a lovely subject. The "Morning," too, is graceful, but the subject has not equal pathos. Looking at these works the glamour of the old artist's genius falls upon us, and we realise that he was not unworthy of the immense fame which he succeeded in achieving.

The "Christus Hall" contains the original models for the marble Christ and Apostles, to see which at their best we must go to the Fruenkirche, for which they were made.

In the fourth room "Venus with the Apple" claims attention, but her attitude is wanting in the grace and simplicity of the antique rendering of a subject which every sculptor in Thorvaldsen's time thought it necessary to essay. They failed to realise that the belief and thought, of which the unapproachable sculpture of the Greeks was the

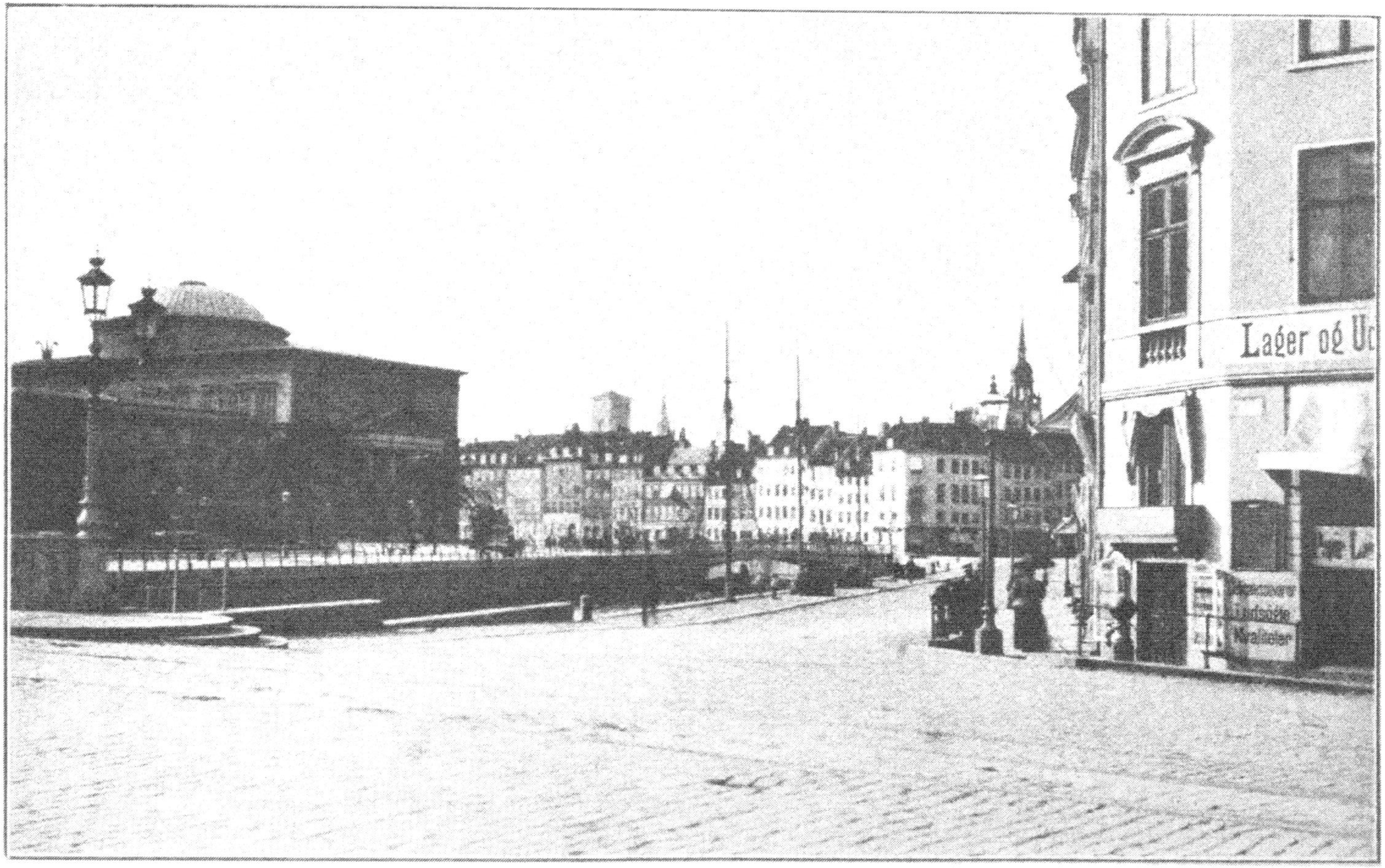
Lager og U

natural outcome, were forever dead, and that works produced under entirely different conditions could only be imitative, and imitations never appeal to the feelings. "Without sincerity of emotion," says a great authority—Lord Leighton,—"no gift, however facile and specious, will avail you to win the lasting sympathies of men."

"Jason," in the fifth room, is one of the best pseudo-classical figures of our time, and is probably the sculptor's finest mythological work. Commissioned in marble by an Englishman, Mr Hope, just as Thorvaldsen was packing up the contents of his studio with the idea of abandoning Rome and returning unsuccessful to Copenhagen, it marks the turning-point of his long and fruitful career.

The draped "Hebe" in the next room is a very graceful figure of a girl.

"Mercury" in room X is not unworthy of the sculptor of the "Jason."

Of course the original model for the statue of Byron at Cambridge is included in the collection. H. C. Andersen relates that, when Thorvaldsen was modelling this statue, Byron commenced to put on an entirely different countenance from that habitual to him. "You must not make these grimaces, my lord," said the artist, and continued his work. When Byron himself saw it he said, "It does not resemble me at all, I look unhappy." "He was above all things so desirous of looking extremely unhappy," added Thorvaldsen.

The sculptor's statue of himself, though interesting, is not equal to many of his other works; the face is dignified but the head and torso are far too colossal for the pitiful little legs which support them.

Thorvaldsen's Museum is also enriched with collections of pictures, gems and curios made by him in Italy, and the furniture of his house in Copenhagen.

My reason for taking the unusual course of giving sculpture instead of painting the precedence is, that Denmark has hitherto produced more remarkable sculptors than it has painters. It will be best here to conclude the subject.

Vilhelm Bissen was born in Slesvig in 1798. He had some little success in his native country, but the example and glory of Thorvaldsen inflamed the imagination of the young Dane, and, like him, he set out for Rome. The great sculptor, then at the summit of his glory, admitted his countryman to his studio; but though the younger man well knew the value of the elder's friendship and advice, he preferred to work alone. Through Thorvaldsen's influence, who had himself too much to do, Bissen received the commission for the fine group of Gutenburg and Faust at Mayence. He soon after returned to Copenhagen, where he executed the great frieze in the Hall of the Knights, and statues of Danish Queens in the palace of Christiansborg (which were destroyed by the fire of 1884), the equestrian statue of Frederick VII. which still stands to excite our admiration, and the bronze statues of Holberg and

Oehlenschläger in front of the National Theatre. His best work is that, however, in which he has departed farthest from the traditions of the classical school—the pathetic "Danske Landsoldat" erected at Fredericia to commemorate Danish victories over the Germans in the unfortunate Slesvig-Holstein war. His biographer, Eugene Plon, to whom I owe some of these particulars, concludes his life of Bissen with the encomium, "*L'œuvre de l'artiste autant que l'existence de l'homme impose l'estime et le respect.*"

The Danish sculptor Jerichau's fine works, the "Hunter and Panther," and "Hercules and Hebe," are well-known in England, and can bear comparison with any work of their class.

As I have before said, the Danes' record in painting is not so good as in sculpture.*

The Academy of Fine Arts was founded in 1754, and the painter Abilgaard, Thorvaldsen's earliest teacher, who had studied in Paris under David, was appointed President, and thus the hard, dry manner of the great Frenchman inspired the first development of Danish art; this influence was of long duration. At the same period Jens Juel, a portrait-painter of considerable merit, flourished. C. V. Eckersberg (1783-1853), called the Turner of Denmark, is regarded by the Danes as the real founder of their school, and he too had studied in the classic school of France. Lundbye,

---

* A careful examination of the Danish Fine Arts Section in the last exhibition in Paris has strengthened this opinion.

Skovgaard, Sonne, Dalsgaard, Vehmehren and Exner painted landscapes and subjects from peasant life in the same manner. Marstrand was a more powerful genius, whose pictures of subjects from Danish history have great merit; two of his largest works may be seen in the Cathedral of Roskilde, and are equal to any painting of the same date. In Carl Bloch Denmark possessed an artist of real power and great feeling; his pictures of the life of Christ in the chapel at Frederiksborg, and the grand altar-piece in Holbœk Church by him, are full of profound religious sentiment, while his " Samson grinding at the Mill," and "King Christian II. in Prison," have equal claims to our admiration as religious and historical works. Bloch and Anton Melbye in a small measure bridge over what Julius Lange, the well-known art critic, justly calls "the abrupt break in the development of Danish national art made by Kröyer, Tuxen, and others."

Otto Bache is a portrait-painter of the old school of no mean power. Michael Anker, born in the Island of Bornholm, and his wife, Anna Anker, devote themselves to painting Danish seamen. In 1880 Anker was awarded the highest honours of the Academy of Arts, both at Copenhagen and Berlin, for his great picture, "Will She clear the Point?" which has been placed among the masterpieces of Danish art in the National Gallery at Copenhagen. P. S. Kröyer is undoubtedly the head of the new school of Danish painters, his study under Bonnat having enabled him to break with the traditions of his predecessors and attain that spontaneity and breadth of colouring which distinguish his work and which have gained for him the medal of honour at the great Exhibition in Paris of 1900. Unhappily this great artist is now suffering from the same terrible malady which darkened the last days of Munkacsy; his whole nation is interested in his recovery, and as he is only in the zenith of his age and his powers, there is ample reason to hope it.* Professor Tuxen is a powerful portrait-painter much patronised by royalty and the upper classes. Ole Pedersen died too young to have produced much; the little he has left is characterised by great delicacy of colouring and sincerity of purpose.

Possessing like ourselves an Academy of Fine Arts, the Danes also naturally have a society of reactionary artists composed of those whose works have been systematically rejected from the annual exhibitions of the older institution, and who have organised an exhibition for themselves, the " Freie Udstilling." At the exhibitions of the former, held in the old palace of Charlottenborg, between 600 and 700 works of art are annually shown, and are well hung and well lighted. The sculpture shows slight evidence of French training, but, curiously enough, the painting has not undergone

* As I write the last lines of this book the good news reaches me that Kröyer is restored to health, and has returned to his home at Skagen. The cause of the malady was overwork.

that influence which has of late years so powerfully affected every other school. Here it may be seen that in painting the Danes are still behind most other nations, though in sculpture and literature they are so conspicuously excellent.

The modern Danish painter is content with the slightest of subjects chosen without effort, or with an affectation of simplicity, which is really the result of much labour; these he renders with more feeling and sentiment than knowledge of technique. He naturally loves low and tender tones; the glory of sunshine and colour does not appeal to him. However, the Danish is already the best of the three Scandinavian schools, and if it continue to retain its marked individuality, and to keep aloof from foreign influence, it has possibly a great future before it. Some of the younger men, it is noticeable, are entirely self-taught, and so are able to look straight into the eyes of Nature without the interposition of a conventional education. Of these I shall write in my notice of two private collections of pictures where their work is best seen; for some of the citizens of Copenhagen, to their credit be it said, have a pronounced taste for buying pictures, and patronise almost exclusively the productions of their own countrymen.

In the Exhibition of 1900 at Charlottenborg the pictures were well hung in a single line; an academical portrait of the late Queen by Otto Bache, and a picture of the Diamond Jubilee of Queen Victoria by L. Tuxen were noteworthy works. The Free Exhibition did not seem to me to justify its existence. I can only compare it to the Grosvenor Gallery in its "greenery yellowy" days, or the Gallery of impressionist works in the Luxembourg; however, it has its admirers.

The Gallery of pictures accumulated by Mr Hirschsprung consists exclusively of works by Danish artists, nearly all of whom are represented, from Eckersberg, with his hard marine subjects, to the last productions of the original painter, Hammershoj. One room is entirely devoted to the paintings of Marstrand, whose illustrations of the comedies of Holberg have much of the spirit of the plays themselves. Besides these, Lundbye and Skovgaard among the ancients, and Kröyer, Zahrtmann, Julius Paulsen, and Viggo Johansen among the moderns, are fully represented. Of Kröyer I have already written; in this interesting collection his progress may be traced from the first dawning of his genius, and his tremendous versatility realised. Zahrtmann is one of the few among Danish painters who is a colourist; the fine pictures of Julius Paulsen are completely French in their technique and choice of subject. Viggo Johansen is among the best of their painters of *genre*, and Hammershoj has a manner entirely his own. This last artist never studied in any school and is in weak health, nearly always the case when a painter confines himself entirely to very low tones; he is a great favourite with a certain clique, who predict for his works wide-spread renown.

Dr Bramsen's collection, accumulated since 1880, is also confined to works by his own countrymen; here the latest and most advanced specimens of their art may be studied. He possesses a masterpiece by Julius Paulsen, "Children being washed," subjects from Skagen by Michael Anker and his wife, and pictures by Philipsen, the only Dane who can be numbered among the impressionists. Dr Bramsen was one of the first to become a patron of Hammershoj, and possesses many pictures by him, all distinguished by simplicity and a certain monotony of low tones, which becomes at last irritating.

To both of these admirable collections access may be had by permission of the courteous owners.

In architecture the Danes have never attained excellence. One of their finest buildings, the Castle of Rosenberg, is the work of an Englishman, Inigo Jones. All the principal edifices are in a style somewhat akin to the Elizabethan in England, and may be described as that of Christian IV. In this style also is Frederiksborg, which is imposing from its size and position, and the Exchange, with its quaint dragon-spire, and the most picturesque of all the time-mellowed brickworn buildings in Copenhagen. The churches in Copenhagen are ugly, and the searcher after the picturesque will have to be content with the quaint old houses which still remain. "The palaces," says Ferguson, "are large, and it may be convenient buildings, but pretend to nothing more."

But perhaps a better era is dawning. The new Town Hall, by Martin Nyrop, only just now completed, has awakened quite a furore of admiration among the Danes. The great tower dwarfs all the spires in Copenhagen; the "Guild Hall" is decorated in the style of the Italian Renaissance. On three sides are open galleries supported by pillars, the portals are very fine, and the grandeur of the main *façade* is enhanced by the castellated wall which rises above the roof, flanked by two small towers. In front of this wall is a flat open space protected by a balustrade supporting a row of life-size gilt figures.

CHAPTER XXI

COPENHAGEN—MUSEUMS

THE National Museum of Copenhagen is of great and unusual interest, not so much on account of its size and variety as for its completeness and perfection of arrangement, due to the energy of the two great scientists, C. J. Thomsen and J. J. A. Worsaae, and to the liberal support they received from the State. It is located in the Prindsens Palais, which, as its name indicates, was once a royal residence, and consists of the Old North Collection, the Ethnographical Collection, the Collection of Classic Antiquities, the Royal Collection of Engravings, and the Royal Collection of Coins and Medals.

A hint for the visitor to Denmark: he must never be afraid to open the doors of museums, offices and shops, which are generally kept shut with a notice on them to the effect that they " are open" or that they "shut themselves." Unfortunately there is no catalogue of the museum either in English or French, and I think I do a service to the Danes in calling their attention to this very inconvenient fact; entrance is free, the arrangements so excellent that no object in the collection can be missed, and it is impossible to go any way but the way one should.

The Ethnographic Museum illustrates the civilisation of the various nations outside Scandinavia. Greenland naturally is particularly well represented by many native-made models, tents, boats, fishing apparatus, etc.; the North American Indian department is also very rich. Africa, Java, Japan, China, the Indian Archipelago, Guinea and many another land have been laid under contribution to render this one of the finest collections of the kind in the world.

The best of the collections and one of the chief glories of Copenhagen is the Museum of Northern Antiquities, founded in 1807, when similar collections were unknown in other parts of Europe; it was brought to its present perfection by C. J. Thomsen, who has here carried out his theory, now so universally accepted, of characterising the three stages of civilisation by their use respectively of stone, bronze, and iron. It contains more than 70,000 objects, and these are being continually added to, owing to the liberality of the Government, which pays the finders of articles of precious metal the full value if they are offered to the museum.

At the entrance are some runic stones; the first room (Age of Rough Stone) contains objects from the kitchen-middens (Kjökken möddinger) or refuse from the meals of the ancient inhabitants of the country, and some very rude stone axes, daggers, and spear-heads. In the third room (Age of Polished Stone) is a collection of amber ornaments, by which it seems that the first care of man, after providing for his sustenance and defence, was to adorn his person.

The room containing objects of the Age of Bronze (to A.D. 250) is particularly interesting. Here should be remarked swords and ornaments of excellent manufacture; the first known garments (of woven woollen material) preserved on bodies buried in coffins hollowed by fire out of trunks of trees; "lure," or peculiar long war trumpets, of which twenty have been found; a magnificent chariot made of wood overlaid with plaques of brass, and some fine wooden shields.

The Early Iron Age (A.D. 250 to 450) exhibits Roman influence, though how that came about does not seem clearly indicated. Silver and glass objects appear, and a rough wooden plough, much like those still used by the natives of Palestine, is preserved. Here is also a find from the oldest royal grave in Denmark, that of King Gorm at Jellinge; as the mound had been previously rifled but little remained for scientific explorers. In the next room, amid many others, are the two celebrated golden drinking horns which were found at Gallehus in Slesvig; unfortunately these are not the originals, which were stolen in 1802 by a goldsmith who had access to the collection and who melted them down, but are reconstructions partly from drawings, and partly from a model in ivory, which was a gift from a Danish king to a Russian Emperor, preserved in the

Hermitage at Petersburg. They consist of an internal tube of gold of inferior quality, outside which is another divided by rings twisted round gold plates. On them are soldered figures representing grotesque men and animals, but no one has yet succeeded in interpreting their symbolism.

The Early Middle Ages (A.D. 1000 to 1250) are illustrated in the upper rooms, which unfortunately are not numbered. Amid many other objects of interest they contain the Dagmar Cross, which belonged to the Queen of Valdemar I.; it is of Byzantine enamel and was found in her grave at Ringsted; an exact copy, with a small portion of the relics it contains, was given to Queen Alexandra on her marriage by King Frederick VII. A reliquary in the shape of an arm, still containing the bone, belonged to King Olaf of Norway, who fell at the battle of Stiklested in 1030. The altar frontals of wood overlaid with gilt copper are, I believe, characteristic of Danish art; one bears the date MCXXIII; on another is a picture of the angel Gabriel drinking out of an ale horn after making his announcement to the Virgin, who is occupied in caressing a foal. The swords in this room are very fine, so also are the antique Church vestments and Norwegian and Icelandic crowns. A huge wooden group, representing the favourite subject of St George and the Dragon, occupies a conspicuous place. In other rooms objects of the period of the Renaissance are arranged—the great national hero's (Tordens kiold) patent of nobility, sword, pistols, autograph, etc., and Tycho Brahe's watch, dated 1597.

The Royal Collection of Engravings contains drawings by Albert Dürer, Marcantonio Raimondi and many Danish painters.

The Collection of Coins and Medals, though including no unique specimens, is remarkable for its universality.

The magnificent art collections formed by Mr Carl Jacobsen, the rich brewer, who may appropriately be called the Tate of Denmark, and Ottilie, his wife, were originally installed in 1888 in a beautiful little building at Frederiksberg named, after his celebrated beer, Carlsberg. When he resolved to present his collection of modern sculpture to the nation, he built the magnificent building called the Ny Glyptothek, which now contains the finest exhibition of modern sculpture in Scandinavia, and presented it to the nation. The remainder of his acquisitions are still in their old place, called the Gamle Carlsberg Glyptothek.

In the Ny Glyptothek we have proof of the Dane's genius for sculpture rather than for painting, for that passionless expression of beauty which resembles the purity of their northern snows rather than for the glow and warmth of painting which is the natural outcome of life amid the sun and colour of the south. It is interesting also to compare here the finest productions of the old Danish sculptors with those of modern French artists, whose influence seems about to reduce or elevate all schools of art to the same uniform level.

As Thorvaldsen and his followers were almost of necessity copiers and imitators of the Greeks and of Canova, so of almost equal necessity modern sculptors are imitators of the great Frenchmen who have known how to regard Nature with an eye untrammelled by the rules of the antique, and so created a new school of sculpture which may be studied here better than anywhere else, except in Paris, as it contains works by Chapu, Falguiére, Dubois, Barrias, etc. But the correctness and coldness of the Greek has appealed most clearly to the Dane; he still adores his great countryman Thorvaldsen, and sees in his work the expression of his own sentiments; the magnificent voluptuousness and genius of modern French sculpture has not yet exercised its dominating influence over him. As it is in art, so it is in life and literature; the Danes of the older generation still retain their honest virtues and their simplicity. A generation has yet to come before that influence, beneath which most civilisations have already bowed, the modern French, shall be, as in art, omnipotent, and as in life, and perhaps in literature, corruptive. From this it may be gathered also that Denmark is still behind England, Germany and other countries in the modern struggle for luxury and extravagance. Germany, which so long influenced completely the little kingdom, has ceased to be a power there owing to the bitterness engendered by the Slesvig-Holstein campaign, and the reaction is towards the imitation of England and of things English.

The Ny Glyptothek is "open to all," on two

days of the week it is free; the rooms with their mosaic pavements, marble columns and profuse decorations are magnificent. A series of galleries is devoted to Danish sculpture, where the pseudo-classical works of Bissen and Jerichau, followers of the school of Thorvaldsen, may be thoroughly studied. Bissen's work greatly resembles that of his predecessor Thorvaldsen; his best productions here are the figures of the "Indignant Achilles," a "Bathing Girl" and a "Flower Girl." Jerichau feebly endeavoured to withdraw himself from the overwhelming influence of the ancient Greeks and of Canova, to which both Thorvaldsen and Bissen owed their inspiration; consequently his work, though not so successful, has more originality than that of the two earlier masters.

Among the sculptures are a reproduction of Leighton's "Athlete," which might itself have been the work of a Dane, and his bust by Brock.

In the rooms devoted to French sculpture we have some of the finest works produced by the modern French school. Barrias is represented among many other statues by his magnificent "Spartacus" and "First Funeral," Dubois by his "Eve" and "Florentine," and Chapu by his "Joan of Arc," "Princess of Wales," and "Princess Dagmar." Falguiére, Mercier and other artists are also well represented.

The upper floor is occupied by a small picture-gallery, which includes paintings by Bouguereau, Kröyer (the greatest painter Denmark has yet produced), Otto Bache (an equestrian portrait of the King), a "Beggar" by Bastian Lepage, Millet's celebrated "Death and the Wood-cutter," several royal portraits by Tuxen, and a well-known Rembrandt (a boy reading); Jacobsen has also been fortunate in securing one of the rare works of Spanish sculpture, "A Monk reading," by Alonzo Cano. Altogether this grand collection of works of art does infinite credit to the generous donor, and to the city which has the good fortune to possess it.

The Gamle Carlsberg Glyptothek is devoted to antiquities, many of which are unique, but it is not to be expected that any collector in our own days should become the happy possessor of *chefs d'œuvre* such as adorn the galleries of older formation. Still, Mr Jacobsen has been fortunate in securing some very fine specimens of Greek sculpture, and of the art of most ancient civilisations. Unfortunately, at present the rooms are not numbered, and there is no catalogue except in Danish.

The galleries are fine, the mosaic floors magnificent; round most of the rooms run friezes representing scenes from Greek or Scandinavian mythology. I only mention a few objects among the many of which the collection consists. In the entrance hall are two colossal lions; the room beyond contains a fine marble Amazon said to be by Polycletes, statues of Jupiter, Apollo, certain of the Muses, and other works, probably Greco-Roman. In a smaller room further on is an early Greek draped female figure, and a number of small busts, and in yet another decorated with a frieze, the subject of which is the "Twilight of the Gods," by Freund, are a Greek altar, and a draped female figure strongly resembling the Venus of Milo. Passing, between two caryatids and ascending a few steps we reach the vestibule which contains casts of the marble statues of the two Princesses which have now found places in the Ny Glyptothek. The apse, with its fountain lined with verdant maiden-hair fern, its marble columns and cushions thrown on the floor for seats, forms a charming vista. Turning to the right we enter a long room with a good marble vase in the centre, and the fragment of a draped female figure, probably of the finest period of Greek art. Opening out of this is the Empress Saloon, round which are placed some good examples of Greek sarcophagi, and statues of emperors and empresses; one of the ladies has had the bad taste to cause herself to be represented in the character of Venus and yet to retain her very tightly-curled wig! In the centre of this room is a good example of antique mosaic. A series of cabinets follows, one containing a singularly graceful marble fragment of a girl's back, and a number of Tanagra figures; another, the largest collection in existence of busts and antiquities from Palmyra, which is of exceptional interest. The room devoted to Egyptian antiquities contains interesting specimens of granite sphinxes, statuettes, mummies, a statue of Anubis in black granite, a head of Ammon Ra, Osiris in red granite, a group of a prince and his mother, and vases of alabaster.

To the left of the entrance is a room containing Roman busts, a noble draped female figure, and a kneeling slave in porphyry; another with numerous busts, a red porphyry hippopotamus, and a granite bath; and further on another collection of busts, of marble columns, and a group of "Bacchus and a Satyr." A lower room is devoted to Etruscan antiquities from tombs at Vulci, Cervetri and Chiusi; here are stone coffins with figures on the top holding vases in their hands as if to indicate that they had drained the cup of life to the dregs; one figure from Città della Pieve still retains traces of painting and gilding. The happy idea of decorating this room with copies of paintings taken from Etruscan tombs has been well carried out; those mysterious and vivid pictures which none may understand and which time surely steals from us when we have at last discovered them. A small room containing fragments completes this interesting collection.

Near the Ny Glyptothek is the Danish Industrial Art Museum where fine specimens of wood-carving, mostly German, iron-work, watches, furniture, Ceramic ware, musical instruments, silversmiths' work, glass, engraving, and bookbinding may be studied. It possesses also a beautiful collection of "vieux Danois" porcelain, from the manufactory, founded in 1775 by F. H. Muller, which a few years afterwards became the Royal Copenhagen Porcelain Manufactory.

The traveller really interested in the rough and picturesque remains of the times which succeeded the still rougher days of the Vikings should not fail to visit the Danish Folk Museum, an offspring of the Historical Exhibition held in Copenhagen in 1879. On account of the interest in peasant life awakened by this section, it was determined to carry it on in a permanent form; the present collection is the result, and though much crowded for want of space, it contains many objects of extreme interest.

Certain rooms are arranged as rooms were several hundreds of years ago, and fully illustrate the home life of the inhabitants of Holstein, Aalborg, Samsö, Mid Zealand, North Zealand, and Rosnoes in Scania; the long narrow tables with their cloths, the seats beside them, fireplaces looking as if the fire was just extinguished, the crockery on the shelves, old Bibles opened as if the readers had just risen from their perusal, quaint wardrobes, cradles, clocks, warming-pans, all are in their places; especially curious are the carved bedsteads resembling those of Brittany, to be shut in which must have been to be nearly suffocated, and the carved boards with handles used by the old housewives to smooth their linen. The place has rather the air of a series of old-fashioned rooms than of a museum. Unfortunately here, as elsewhere, there is no catalogue in English. The Danes do not take any special pains to render their country attractive to strangers, which is one of the reasons why it still retains its almost primitive charm; still, I think they would do well to endeavour to attract to their far healthier and less overcrowded shores the English travellers to whom, for obvious reasons, France and the Riviera are for a time less agreeable than they might be.

The most interesting building in Copenhagen is the Palace of Rosenborg, founded by Christian IV. and partly designed by the King himself. After its completion in 1624 the castle, which is built in the style of the Dutch Renaissance known in Denmark as that of Christian IV., served as a residence for the royal family. Since the time of Frederick III. it has been used as a royal museum, thus carrying on chronologically the collection of historical treasures from where the Ethnographical Museum leaves off. The pointed towers and gables of the old castle rise picturesquely from masses of tree foliage and curious old houses. For the convenience of the visitor it may be added that the director who conducts parties through the rooms gives an admirable description of its varied and most interesting contents in English if desired. An English catalogue may also be had.

The lower rooms date from the period of Christian IV. and are still just as he left them. After passing through an ante-chamber, the visitor enters a room, the walls of which are painted by various Dutch artists, where he may see the sword of Tordenskiold, and the celebrated horn of Oldenburg. An old legend relates about this horn that one day in the year 989 it was handed, filled with a refreshing beverage, to Duke Otto I. of Oldenburg, who had lost his way and was thirsty, by a nymph who stepped out of a mountain to do so. The fact probably is that it was made in 1474 for Christian I., who vowed to present it to the Cathedral of Cologne if he won a certain battle; as victory however did not attend his arms, the King judiciously retained the horn. If this be so, we get an explanation of its symbolism, of the towers and battlements on the lid, and of the six shields bearing the three Danish lions, the Papal mitre, the German eagle, the Brabant lion, the Flemish lion and the Burgundian lilies. Cologne was, moreover, the city of the Three Holy Kings, and their names are also found on the horn.

The next room, where rococo and renaissance ornament are blended, was the King's study; there is a peephole in the door through which he was accustomed to survey his visitors; his writing-table is as he left it. It also contains, among other objects of interest, a silver fountain six feet high for washing hands, with a reservoir for rose water above, and a jewel-box of silver presented by Queen Anne of England to Queen Sophia Amelia of Denmark; through large crystals in the lid and sides light is thrown on the beautifully-chased bottom, and the whole is covered with diamonds. Sumptuous, too, are a saddle and bridle covered with pearls and diamonds which were presents from Christian IV. to his son on the latter's marriage; a curious brass figure of that King on horseback, which takes to pieces and forms drinking cups, also stands here. The furniture is of the period, black wood inlaid with silver.

In the dark room which adjoins, Christian IV. died. Beyond is a bedroom with a very fine ceiling, some cups made of tusks of the narwhal, a material which is worth its weight in silver, and the "Wismar cup" of worked crystal, one of the finest objects of the kind in the world.

In the next room we have a specimen of pure rococo—a style which comes so near being beautiful and yet is so irritatingly bad; the unpleasant ceiling is of carved plaster. Some ivory cups and a large ivory model of a frigate are among the contents.

The great dining-room has a silver screen and plate-warmers in front of the fireplace, and contains also in glass cases costumes worn by various kings and queens. In the corridor are painted shields and portraits in which the Danish family colours, red and yellow, are conspicuous.

On the floor above are the bed of Frederick IV., the fine embroidery of which has been most skilfully restored, and a good portrait of the same monarch by Rigand. On the walls are some very rare and priceless specimens of what may be termed Gobelin appliqué tapestry. The mirror room is a curious freak; in a glass above you get a top view of yourself, in a glass below you seem to be standing at the bottom of a well, while yet you see yourself all round.

The reception-room contains a silver throne used by kings when they administered justice, cups made of porcelain and gold and silver by an art which is now lost, and porcelain cups which, on account of their rarity at the time, were lined with silver to protect them. Here also are the three splendid cups, "Holstein" "Eider" and "Homage"; the first is a family cup, the two latter commemorate the re-union of Slesvig in the reign of Frederick IV. in 1720.

A rococo room follows, wherein stands a huge cabinet piano in which is not a single straight line; it is difficult to imagine anyone having been in the least degree pleased with its tone.

All Danish kings and queens are taught the art of turning, and here is to be seen the lathe of Queen Sophia Magdalene. Some silver-gilt figures of soldiers on camels are toys which have belonged to royal children, a set of the earliest Danish porcelain, and a collection of ninety rings worn by various kings, are in one room; in another are portraits of the unfortunate Caroline Matilda, sister of George III., for whom the Danes have ever a warm place in their hearts, of her insane husband, and of the unhappy Struensee;

Copenhagen—Museums

also a profile portrait made entirely of diamonds. By way of contrast, the cotton umbrella, decidedly of the Gamp pattern, which belonged to Frederick IV. stands in a glass case. The clothes of several kings are still preserved in a room where, standing on a table, are photographic portraits of the Prince and Princess of Wales taken on the occasion of their wedding, and so we are brought from the times of Christian IV. to the present day.

The crowning glory of the Castle of Rosenborg is its magnificent Riddersal or Knights' Hall, one hundred and fifty feet long, still used on State occasions. It is lined with Dutch tapestry of the seventeenth century representing battles with the Swedes; at one end is the silver font in which all Danish royalties are baptised, and at the other a velvet canopy, underneath which stand the coronation chairs of the King and Queen, which are for these occasions removed to Roskilde Cathedral, where the ceremony takes place. Before them three life-sized silver lions, representing the Sound, the Great Belt, and the Little Belt, keep watch and ward.

In a cabinet opening off the Riddersal is an unequalled collection of old Venetian glass, which comprises specimens of thread glass and that unequalled ruby glass, the making of which is now a lost art. The arrangement of this glass is exquisite and original. Another cabinet contains a collection of porcelain, among them that which is called Flora Danica, each piece of which is adorned with a Danish flower beautifully painted and named.

The old gardens of Rosenborg are a favourite resort of the Danes, for though Christian IV. built his castle outside the walls as a place of retirement, it is now engulfed in the city itself.

The New Picture Gallery opened in 1896 does for painting what the Glyptothek does for sculpture, by offering an opportunity for the study of the development of Danish pictorial art from its first early efforts to the present day. Sculpture is also represented there by, among other works, a fine "Susanna" by Saabye, a very modern lady by O. V. Bissen, and a "Discus Thrower" by Hasselriis, while on the ground floor is a fine collection of casts. It is unfortunate that the bronze group which stands in front of the museum is not worthy of the position it occupies.

The building itself is fine, and the entrance, with its broad granite steps and groups of statuary, imposing. The names of the artists are in all cases indicated on the frames of the pictures. The collection of old Masters, chiefly of the Dutch school, does not present any particular interest if we except the Rembrandts, and even they are not fine examples of the master. In the Danish school are works by Eckersberg which one might almost suppose to be copies of David, black and green landscapes by Skovgaard, cattle-pieces by Lundbye, who at least knew how to suffuse his scenes with a radiance which recalls the pictures of Both, and amusing scenes of peasant life by Exner, who excelled in this branch of art. Bloch's large picture, "Christian II. in Prison," where the king is represented walking round the table which he pressed with his thumb and so left a mark on the hard wood, created a great sensation at the time it was first exhibited, and shows a marked advance on the mahogany tones of the same artist's "Samson Grinding at the Mill."

Kröyer is represented by many pictures, among which are two fine paintings of animals; in a "Street in Torella" and "Haymaking in Canto d'Antini" by him we have works glowing with colour and truth worthy of the best efforts of the modern school.

"Cattle" and a "Huntsman and Dogs" by Bache, a landscape which, though soft and dewy, is very green by Edv. Bergh, a portrait by Y. R. Bergh smelling strongly of Paris, a picture of peasants by L. Tuxen, "Cows" by Riis, a "Beech Forest" by Larsen, "A Mining Accident" by Henningsen, full of feeling, in which the northern type of the personages is well-defined, a landscape by Golf. Christensen, and a fine picture of the "Plains of Sardis" by Jacobsen are among the chief treasures of this very interesting collection.

Count Moltke's gallery of pictures of the Dutch school is small but interesting. A portrait of an old woman with shimmering, transparent shadows, by the master-magician, Rembrandt, three Ruysdaels with sombre trees watching over solid water and aggressive foam, a charming little Metzu, in which the sleeping woman's head rivals in tenderness anything this artist has ever produced, some celebrated Teniers and two Greuzes, as sweet and characterless as is usual with this artist, are the most noteworthy works.

And here I wish to pay a tribute to the courtesy and kindness of the Danes, which is but justly due. At the National Museum, seeing I was a stranger interested in the exhibits, one of the staff was good enough to point out those of greatest interest. At the University a professor showed me the rarest codices of the Sagas and other Icelandic MSS. at my simple request, and at Rosenborg, where the ticket costs six kroner and is available for a party of twelve,* a Danish lady who was entering, seeing I was a stranger, invited me to join her party. Would English people have done as much?

* This is no longer the case; tickets of admission may be had at the castle itself for one krone each—1901.

CHAPTER XXII

THE ROYAL PORCELAIN MANUFACTORY—MANUFACTURES AND TRADES

THE originality and elegance of Danish porcelain have deservedly gained for it a world-wide reputation; in fact, it is the best and most characteristic production of the country. "To understand the glorification of which pure porcelain, as a material, is capable, one has only to examine the display of the Royal Copenhagen Manufactory, consisting exclusively of hard porcelain. The ware is a dazzling white, the glaze perfectly tender and clear, the forms are simple to severity and the colours delicate and sweet. Gold is absolutely ignored. The charm of this ware is its perfect simplicity and artistic truth. Upon some pieces the colours have been allowed to flow at the caprice of the fire, others have a wonderful crystalline effect, as of frost upon a window pane."*

Permission to visit the factory is not easily obtained; a slight description of it may therefore prove of interest, for few can look at the beautiful exhibition in Amagertorv without being

* *Pottery Gazette.*

interested in the process by which these quiet and simple forms so delicately decorated are produced.

The principle upon which the art-directors work is that no more should be demanded of the material than it is capable of producing—one style of work is proper to the goldsmith, another to the jeweller, and so forth; but that little must also be the best possible quality. The designers execute their own designs, which are never repeated, but carefully signed and numbered; the manufactory therefore rather resembles a vast studio than a manufactory, and the *employés* are artists rather than workmen. Every pattern is copied from Nature by hand; I saw one girl diligently modelling the claws of a frog, another copying the folds in the skin of a lizard; conventional ornament and printing by machinery are utterly ignored. The Germans have tried to imitate this ware by machinery but unsuccessfully, as even the ordinary blue fluted household crockery is painted by hand in Denmark.

Many women, among them students of the Royal Academy, are happily employed here; they have a good position in society, are paid, comparatively speaking, well, and are at liberty to choose their own subjects for designs. While they work one of their number reads aloud; around them are objects of utility in their art—flowers, birds, fish, casts, and other such things. They study in the garden belonging to the establishment and in the Zoological Gardens almost adjoining, and every year enjoy a holiday of from one to two months, during which they travel to Italy, Spain, etc., to examine the faience of those countries. Their hours are from nine to three, and as the girls sit at their work, copying the natural objects before them, it is apparent that their lives are happy, and that here at least some women have found their right places in existence.

As the courteous director, whose heart and soul seemed in his work, led me from room to room, saluting and being saluted, and introducing each of his numerous *employés* by name, it was easy to realise the social life of the workers of mediæval Italy which rendered possible their wonderful art-productions, and which is so far removed from the manufactory systems of the present day.

The substance of which this porcelain is made is a mixture of feldspar and quartz, found at Kaolin in Norway, ground together. The objects are baked in terra-cotta forms in an oven heated to 800 degrees. The design is then painted on them before glazing, never after; then they are again put in a furnace heated to 2000 degrees. Under the pressure of this tremendous heat many pieces warp or crack. It is considered fortunate if, out of twenty, two or three only are quite perfect; the imperfect are always destroyed. Three colours only can survive this last baking, and even they change a little; from them are produced all the soft grey hues which distinguish this kind of pottery. The secret of the colouring has not been discovered.

As I have said, the very finest specimens cannot be repeated; there is an inferior quality of which several copies are made, but always by hand; the little reproductions of Thorvaldsen's works so common in Denmark are also hand-made. Every piece when finished is numbered and valued. A little vase of the best workmanship is worth about fifty crowns; I saw a coffee service of eight or ten pieces which it had taken five years to bring to perfection, and which was valued at one hundred and fifty crowns. For fifteen years new effects produced by the crystallisation of portions of the *pâte* have been studied, which, when brought to perfection, will be at once novel and beautiful.

One magnificent set of porcelain is called the Flora Danica, because on each piece a different Danish flower is painted and named. China resembling Dresden is also manufactured here. The common blue-fluted or Muschel ware, called by the Danes "Copenhagen china," is, as I have before remarked, also painted by hand; the pattern is an adaptation of a Japanese design.

The mark of the Royal Danish porcelain is three waving lines, which represent the Greater and Lesser Belt and the Sound.

The Royal Manufactory is not alone in producing beautiful specimens of the Ceramic art. Kahlen of Nœstved has brought to perfection a faience whose characteristic lustre-glaze rivals in depth and colouring the metallic glow of the old Spanish-Moorish pottery, and which is original as well as of genuine artistic value.

*The goldsmith's art has attained such perfection as enables it not only to satisfy home requirements, but also to compete in the markets of the world with productions that attract the attention of all interested in such matters. There still exist specimens of original Scandinavian work, such as the Gunderstrup vessel, and the two golden horns of Gallehus. Gold ornaments and money brought by Svend Tveskœg from England and Ireland greatly influenced the goldsmiths' efforts here, as the same countries have also done in later days; the first Danish coins bore the impress of English mint-masters. The influence of Germany succeeded, and its magnificent development may be studied in the Oldenborg horn at Rosenborg Castle. At present, while influenced by the dominating ideas of the art industries of other nations, it preserves in addition a character which is peculiarly Danish.

The export of butter from Denmark, with a population somewhat exceeding two millions, is more than 100,000,000 pounds per annum. The laws against the adulteration of this article are extremely severe; qualified inspectors are appointed by the Home Minister, and infringements of the Act are punished by heavy fines and even imprisonment. It thus happens that in eight

---

* For many of the following facts as to trade and manufactures I am indebted to the Danish *Export Review*.

years only two samples have been found adulterated by two small local dealers. Exhibitions of butter are held monthly at the cost of the Government, in which nearly 50 per cent of the dairies participate; the quality of their goods is thus fairly judged, and they are in this way enabled to remedy the defects. *

In most of the pastoral districts there are co-operative dairies for the manufacture of butter and cheese. To these the farmers bring their milk and cream. Better machinery is used than one farmer alone would be able to procure, and cleanliness, the best methods of work, and skilled supervision combine to render the results as perfect as can be. It is impossible to insist too strongly on the sanitary advantages thus obtained.†

---

* The prevalence of small holdings in Denmark, rendered practicable only by co-operative methods, has checked a steady rural exodus, and turned back the tide of emigration which was flowing to the towns. Though by far the greater area of Denmark is occupied by "peasant farmers," holding less than 100 acres, the tendency increases to cut up even these farms into still smaller holdings, and for every "peasant farmer" there are already two small holders farming from two to eight acres. It is only the product of milk for the co-operative dairy, and of eggs for the co-operative collecting and export agency, which enables these people to live as they do.

A. M. BRICE.

† On an average 150 small farmers combine together to establish a dairy, subscribing between them £1200, that is £8 each, this enough capital for a dairy of 850 cows.

A co-operative society has also been formed for organi collecting for export. Local societies are established al country, whose members engage to deliver fresh eggs. fined £5, 6s. for every bad egg delivered after fair warni

A deduction is also made for dirty eggs, but no w eggs is allowed. The eggs are all marked with t number of the member and the local society, so the s egg can be ascertained.

PROFESSOR DIMOND.

The celebrated "Red Danish" dairy cattle came originally from Slesvig, and are found almost exclusively in the Danish islands.

The method of supplying Copenhagen with milk is extremely well organised; in this matter the Danes are the pioneers of the world. The milk is brought from the farms packed in ice; on its arrival in town its temperature is tested, and all that is not of a certain degree at once rejected: during the night it is filtered through two layers of gravel, and afterwards through several thicknesses of cloth, placed in sterilised bottles, the contents of every one of which is tested by an expert, and sealed before it is delivered to customers.

In the manufacture of beer the Danes have obtained great celebrity. The enormous fortune amassed by the brewer Jacobsen, who has used his wealth so nobly for the adornment and enrichment of his native city, serves to show how highly it is appreciated, not only in Denmark but throughout Europe. Their method of working the yeast is the subject of study by all interested in the matter, and the establishment of a laboratory, frequented by students of all nations for this purpose, is another proof of the extreme care with which the Danes foster native industries, of which there is probably no example over which a properly-constituted body under royal sanction does not watch to protect its interests. They were the first to produce fermentation from one kind of cell only, a discovery made by Hansen, who carried out his theory in spite of the adverse criticism of Pasteur.

The brewing of the national beverage, beer, has naturally reached large dimensions, and Danish beer is exported to every quarter of the globe. The cellars of the great brewer, Jacobsen, which are probably the largest in the world, extend for several miles underground, and contain many thousands of huge barrels; one of his employés who had been there for more than three years, said he did not yet know his way over them, so vast are they.

Danish horticulture did not become of any importance in the life of the community till towards the close of the eighteenth century. At this time reforms of vital importance took place (the abolition of serfdom) by which the condition of the hitherto oppressed peasantry was considerably improved. About 1870 various Horticultural Societies were established, with the result that now Denmark, besides supplying its own needs, exports apples, white cabbages, cucumbers, flowering shrubs, roses, lilies of the valley, Christmas roses, and cyclamen of the very finest quality. Seed-culture is the subject of serious study under scientific guidance, and seed-corn, notably the square head wheat, is a Danish speciality.*

---

* There are twelve agricultural schools and a Royal Agricultural College. The State has also provided ten expert specialists to give personal advice to all who may ask on various subjects, such as disease of crops, agricultural machinery, breeding of stock, etc. Besides these there are two directors of field experiments and an agricultural commissioner in London, and a veterinary commissioner in Hamburg, the total annual grant from the State paid in salaries being £8300. There are also twenty-seven experts appointed by various agricultural societies who are partly paid by the State.

PROFESSOR DYMOND.

Manufactures and Trades

About four hundred distilleries are occupied in the production of "akvavit," a white spirit much drunk in the country.

The breeding of horses and ship-building are branches of industry carried on with considerable activity.

The Greenland trade always has been, and still is, monopolised by the State, and only Government vessels are allowed to sail in Greenland waters. This old-fashioned isolatory spirit is naturally disliked, but its advantages are that it protects the Greenlander from being deceived by unscrupulous merchants, and prevents the importation of intoxicating liquors, which would ruin him, as unfortunately the North American Indians have been ruined. For foreign travellers also Greenland is a closed country unless the traveller in question has beforehand obtained permission from the Danish Government, which is however very seldom given, and only in those cases where the person concerned is backed by his own Government. The exportations from Greenland consist of seal-oil, seal-skins, bear and fox skins, eider-down, feathers, tusks of the narwhal, and small whalebone. Unfortunately the quantity of eider-down exported has decreased very much in quantity during the last few years; at present only about one hundred and fifty pounds of pure eider-down are produced annually.

No manufactories whatever exist in Iceland, and the fine arts are not cultivated; its principal exports are sheep, fish, and the sturdy little ponies so often seen in the streets of Copenhagen. It is hoped the present influx of travellers, whose attention is gradually being drawn towards its peculiar and beautiful scenery, will greatly ameliorate the condition of the islanders.

With respect to Bornholm, a lovely little island in the Baltic, which belongs to Denmark, two-fifths of the population are engaged in agriculture. Herrings, granite and kaolin are exported thence. It may be added that a visit to this island, with its characteristic natural beauties, curious fortress, churches, cheapness and freshness, will well repay the traveller to its distant shores.

CHAPTER XXIII

MODERN DANISH LITERATURE

THE introduction of monkish literature which accompanied the diffusion of Christianity, and the increasing influence of Germany in Danish affairs, together with the internal and external dissensions from which Denmark suffered, hindered for a long time the intellectual development of the people. The language gradually differentiated from the old Norse, and we find the separation had made rapid progress so early as the thirteenth century, when the Provincial Laws were written, which are the oldest books in vernacular Danish. The descendant of a Scotchman, Thomas Kingo, was the first to write Danish with ease and grace; in 1674 he published his *Aandalige Sjungekor* (The Spiritual Choir), consisting of psalms and hymns, which are still in use, and are perfect examples of devótional songs: with this single exception there is no name in literature at that period which deserves record in so short a notice as this. However, Tycho Brahe, at the observatory Uranienborg, which he had built on the island of Hveen, given him by Frederick II., pursued his astronomical studies; in 1572 he discovered a new star, and during thirty years made those regular observations of the movements of the planets which enabled Kepler to formulate his celebrated laws.

The history of modern Danish literature might be roughly divided into three epochs, each introduced by a great dramatic writer, who is the "guide, philosopher and friend" of his countrymen for the time being, and who moulds and directs their literary tastes and pleasures. Such a man was Holberg, the first of these dominating geniuses; he was succeeded four years after his death by Heiberg, who again found a successor in Hostrup, an author, who, if not the equal of these other great men, still carried on not unworthily the great traditions of the Danish stage.

Holberg is justly regarded by the Danes as the creator of their modern school of literature. Born at Bergen, in Norway, in 1684, he, like so many of his countrymen, lived in Copenhagen and wrote in Danish. His productions are but little known in this country, but in the north of Europe few names are held in higher esteem. His works are principally comedies, of which Oehlenschläger remarks, "If Copenhagen had been buried beneath the ground and only Holberg's comedies had remained, we should nevertheless have known the life that stirred within its walls, not only in its broad outlines but also in many of its minutest details."

His first work, *The History of Peter Paarsins*, as he himself tells us in his autobiography, was immediately successful. "The Danes," said the critics, "have at length a poem in their native language, which they need not be ashamed to show to Frenchmen and to Englishmen." The first of his comedies was *The Pewterer turned Politician;* this was succeeded by thirty others, which are as popular on the stage now as they were a hundred and fifty years ago. *Niels Klim's Journey to the World Underground*, a satirical romance, created an extraordinary sensation; in it he expresses in a humorous manner his idea on the state of things in the world—a state which reminds us of some of the features of our present advanced period. "Foreigners were surprised," he says, "on entering any house, to find the mistress in the study, and surrounded by papers up to her ears, while the master was bustling about in the kitchen and busy in scouring pots and pans. And to which house soever I went and desired to speak to the master, I was certain of being shown into the kitchen." Among Holberg's other works are a *History of Denmark* and a *History of the Jews*.

Mr Gosse, writing on the Danish National Theatre, says: "Of all the small nations of Europe, Denmark is the only one that has succeeded in founding and preserving a truly national dramatic art. This foundation she owes entirely to Holberg."

Molte Brun (1775-1826), the famous geographer, though living in France and writing under a French name (Malte Brun), was really a Dane. The German Klopstock was summoned to Denmark by Frederick II. and is mentioned here because he exercised a most powerful influence over the literature of the country.

The brothers A. S. Oersted (1778-1860) and H. C. Oersted (1777 - 1851) have rendered Denmark illustrious both in science and literature. The former was a celebrated juris-consult and statesman, but his fame is completely eclipsed by that of the latter, whose name ranks among those of the greatest scientists of the world. A natural philosopher and chemist, he carried on the studies of Volta, and in 1820 made the great discovery of electro-magnetism, which at first appeared trifling, but which initiated a complete revolution in means of communication, leading finally to the invention of the electric telegraph. The quiet and modest man of science had not at first an idea of the importance of his discovery, but when he published it in the form of a Latin tract, the fact quickly spread, and honours were showered upon him as well by his own country as by the rest of the world. The Royal Society of London was the first to recognise his genius, and sent him its gold medal, he received that of the Institute of France in 1822; he was made a member of nearly every existing scientific society, including those of Sweden,

France, England, Germany, Italy, Holland, Belgium, India and America. He also founded in Copenhagen a society for the propagation of natural science. His character was of the noblest; he was an enthusiastic admirer of all that is good and beautiful, and forbearing to his fellow-men. He was not exclusively a great scientist and naturalist, but also a poet and *littérateur* of no small merit. His principal scientific works are *Bidenskaben om Naturens almindelige Love* (The Science of the Common Laws of Nature), *Naturens mekaniske Del* (The Mechanics of Physics), and *Aanden i Naturen* (The Spirit in Nature), only some of which are translated; his purely literary works are, among others, *To Kapitler af det skonnes Naturlære* (Two Chapters on the Physics of the Beautiful), and *Naturvideu-skaben i dens Forhold til Digtekunst og Religion* (The Science of Nature with regard to Poetry and Religion).

One of the very greatest names in Danish literature is that of Johannes Ewald (1743-1781), a poet who suffered much and died young, and who, while perishing like Heine by inches, composed his masterpieces. He was influenced successively by the works of Corneille, of Klopstock and of Shakespeare, and finally by the *Ossian* of Macpherson. Gaining a precarious livelihood by writing songs and poems for the fisher folk among whom he resided, he lived and died poor. One of his songs alone would have been sufficient to secure him immortality — the glorious National Hymn of Denmark—"Kong Christian stod ved hoien Mast," which was written for the character of Knud in his dramatic poem "The Fishers," a piece received with unbounded enthusiasm at the Theatre Royal, Copenhagen, in 1778. The poet himself was present but this recognition of his genius came too late. There is a spirited translation of the song by the multi-lingual George Borrow, but its effect is destroyed by the lengthening of the last line of each verse, which in the original, consisting of two syllables only, strikes the ear short and crisp like the blows of a hammer on the anvil, or the sharp report of cannon. In Longfellow's translation the fire and force of Ewald's great poem are nearly preserved:—

> " King Christian stood by the lofty mast
>   In mist and smoke:
> His sword was hammering so fast
> Through Gothic helm and brain it passed;
> Then sunk each hostile hulk and mast
>   In mist and smoke.
> 'Fly!' shouted they, 'fly, he who can!
> Who braves of Denmark's Christian
>   The stroke?'
>
> Niels Juel gave heed to the tempest's roar
>   Now is the hour!
> He hoisted his blood-red flag once more,
> And smote upon the foe full sore,
> And shouted loud, through the tempest's roar,
>   'Now is the hour!'
> 'Fly!' shouted they, 'for shelter fly!
> Of Denmark's Juel who can defy
>   The power?'

North sea ! a glimpse of Wessel rent
    Thy murky sky !
Then champions to thine arms were sent ;
Terror and Death glared where he went ;
From the waves was heard a wail that rent
    Thy murky sky !
From Denmark thunders Tordenskiold
Let each to Heaven commend his soul
    And fly !

Path of the Dane to fame and might !
    Dark-rolling wave !
Receive thy friend, who, scorning flight
Goes to meet danger with despite,
Proudly as thou the tempests might,
    Dark-rolling wave !
And amid pleasures and alarms
And war and victory, be thine arms
    My grave ! "

The songs of Ambrosius Stub, a poor peasant whose poems are now being collected with great difficulty, and who was rather an improvisatore than a writer, are infinitely sweet and tender, and have gained for him the name of "the first swallow of Denmark." Are not the following lines by him dictated by the same feeling as that which inspired Odin the Old in writing his "Havamal"? for the old Norse spirit dieth not.

"To be well born is good,
    But better still well taught.
Well-married is life's joy,
    Die well, all else is naught." *

---

* In making the studies necessary for the few notes on Danish Poets which follow, I thought the greater part of the existing translations of their works so inadequate (some are not even to be found in English) that I have felt it best to translate afresh the

Of course the English fails to give the force and terseness of the original.

John Herman Wessel (1742-1785) is celebrated for his tragic comedy, *Kjærlighed uden Strömper* (Love without Stockings), a trenchant satire on the stilted heroics and classical writers of the French stage. Its effect was to cause the ejection of French plays, and even the Italian opera, from the Danish theatre, and to supply their places, the composer Hartman, who died in 1900, set native dramas to music, and thus originated the Danish school already so fertile in results. Owing to a painful illness Wessel completely lost the gaiety and genial humour which had rendered him so popular, and a settled melancholy took possession of his whole mind. The lines which he wrote as his own epitaph describe truthfully the character of the poet, and may be translated thus:—

> "He ate and drank, ne'er gay did feel,
> His boots were ever down at heel,
> He never wanted work or strife,
> At last he did not e'en want life."

The following humorous poem by Wessel has given subject for laughter to generations of Danes:—

specimens given in illustration, and this I have done with the assistance of a Dane, to whom I wish here to express my obligation. The poetry of Denmark is a literature so rich, so little known, and so original, that I would gladly have given more space and time to its study had the scope of this book permitted.

THE SMITH AND THE BAKER.

"There was a little town, a smith lived in it too,
 Who dang'rous was when hot he grew.
 An enemy he had; that one can get alway.
 (I haven't one; and may
 As much my reader say!)
 By evil chance of both, the same
 Unlucky inn within they came.
 They drank (myself in inns drink ever,
 For other object go there never,
 Remark, my reader, though,
 They're always honest inns to which I go).
 They drank, I said,
 And after many quarrels, hot of head
 Smith struck his foeman's eyes between.
 So heavy was the stroke
 That he saw daylight not
 Nor after has it seen.

 Quickly the smith they do arrest,
 A doctor likewise gives attest
 That he a violent death had met by blows.
 The murd'rer is examined and avows
 His hope is that he might to heav'n go
 And there get full and free forgiveness of his foe.

 A joke now list! upon the day
 When final judgment they shall say
 Stepp'd forward four good citizens
 Before the judge, the clev'rest speaker then
 Him to address began:
            "All-wisest hear!
 The welfare of our town to you is dear,
 The welfare of our town doth claim
 That we shall have our smith again;
 His death shall not revive the dead man ever,
 And surely for his crime 'tis hard so much to give.
 We never more shall get a smith so clever
 If you don't let him live."

 "Consider then, dear friend, life must for life atone—"
 "Here lives a baker poor and lame
 Whom soon Old Nick will surely claim.

E'en two we have: if you the eldest took of them,
Life would for life be duly paid."

"Yes, surely," said the judge, "that's really neatly said.
The cause I now must verily postpone.
We ought, on such important cases, think with care.
Would that our smith's existence I could spare!
Good-bye, good folk, I'll do all that I can."
"Good-bye, all-wisest man!"

He now skims through the law with utmost care,
But in itself finds nothing there
Preventing for a smith's a baker's execution.
He forms his resolution.
And then pronounced his doom severe
(Who that will hear it, come and hear!):
"Jens, blacksmith, I refuse
By all means to excuse,
And here in court he has confessed
He Anders Pedersen has sent to heav'n blessed.
But in our town one blacksmith sole we find
And I should be quite out of mind
If I could wish to see him dead.
But here are two who can bake bread;
So this my sentence is:
The oldest baker suffer shall for this
And for the murder done shall life for life atone
To him as a deservèd penalty
For such as he, a warning and example dread."

The baker wept most piteously
As he away was led.

MORAL.

For death you always should prepare!
It comes when least of all you think it there.

I have been fortunate enough to hear from a direct source a hitherto unpublished anecdote of Wessel. He went one day to a christening, at which ceremony it was in his days the custom to make a collection. The bag accordingly came round, and Wessel, having but eight skillings in his pocket, deftly slipped his hand into his neighbour's and extracted four more, which he put in it, explaining his reason as follows:—

> "As in all other things so also in my giving
> From ordinary folk I always differ will,
> They offer little of the much that they are having,
> I offer you all mine, of theirs a little still."

Jens Baggesen (1764-1826) is the greatest satirist Denmark has produced, and also one of the most prolific of poets. His satire, *Gjengengeren og han selv, eller Baggesen over Baggesen* (The Ghost and himself, or Baggesen upon Baggesen), is a violent attack on things and persons in general, and the work by which he will be best remembered. He became embroiled with the great Oehlenschläger in a quarrel in which the whole intellectual world of that time took part. The wit and humour of Baggesen would no doubt have triumphed if his irritable disposition had not caused him to answer the attacks made on him in a manner little becoming one who sacrificed to the graces. The following lines are by him:—

> "Ah, nowhere is the rose so red,
> Nowhere so small the thorn,
> Nowhere so soft the downy bed
> As those where we were born."

In a galaxy of poets which would have done

honour to any country and any age, the greatest name is that of Adam Gottlob Oehlenschläger (1779-1850), of whom it has been said that "the old Scandinavian mythology lived in his hands as the Greek in Keats's." "For the north he is of equal importance as Goethe was for Germany; in his best works he is so penetrated by the spirit of the north that the same has, as it were, through them, ascended for all nations."* His great work, *Nordens Guder* (The Gods of the North), is, he himself tells us, an attempt to combine the legends of the Eddas into one connected whole. The result is magnificent. Oehlenschläger has entered most completely into the spirit of these grand poems, and has written as a poet who was at once patriot and scholar alone could write.

His literary output was immense, but I have only space to mention *Hakon Jarl*, *Aladdin*, *Helge*, *Coregio*, and his last grand composition, *Regnar Lodbrok*. His works have a great and imperishable value for Denmark on account of their national character, and have gained for him the name of its Shakespeare, but it is difficult to give an idea of his style in a small space. Perhaps Thora's soliloquy over the dead body of Jarl Hakon, which has been so inadequately rendered in Longfellow's *Poets and Poetry of Europe*, will serve as well as any other excerpt.

* H. C. Andersen.

Scene—The Subterranean Vault.

The lamp still burns in its former place. Two retainers enter, carrying a black coffin: they place it silently down in the middle of the cavern and go. Thora comes slowly in with a naked sword and a large wreath of fir in her hand. She stands long and considers the coffin. At last she says :—

" Now art thou then enshrinèd, Hakon Jarl,
 In Thora's coffin, in the coffin Thora
 Had made for her. This had I least expected :
 May in the grave have peace thy bones so weary !
 If thou hast sinnèd thou hast dearly paid it
 And no one more shall waste a vile and cruel
 Or heedless word which thy renown can sully !
 As in thy life so in thy death I love thee.
 A short time hence thou shinedst in the North
 As does the sun which warms where'er it gloweth,
 Now have the hosts of heroes all forgot thee
 And sworn allegiance to a foreign light ;
 Now only throbs a woman's modest heart
 In quiet misery at thy remembrance ;
 So then let her the honour to thee render
 The which thy men in pleasures have forgot."

(She lays the wreath and sword on the coffin).

" Take from thy Thora's hand a vig'rous wreath !
 A wreath of Norway's haughty pines be woven
 Around thy mighty hero-sword ; betok'ning
 Thou wast true Northman and a noble chief,
 A blossom beaten down by winter frost !
 Erewhile the northern chronicles will tell us,
 When time's rude hand has rubbed the colour off
 And but the grand contour shall linger still,
 He was a wicked and a cruel pagan !
 And men will shudd'ring mutter then thy name.
 I do not shudder for I know thee best,
 The noblest gifts and greatest heart on earth
 Fell victims to the errors of the times.
 Then sleep thou well, my Hakon ! sleep thou well !

> Thousand good-nights. On high may vict'ry's Father
> Make glad thy giant soul. Now go I shutting,
> But when yet once again this door shall open
> Then Thora's slaves shall bear her body here
> And place it by her noble Hakon's side."

The most characteristically Danish of the poets who have hitherto written in Danish is Steen Steensen Blicher (1782-1848). His poems describe the wild scenery of Jutland, where he lived; he also translated Macpherson's *Ossian*.

Bernhard Severin Ingemann (1789-1862) is said to have taken Sir Walter Scott as his example, but unfortunately he did not possess the great Scotchman's gift of humour; his novels, however, are exceedingly attractive on account of their graphic descriptions of the most glorious epoch of the Valdemars. His great poem, "Holger Danske," relates the adventures of a king named Holger who was the co-temporary of Charlemagne and who is the national champion of Denmark. He is said to have eaten of the fruit of the trees of the sun and moon, "and men say tho that kepe the trees and eten frewght of hem, they leve CCCC or V yere," therefore he is not believed to be dead but to lie wrapt in slumber in the dark vaults of Kronborg and to come mounted on his white steed on all national emergencies; as the ballad says,—

> "Thou know'st it, peasant! I am not dead.
> I come back to thee in my glory,
> I am thy faithful helper in need
> As in Denmark's ancient story."

Ingemann's religious poems are remarkable

for a rare healthiness and simplicity, of which the following may perhaps give some idea:—

"O blessèd the soul which our God's peace can own,
  Though we judge not the day till the sun has gone down.

  Good morn! on the branch sings the little bird, yet,
  In the bars of a prison oft sees the sun set.

  The flowers breathe out perfume at dawn as they bow;
  Yet oft before eve 'neath the hailstorm lie low.

  Oft the infant that plays in the morning sun red;
  When the ev'ning has come lieth silent and dead.

  So happy a soul on the earth does not live,
  That his fate may not change between morning and eve.

  Yet blessed the soul that our God's peace doth own,
  Tho' not one knows the day till the sun has gone down.

  The children of God may rejoice like the flow'r
  E'en tho' they lie crushed in the still ev'ning hour.

  Good morning we sing with the bird glad and bright,
  Tho' we linger ourselves in a prison at night.

  Like a child I can sing in the morning light red,
  E'en tho' before night I lie silent and dead.

  God's peace and good-night! as the ev'ning clouds roll:
  God Almighty Himself preserve each passing soul!

  O blessèd, most blessèd the soul which has peace!
  God's peace is the soul's sun which never shall cease!"

The poetry of Denmark is emphatically strongest in lyric poems, and among the names of those authors who have most enriched this branch of literature that of Christian Winther (1796-1876) ranks high. He is above all the interpreter of Northern nature, of which his accurate descriptions have a peculiar charm; when he attempted to describe that of the south he was less successful. His principal works are "Hjortens Flugt" (The Flight of the Stag) and "Træsnit" (Woodcutting), a series of idealistic poems on rural life. I have ventured, though he is almost untranslatable, to attempt a version of the following lyric by him which is extremely popular in his own country:—

FLY, BIRD! FLY!

Fly, bird! Fly over Furresö's wavelets!
Soon comes the night without ray,
Soon dies the sun 'neath the dim dark'ning forest,
Day it is stealing away;
Off to thy home, to thy feath'ry mate, hasten,
Flee, to thy gold-beaked, flee;
When thou again shalt come back on the morrow,
All thou hast seen tell to me!

Fly, bird! fly over Furresö's billows,
Both of thy pinions outspread!
Then if two lovers thou see'st, thou shalt follow,
Deep in their souls thou shalt read.
I am a singer and ought to know truly
Love that can flatter and bless,
All that a heart can contain or can suffer,
Surely my voice should express.

Fly, bird! fly over Furresö's murm'ring,
Love calls thee home to thy nest;
Then if two lovers thou see'st, thou shalt follow,
Sing out thy love at thy best!
If I, like thee, could take wings through the ether,
Well do I know where to rove;
Now I but dream and but sigh in the forest,
Such is the fruit of my love.

Fly, bird! fly over Furresö's waters.
Far, far away in the sky!
Lone in the woods on the farthest shore walking
See thou my fairest pass by.
Yellow-brown locks in the zephyrs are flutt'ring,
Light is she, straight as a reed,
Black are her eyes and her cheeks have their roses,
Her shalt thou know with all speed!

Fly, bird! fly over Furresö's foaming,
Deeply its breath draws the night!
Whisper the trees with an anxious low murm'ring,
Bow to her, greet her good-night!
Hast thou not listened to manifold sadness
E'en where thy feathered mates stay?
Say thou good-night to my quiv'ring heart's treasure,
Say it, thou surely can'st say?

Of all names in Danish literature the one best known and loved by us in England is that of the author who has peopled our nurseries with elves and fairies and filled our schoolrooms with romance—Hans Christian Andersen—the darling also of his own countrymen, to whom, when he walked the streets of Copenhagen, everyone who knew his appearance touched his hat and said, "God bless you!" He was born in 1805 at Odense, in the island of Fyen, and early distinguished himself by his taste for theatrical pursuits. At the age of fourteen years, as he tells us in his charming autobiography, he made his way to Copenhagen friendless and alone; he passed away at the age of seventy, just after the festivities of a whole nation had done honour to his birthday. "He could not have died at a moment when his fame, spread from one end of the world to the other, was more living, and in dying he took from among us the most popular of all contemporary writers of the imagination."*

A few anecdotes concerning this favourite author may interest English readers. One of Andersen's characteristics was an abnormal dread of illness, death, and of being buried alive. It is related of him that every night before going to sleep he placed a paper beside his bed on which was written, "I am not really dead but only in a lethargy. Do not bury me alive." Once, dining with a friend, he happened to knock his head (he was a very tall man and enjoyed the soubriquet of "Long Andersen") against a chandelier, and though but slightly injured, thought so much about it that his host feared he was about to faint. It was necessary to do something to pacify the suffering genius, so he asked him to take a little of that innocent medicine, "Hoffman's drops." The son of the host brought it. "Are you quite sure," said Andersen, "that this is not poison?" "Of course it is not." "Would you mind taking a little first just as a guarantee?" said the celebrated writer of fairy tales to the little boy.

He had great facility in cutting out objects with his scissors, and his subjects were nearly always the storks and dancers about which he has written so much. He represented them on one leg—perhaps he felt the resemblance which exists between the bird and the short-petticoated pirouetter on the stage.

* E. W. Gosse.

Going to a barber's to be shaved, he remarked to the operator, "Remember whom you have under your razor." *

Andersen's epigram on Thorvaldsen may be translated as follows:—

>"'How much in Homer will you take?'
>And papers they expected;
>But you, in magic clay to make
>The Iliad whole, selected."

His novel, *The Improvisatore*, is a work containing many beauties, but the reader feels that Andersen was not a *born* novelist, though he says of himself, with naïve egotism, "Criticism was silent, but I heard around me that interest for my work and delight at the same were predominant."

Browning, writing of Andersen's *Improvisatore*, says, "The writer seems to feel, just as I do, the good of the outward life; and he is a poet in his soul. It is a book full of beauty and had a great charm for me." With finer criticism Mrs Browning says, in those wonderful letters of hers written before she became the poet's wife, 'But they do fret me, those tantalising creatures of fine passionate class, with such capabilities and such a facility of being made pure mind of. And the special instance that vexed me was that a man of sands and dog-roses and white rock and green sea-water just under, should come to

* "*Minder fra mine Forældres Hus*" by Arthur Abrahams. Cand: Phil.

Italy, where my heart lives, and discover the sights and sounds—certainly discover them. And so of all Northern writers."

Mrs Browning's last lines before her death were written to Andersen, as he was never tired of telling his friends :—

> "'Now give us men from the sunless plain,'
>   Cried the South to the North.
> 'By need of work in the snow and rain
> Made strong and brave by familiar pain,'
>   Cried the South to the North.
>
> The North sent therefore a man of men,
>   As a grace to the South.
> And thus to Rome came Andersen.
> 'Alas, but you must take him again!
>   Said the South to the North.'"

It is interesting to notice to how many very great men this little country of Denmark has given birth. The population is less by much more than two millions than that of London alone, yet it has produced men who have nobly distinguished themselves in every branch of literature, and of this J. N. Madvig (1804-1886) is one of the most brilliant examples. There is no greater name in the annals of philology than his: he devoted himself to the study of Latin, and it is said of him that he wrote that language better than Cicero himself, for Cicero might sometimes be negligent in his style, but Madvig never. He was Rector of the University of Copenhagen and there founded a school of followers who have caused Danish philologists to be renowned all over Europe for their erudition and thoroughness. Madvig was also one of the greatest of emendators of Latin texts, and during some part of his life occupied himself with politics. He first published his *Opuscula Academica*, afterwards *Emendationes Livianæ*, and finally his greatest work, *Condition and Administration of the Roman States*.

Johan Ludvig Heiberg (1791-1860) was the greatest writer of comedies after Holberg that Denmark has produced. The peculiarity of his plays consist in the manner in which he blends words and music, which has become characteristic of the Danish Theatre. His best known plays are *Elverhoi, Kong Solomon og Jörgens Hattemager, Aprilsnarrene, Recensenten og Dyret* and *De Uadskillelige*. *En Sjæl efter Döden* is a striking satire on some forms of religion and protestantism in nature, which discloses the philosophic opinions of the poet in a practical form. Heiberg also takes high rank as a writer on æsthetics. He was manager of the National Theatre and married the most celebrated actress Denmark has produced.

I have endeavoured to translate one of Holberg's finest poems; the original is in rhymes which I was unable to preserve in such a manner as to do justice to the beautiful thought it contains. I hope the reader will agree with me in preferring reason to rhyme:—

FROM "PROTESTANTISM IN NATURE"

The God thou seekest is thy proper God:
What wouldst thou more?
He is not from all other things detached
'Mong others, various.
Thou feelest Him each time thy heart is throbbing
With sacred joy;
Like an eternal voice 'midst highest thinking
Thou hearest Him.
Already when thou seekest thou hast found Him,
Already when thou askest thou art answered.
In all her splendour Nature when adorned,
Too mean is ever
With quiet diligence a worthy garb
For Him to offer.
But void and soulless is she therefore neither
And not forlorn
She looks towards the sun with thousand glances
From dusty night;
With thousand tongues her strivings she declareth
Unconsciously His word her lips express.

To Frederick Paladan Müller (1809 - 1876) belongs the honour of being the finest satirist Denmark has produced. His great work is "Adam Homo," adjudged by Dr Brandes to be the "most manly work written in Denmark." The eminent critic thus continues: "'Adam Homo' is, above all that Paladan Müller has written, a Danish epic. Not only is it characteristic in its moulding, but it also gives a faithful picture of our national peculiarities and sins. I have, in my treatise on *Naturalism in England*, endeavoured to show its position in European literature, and especially its *rapport* with Byron's kindred poem, "Don Juan." This observation gave the poet an opportunity of replying, which reply, together with an answer from me, is to be found in the February and March numbers of the *Nineteenth Century Review* for 1876. But though it was not then thought that 'Adam Homo' would have become what it has become had not Byron's work preceded it, the Danish poem, notwithstanding, possesses such taste and smell of the soil which fostered it that already, by its originality, it is able to maintain its place among the few epics of the first rank which Europe has produced during this century."

FROM "ADAM HOMO"

O far-off childhood's home which we forsook,
Which we forsook and is in mem'ry sleeping:
Where is the peace which blossomed from thy root
And which beneath time's heavy mould is keeping?
A hope art thou which tempted forth our foot
Fair hopes of future paradise repeating
By promises that bid us wander bolder,
"All surely shall be yours when you are older!"

We grow, and blind we are our path pursuing
Upon the word of hope we still rely;
And by-and-by is changed to mem'ry ruing
The splendour of the world for which we sigh,
At once we stop and all our past reviewing
See but the traces of the hopes that die:
We hear a voice behind us calmly saying,
"Your paradise was when in childhood playing!"

Still are we wanderers, still we forward go
The way already downward is descending,
A few poor flow'rs upon it only grow,
Beneath day's heat and burden we are bending,
And still for our lost treasure are contending
There is the night and death to which we're going,
But where is childhood's home? where morning's glowing?

It is pleasant here to be able to mention a female writer—the mother of J. L. Heiberg, Countess Thomasine Gyllemborg - Ehrensvärd (1773-1856), the first great authoress Denmark can boast. She published a number of novels, distinguished for their style and wit, anonymously; the authorship was not known till after her death.

Bishop Grundvig (1783-1872) exercised a most important influence over the intellectual life of Denmark, and is denominated by his countrymen the profoundest thinker of the North. He has created a certain party in religion which endeavours to follow out his principle; this is that for those who believe in what he calls the "three words of Christ," or first sentence of the creed of our English Church, there is no condemnation; all other dogmas are of infinitesimal importance. His doctrines are extremely broad; he deprecates the too-early education of children of tender years and prefers it should take place in youth. He also wrote on mythological subjects, composed poems, and translated Saxo's *Chronicle*, the *Heimskringla*, and Beowulf's *Drapa* into Danish.

Soren Aaby Kjerkegaard (1813-1855) was undoubtedly one of the noblest thinkers of Scandinavia; his writings are narrower but more trenchant than those of the great bishop. His powerful satire is directed against priestly beliefs and dogmas, for which he wished to substitute the pure religion of Christ. It is commonly thought that the study of Kjerkegaard has influenced the thought and writing of Ibsen, but the connection between their principles is more ideal than real, and Ibsen himself denies ever having read the works of Kjerkegaard. Yet no doubt, indirectly, it has done so, for the priest Thorvald Lammers, who lives at Stavanger, the birthplace of Ibsen, and who was his model for " Brand," was a disciple of Kjerkegaard.

Parmo Carl Ploug (1813-1894) devoted himself to advocating the political union of the Scandinavian kingdoms, first as a student and afterwards as the editor of *Fædreland* (Fatherland), a cause which has had no more persevering and ardent partisan. His political writings are considered models of Danish prose. He was, above all, a writer of occasional verses, which have been collected under the titles of *Poul Rytter's Viser og Vers* (Paul the Rider's Songs and Verses), *Samlede Digte* (Collected Poems) and *Nyere Sange og Digte"* (New Songs and Poems).

Hans Vilhelm Kaalund (1818-1885), after essaying the professions of medicine and art, found his real vocation in literature. His principal works are "Et Foraar" (A Spring), "Fulvia," a dramatic lyric, and "Et Efteraar" (An Autumn). He is to be noticed as the first Dane who has written fables after the manner of Esop, La Fontaine, and Gay, with whom he takes rank; these poems are distinguished by their freshness, wit, and healthiness of sentiment. Kaalund is never vulgar, never coarse, but drives his point home with refined wit and piquant irony. The following are examples:—

THE GOLDFISHES.

A twofold bubble made of crystal all
  Was sparkling brilliantly in sunshine glowing,
On marble table in the splendid hall
  The fragile work its splendid form was showing.

The inner globe was fashioned hollow, while
  Cool water in the outer one was streaming;
In that a fine canary did beguile,
  In this a pair of golden fish were swimming.

They turned and turned around their little space
  Straight outward at the world to look rejecting,
The same round course, the same slow stupid pace
  They kept as if too haughty for reflecting.

A fashionable life! court did they pay
  And wagged their fins and tails within their hollow;
But right from free fresh nature, peeped one day
  Into the hall a poor and tiny swallow.

It saw the fish their backs forever bow,
  It saw the pastime of the bird so yellow,
And thought, exulting in its freedom's glow,
  "Good Heavens! fishes are but stupid fellows!"

O say, my dear, and have you seen fresh-eyed,
  Within saloons where high-life gathers, ever
Society's formality and pride?
  And tell me, thought you like the swallow never?

THE RATTLE.

"I," loud a rattle shouted
(And deafened all about it),
"Make silent wisest men!"
What do you then announce, dear?
It must be pearls I think, there,
Let's see—trash was it then.

THE CRITIC.

That man a critic now we dub
  Who but "you fool" can write, as we
Employ for brooms the little shrub
  Which has not pith to grow a tree.

In modern days the most celebrated names in Danish literature are not inferior to those of their great predecessors. Johan Christian Hostrup, whose death in 1900 was so widely lamented in Denmark, succeeded to the throne of Holberg and Heiberg, and was the most popular writer of comedies in Copenhagen. His witty and delicate plays are interspersed with graceful songs and are extremely successful. Some time before his death he was seized with unnecessary remorse that he had written for the stage and became a priest.

Among his other works Carl Hertz wrote a drama, *King Rene's Daughter*, which has been translated into most European languages.

The works of Sophus Bauditz are remarkable for their purity and genial humour. He is an excellent *raconteur*.

J. J. A. Worsaae (1821-1885), the greatest archæologist of the north, began his studies by travelling extensively in Sweden, Germany, Bohemia and Austria. In 1846 he was commissioned by the Danish Government to proceed to England, Scotland and Ireland in order to examine the Danish remains in those countries, and on his return was made inspector of antiquities and a member of the Committee for their preservation; after a journey to Rome and

Naples he was also appointed Inspector of Rosenborg Castle. On the death of Professor Thomsen he became Director of the Museum of Northern Antiquities and the Ethnographical Museum, in the interest of which he undertook excavations which threw much light on the knowledge of pre-historic times. For this work he possessed especial qualifications, both scientific and practical, together with clear intuition and sharp faculties of observation and combination. His power of work was enormous, and he had the gift of presenting its results, by pen as well as by speech, in a delightful manner. Worsaae had his special method of work; he led the way to the comparative method of research for pre-historic antiquities, and may be considered the founder of that science. Besides writing for scientists he was also a popular author—his patriotism and poetical mode of expression being very pleasing to the general reader. He even wrote for almanacs. *Danmark's Oltid oplyst ved Oldsager og Gravhoje* (The Antiquity of Denmark shown by its Antiquities and Grave-hills), *Minde om de Danske og Nordmændene i England, Skotland og Ireland* (Memorials of the Danes and Northmen in England, Scotland and Ireland), *Den Danske Erobring af England, og Nordmandiet* (The Danish Conquest of England and Normandy), and *Nordens Forhistorie* (The Pre-historic North) are the chief among the many writings due to the pen of an antiquarian to whom his country owes the splendid arrangements of its scientific and historical collections, and many works accepted as authoritative by all European nations.

Since the establishment in the fifteenth century of a German dynasty, German literature and thought have had a predominating influence in Denmark. The language used by the Court and the upper classes was German. The poet Klopstock, subsidised by Christian VII. to reside in Copenhagen, was the leader of the literary movement there; even the present King used German during the first years of his reign, and to this day speaks Danish with a German accent.

But with Dr Georg Brandes (born 1842), an author whose merits are more appreciated in England than in Denmark, a reaction set in, the importance of which it is impossible to overestimate, and which owes its inception entirely to him. A critic of singular acumen, and having the faculty of his race (he is a Jew) for assimilation rather than for creation, he succeeded in awakening intense enthusiasm in the youth of Denmark, and in founding a school of writers who derive their inspiration from French sources.

The greatest of these is Holger Drachmann, one of the most striking personalities in Denmark. Beginning life as a marine painter, he has lived for years among the sailors and fishermen of Skagen, that desolate point of land where the North Sea, the Skager Rak and the Cattegat meet. Novels, dramas, essays, and some of the finest lyrics ever written in the Danish tongue—and the Danes are past masters of lyric poetry—testify to the genius of Drachmann; he has also rendered Byron's "Don Juan" into his native language with such aptitude and vigour that it is almost impossible to believe the poem a translation.

Speaking at the banquet given in his honour during a recent visit to London, "I have," he said, "read and studied your literature considerably — a literature which has greatly influenced me in my hot youth." "Come over and visit us," he continued. "Come to Denmark and try to speak to us in our language. You will find us patient enough and anxious to meet you half-way. For the languages of the two countries are very much related to one another, and, like lovers, they stretch their hands across the North Sea."

It is almost impossible to translate Drachmann's poems, but it is hoped the following attempt may not be found wholly inadequate:—

THE MOUNTAIN RUIN.

On high above the narrow vale I'm sitting,
  Which lies in mist the lofty mount below,
  The sun as in a spring of blood sinks low,
And purple shadows long are upward flitting.

Already o'er the river's waves they're creeping,
  The mountain's steep and rocky wall they breast
  Where th' ruined castle, once the eagle's nest,
By time forsaken, watch and ward is keeping.

By time forsaken which we're "golden" calling
  Because 'tis seen in mem'ry's ev'ning glow,
  Its crown of battlements is fading slow,
To pieces is the mountain ruin falling.

Down in the valley, where the river's flowing
　With constant murmur and with constant groan,
　Piece after piece its brickwork, lime, and stone,
As if in play, the watch-tow'r old is throwing.

And as it plays, the mountain darker growing,
　And shadows hide below the glowing streams,
　About the sea of blood the river dreams
Which ran of yore—and now is thicker flowing.

Then shakes the tower—but it is with gladness
　For "sentimental" was not that old life ;
　It fostered men and hardened them in strife,
But left to women all the task of sadness.

Yes, shakes the tow'r as in the joy of feasting ;
　A feast it was when spearmen forth did ride
　To steal the gold, to steal themselves a bride
And drink with armour-coated guests unceasing.

How then within the hall there was carousing !
　How sparkled wine around the haughty lips
　'Mid sound of song—down where the valley dips
Mid echo from the nightingales arousing.

Because the knight who rode his steed unbroken
　Along the rugged path beneath the wall,
　Demanding toll as if by right, of all,
Left to a singer wide his portal open.

With feathered hat, there stood the minstrel gaily,
　A knowing wand'rer, light of foot and mien,
　Portcullis up ! the stranger entered in,
Drank with the knight, and sang unto the lady.

Yet oft it happened when the singer's sighing
　Too boldly rose, his heart too warmly beat,
　The knight drew forth his sword in sudden heat
And in his life-blood soon the guest was lying.

Then o'er the mount a double darkness shaded ;
　The knight set quickly out for Jordan's flood,
　But in her lofty bow'r the lady stood
Before the window, pale, too early faded,

> Slowly the wall with subtle feet and airy,
>   Month after month in beating wind and rain
>   The sombre ivy crawled, and thrust amain
> Through rift and fissure, all its roots so wary.
>
> Then sat I high above the valley darkened
>   Which lies in mist the lofty mount below.
>   The sun as in a spring of blood sank low,
> And to the sounds of distant songs I hearkened.
>
> They mixed themselves amid the river's weeping,
>   And with the shadows climbed the mountain's breast,
>   Where th' ruined castle, once the eagle's nest,
> By time forsaken, on its guard post's sleeping.

The success of Drachmann has procured him numberless imitators.

Other followers of Brandes are Carl Gjellerup, a poet resembling, but without the same erudition, our own Swinburne, who is his favourite author; J. P. Jacobsen, whom I shall mention in fuller detail further on; Schandorf,* a novelist of great power; Peter Nansen, Carl Ewald, Svan Lange, Rode, and his own brother, Edvard Brandes, all novelists.

Brandes hoped at one time to succeed Hauch as Professor of Esthetics at the University of Copenhagen, but his well-known atheistic and revolutionary tendencies hindered the realisation of his desire, and, disappointed, he retired in 1877 to Berlin, where, for he speaks and writes German as fluently as Danish, he lectured on literary subjects to crowded audiences. In 1883 he returned to Copenhagen, where his friends and admirers united to assure him a revenue of

---

* Schandorf died early in 1901.

4000 crowns per annum. Much of his unpopularity in Denmark arises from his want of patriotic feeling, which he once expressed by the phrase, "Denmark s'efface," a saying as far removed from good taste as from the truth regarding a little country which has contributed more than its quota of great men to the century which is just past.

It is yet too soon to form a definite appreciation of the work of Georg Brandes; his last word has not yet been said, and as he is still in the prime of a life spent in the midst of fierce and heated controversy, much may yet be expected from him. So far the greatest result of his labours is the enthusiasm for literature he has awakened; he has taught people to think for themselves rather than to accept the dictum of others. He set himself to become a reformer, and he has shared the common fate of reformers who, against their own will, are often carried by circumstances further than they originally intended to go. He endeavoured to remove the accumulated dust of ages, and in so doing rudely broke the windows of the chamber and let in too strong a blast of air, which whirled it up only to gather again. In endeavouring to amend things he has acted like the servant who, in arranging a study, throws away all the loose papers she can find, but who, in so doing, destroys perchance her master's best treasures, his record of his memories, his thoughts and his dreams. Such assuredly was not his intention, but in the whirl of enthusiasm he awakened, this result was probably inevitable.

His chief works out of many are, *French Æsthetics in our Times*, *The Principal Sources of the Literature of the Nineteenth Century*, *Danish Poets*, a *chef d'œuvre* of psychological analysis, *A History of Modern Scandinavian Literature*, and many biographies, including that of Lord Beaconsfield.

Modern Danish literature boasts also Vilhelm Bergsoë, a novelist, and Ernst van der Recke, a lyric and dramatic poet, neither of whom have submitted to the powerful influence of Brandes.

To continue this list of the best modern writers, Rudolf Schmidt is a philosophical and dramatic writer whose play, *The King Transformed*, has become celebrated, and who made the preacher, Edward Irving, the subject of another called *The Awakening*. Edgard Höyer is the only living Danish author who has had the good fortune to attain popularity in countries other than his own; his play, *The Jensen Family*, has been produced in many countries, especially in America, with great success.

Amalie Skram is a realistic novelist of singular strength and powerful genius; though born in Norway she claims the right of being called a Dane, as she has married an author of that nationality, writes in the Danish language, and lives in Copenhagen. One only of her books, *Professor Hieronimus*, described by Björnson as "an epoch-making work," is accessible to the

English reader. This is a *roman à clef*, and of course has an interest for the Danes apart from its literary qualities. To quote Björnson again: "Those who in the name of humanity are opposed to the too arbitrary power of asylums, have, in this masterly picture of the interior of one of these, a weapon of insuperable strength." For "seeking quiet and treatment for a nervous affection, Amalie Skram of her own free will became the inmate of a lunatic asylum, and thus had a chance of studying one of those specialists in mental disease who are too apt to mistake rebelliousness for a sign of mental derangement. Of this doctor, of the patients, the nurses, her whole environment, she gives a picture so vivid, of such absorbing interest, that it can vie with the most thrilling romance." "In the whole of Europe," says Laura Marholm Hansen in her book on *Modern Women*, "there are only two naturalists and they are Emile Zola and Amalie Skram."

Though far from being the equal of Jacobsen in ultimate psychological analysis, she is yet a profound observer of mental phenomena, and knows how to surround her personages with an atmosphere which, if less refined, is quite as realistic as his. In fact, the writings of these two authors may be taken as typical of modern Danish novels—novels which are very much what Brandes, inspired by French writers, especially by Flaubert, has made them.

With the names of Eirik Pontoppidan, novelist,

of Urik Christiansen, dramatic poet and director of the Royal Theatre, of Otto Benzon and Esman, both dramatic poets, and of Gustav Wied, humorist, the list of modern authors of note concludes.

I have said that J. P. Jacobsen claims more than a passing notice. Just before the commencement of the last third of the century which has now closed, the whole reading world of Denmark was startled by the appearance of a book so new in its methods, so profound in its analysis of character, so marvellous in its descriptions of Nature, that it immediately took rank amid the classics of the country and its author leaped at once into immortality. The book was the great historical romance, *Marie Grubbe*, the writer a young man stricken with a mortal disease — Jens Peder Jacobsen.

Born at Thisted, a town in the province of Jutland, where he also died in 1885, Jacobsen from childhood devoted himself to the study of natural history, gaining a gold medal at the University of Copenhagen for a treatise on the subject. The effect of this early bias is perceptible in his observations and descriptions of natural objects. While still young he became a convert to Darwinism, and remarking that the theories of the great scientist were little known in his own country, he translated *The Origin of Species* and *The Descent of Man*, while he also endeavoured to spread their principles by his own fresh and powerful writings.

However, he soon abandoned these studies. Inheriting conspicuous talent for poetry from his mother's family, he yet failed to find a satisfactory form for the expression of his genius till he came in contact with the celebrated critic, Dr Georg Brandes, one of his warmest admirers, and who was endeavouring to replace the obsolete school of Oehlenschläger, Holberg and their followers with a new one which should draw its inspiration chiefly from the French. The writings of his great fellow-countrymen, H. C. Andersen, had at first strongly appealed to Jacobsen, but then the new Shakespearian revival, and above and before all the study of the works of Flaubert and Beyle, assisted him in forming that unapproachable style which has placed him at the head of all modern Danish novelists. In the words of Mr Edmund Gosse, one of the few Englishmen of letters who has made a study of Scandinavian literature, "all competent Danish critics agree in saying that no artificer in prose has ever used the Danish language so subtly as did in his brief career this brilliant 'inheritor of unfulfilled renown.'"

Marie Grubbe was followed in 1876 by *Niels Lyhne*, and in 1882 by *Mogens and other Stories*. After Jacobsen's death a few scattered poems and prose sketches were collected and published, and these complete the list of his works.

Though he died young, and in spite of a limited literary production always interrupted by illness, Jacobsen nevertheless created in Denmark the modern psychological romance, the new and more artistic novel; he holds the same rank among Danish novel-writers as Holger Drachmann among poets—that of master. He unites to the objective studies of a naturalist a profound knowledge of human emotions. He understands how to follow, with the deepest comprehension, the finest feelings of the heart, the budding desires and dreams of the soul; and these have never been expressed in Danish more strongly or more richly than by him. Light, hearing, colour, odour, he knows how to render them all in words which he selects and combines as a painter chooses and mixes his tints. He has the magic power to cause the flowers to exhale their perfume, the sun to shine, the rain to drip, the wind to whisper or howl, with a reality unknown and unimagined before in literature. *Marie Grubbe* is Jacobsen's greatest work, but English people who wish to become acquainted with his style may do so by reading *Niels Lyhne*, which has been well translated under the title of *Siren Voices*. The following description by him of a shower of rain is a fair specimen of that minuteness and accuracy of observation in which he surpasses Richard Jefferies himself:—

"Everything gleamed, sparkled, sprouted. Leaves, branches, trunks, everything glistened with wet; every little drop that fell on the earth, on the grass, on the stile, or wherever it might be, was spluttered and sparkled about in thousands of fine pearls. Small drops hung a little while, then became large drops, dropped down here, joined other drops, became small streams, were lost in small furrows, ran into large and out of small holes, sailed away with dust, with splinters and bits of leaves, ran them aground, set them afloat, whirled them round and set them aground again. Leaves which had not met together since they lay in the same bud met again in the dampness; moss that had turned to nothing with dryness swelled up and became soft, crisp, green and juicy; and grey lichen, that had almost turned dry as snuff, spread itself out in graceful folds, stiffening like brocade and with a gloss like silk. The convolvuluses let their white cups be filled to the brim, clinked together, and poured the water at the feet of the nettles. The black snails crawled amiably along and looked appreciatively up at the sky."

Jacobsen has written a few poems distinguished for their grace and elegance. Here is one taken from his tale, *Mogens*:—

"Thou flow'r in dew,
Thou flow'r in dew!
Whisper th' dreams thou art dreaming!
Is there in them the self-same air
The self-same wonderful fairy-land air,
As my seeming?
There does it whisper and sorrow and weep
Through perfumes that die and through colours that sleep?
In longing,
In longing I linger."

He has had many imitators, but, needless to add, unsuccessful ones.

Outside the domain of pure literature Denmark boasts at present, Professor Hoffding, a psychologist and metaphysician, Johan Steenstrup, Karl Erslev, Fridericia, and Edvard Holm, historians, Wimmer, Thomsen, philologist, Julius Thomsen, the great chemist whose theories and discoveries in thermo-chemistry are of worldwide reputation, and Paul de la Cour, some of whose discoveries in electricity antedate those of Edison, and are said in Denmark to have been appropriated by other nations without due recognition of the real inventor.

Though the best works of English writers are now accessible to the Dane in his own tongue, it is very much to be regretted that we have so few translations of theirs as to render a just appreciation of Danish literature very difficult indeed to those unacquainted with the language. To most of us, such masterpieces as Kjerkegaard's *Oehblikke*, Heiberg's *En Sjæl efter Döden*, and Paladan Müller's *Adam Homo* are sealed books, though the Dane may rejoice over the latest productions of Kipling's genius, as indeed he does, in his own language; many also know their Shakespeare better than most of us. The French are more fortunate in this respect; they are better acquainted with Danish history and literature than we are, though surely, to a cognate race like ourselves, they should prove of far greater interest than to the alien Gaul. The Americans also have devoted much more attention and study to these subjects than we have done hitherto.

The works of Ibsen, Björnson and Jonas Lie do not come within the limits of this book, because, though they write in Danish, these world-famous authors are of Norwegian origin and live in Norway.

CHAPTER XXIV

ANCIENT SCANDINAVIAN AND OLD DANISH LITERATURE

THE author of an artist's book would not have been so daring as to venture into the thorny paths of literary criticism had she not had an adequate "purpose" like any modern novel-writer in so doing, in fact, she has two — first to show the close connection between English and Danish traditions, and secondly, to draw the attention of readers to the ancient and modern literature of the Danes, a literature which has hitherto been most unaccountably neglected except by the elect few.

The slight sketch of modern Danish literature which seems necessary for a proper understanding of Denmark to-day must of course be accompanied by some remarks on the old Icelandic literature with which it was identical until the eleventh century.

Passing over the names of certain primitive Icelandic skalds, we come at once to the crowning glory of Scandinavian literature—the Eddas.

The great critic, Dr Horn, is of opinion that "if any single country is to be claimed as the special home of the Eddas, Denmark would seem to be chiefly entitled to that honour. The majority of them relate to Denmark. This assumption is also supported by the fact that, according to the incontrovertible testimony of Northern antiquities, there existed in the Middle Iron Age a rich and varied culture in Denmark in that very time to which doubtless the bloom of Norse poetry is to be referred. Denmark is, upon the whole, throughout antiquity, the one of Northern countries which seems to have acted the most conspicuous part at least in the field of culture, since the waves and movements that passed over the North proceeded from Denmark, or at least reached this country first."

No praise has seemed too extravagant for these venerable works by those who have studied or translated them. "An acquaintance with the ancient runes," says Rasmus Anderson "with the Eddas, with the Heimskringla, and with all the old saga-lore, should be the pride of every Englishman and American." The poet William Morris, who among his countless avocations gave much time to the study of Scandinavian literature, writes: "The Volsung Tale is the great story of the North which should be to all our race what the Tale of Troy was to the Greeks—to all our race first, and afterwards, when the change of the world has made our race nothing more than a name of what has been—a story too—then should it be to those that come after us no less than the Tale of Troy has been to them."

There are two of these remarkable collections of Scandinavian literature—the Elder or Poetic Edda, or Edda of Sæmund Sigfusson, and the Younger or Prose Edda, or Edda of Snorre Sturlason.

The Poetic Edda was unknown on the continent of Europe till the middle of the seventeenth century, when a parchment copy, now called the Codex Regius, was sent as a present to King Frederick III. of Denmark by an Icelandic bishop. The thirty-nine poems of which it consists seem first to have been committed to writing in the eleventh century; they treat of mythological and religious legends. Its unapproachable sublimity, genius and strength can only be compared to the Hebrew Bible or the works of Homer. The most remarkable poems in this priceless collection are the "Voluspa," or Prophecy of the Volva or Sybil, and the "Havamal," or High Song of Odin the Old.

In the "Voluspa" the Prophetess describes chaos, the formation of the world and its inhabitants, the functions of the gods, their quarrels with Loke, and the vengeance which ensued. She concludes with a description of the world's dissolution, the reward of the good and the punishment of the wicked. The description of the final conflagration is very powerful and will serve as an example of the fire and sublimity of this wonderful poem:—

"The sun turns pale,
The spacious earth
The sea engulfs;
From heaven fall
The lucid stars;
At the end of time
The vapours rage
And playful flames
Involve the skies.' *

The "Havamal" reminds the reader of the Proverbs of Solomon, of Omar Khayyam's immortal Rubaiyat, and, in a lesser degree, of the sweet coplas of Manrique translated by Longfellow. The following verses are a fair example of the worldly wisdom of this old singer — wisdom which the thousand or more years which have elapsed since he sang have not made greater— as neither have they the sayings of Solomon, the strophes of Omar, or the couplets of Manrique :—

"Do not too frequently
Unto the same place
Go as a guest;
Sweet becomes sour
When a man often sits
At other men's tables.

One good house is there
Though it be humble.
Each man is master at home;
Though a man own but
Two goats and a straw-rick
'Tis better than begging.

Never found I so generous,
So hospitable a man

---
* Longfellow's Translation.

> As to be above taking gifts;
> Nor one of his money
> So little regardful
> But that it vexed him to lend."*

The rest of the collection consists of songs on the adventures of Sigurd, Brynhild, Gudrun and Hamdir. Wagner has founded his trilogy, "Das Nibelungenring," partly on the Volsungensaga and the Thidreksaga, another Icelandic narration, which were the origin of the German epic, "Das Niebelungenlied." Iseult in the noble musical drama, *Tristan and Isolde*, was of Viking descent, the Danes having been in possession of Ireland in the ninth century, whence the legend dates.

The second of these collections, the Prose Edda, was composed between the years 1140 and 1160 by Snorre Sturlason, who was educated by a grandson of Sæmond, and can bear no comparison as a literary work with the Poetic Edda, on which it is a kind of commentary. It contains a history of the world, a compendium of Scandinavian mythology, the Art of Poetry, and the Sayings of Brage. The charm this book of varied contents has for us is great, for "the Mythology of the Ancient Scandinavians is well calculated to awaken our interest as the source of our popular superstitions from whence the favourite authors of our early childhood and of our maturer age have drawn their witches, their fairies, their dwarfs, their giants and their

* Longfellow's Translation.

Old Danish Literature

ghosts."* "Jack the Giant-killer," "Cinderella," "Blue Beard," "The Pig that would not go over the Bridge," "The Giant who smelt the Blood of an Englishman," "Puss in Boots," are all creatures of the imagination of the old Norsemen. Some of the finest of the Sagas are contained in the *Heimskringla*, "World Circle" (so called from the first two words of one of the manuscripts), which is a history of the Kings of Norway to the year 1177, written by Snorre Sturlason. This work traces Odin and his Asur from the East, gives us the settlement of Scandinavia, the contests among its petty kings, discovery of Iceland, Greenland and America, and the conquests of Normandy and England.

The discovery of America by the Viking Biarne Heriulfson reads not unlike the tale of a modern explorer—his exploit was the legitimate predecessor of those of Cook, Sturt, Stanley and numberless other intrepid travellers who are the glory of our race. Biarne's father was a Viking also, and Snorre relates that one summer "Biarne came with his ship to Eyrar, where his father had sailed abroad from in spring." He was very much struck with the news, and would not unload his vessel. When his crew asked him what he intended to do, he replied that he was resolved to follow his old custom of taking up his winter abode with his father. "So I will steer for Greenland if you will go

* *Literature and Romance of the North.*—W. Howitt.

with me." They one and all agreed to go with him. Biarne said, "Our expedition will be thought foolish, as none of us have ever been on the Greenland shore before." Nevertheless they set out to sea as soon as they were ready, and sailed for three days, until they lost sight of the land they had left. But when the wind failed a north wind with fog set in, and they knew not where they were sailing to; and this lasted many days. At last they saw the sun, and could distinguish the quarters of the sky; so they hoisted sail again, and sailed a whole day and night, when they made land. They spoke among themselves about what this land could be, and Biarne said that in his opinion it could not be Greenland. On the question if he should sail nearer to it, he said, "It is my advice that we sail close up to this land." They did so; and they soon saw that the land was without mountains, was covered with wood, and that there were small hills inland. This voyage and discovery of America is supposed by northern antiquaries to have taken place in the year 986.*

The hardy adventurers who had thus caught the first recorded glimpse of the great new Continent, returned in safety to their native land, where however, amid the excitement caused by the report of the discovery, "People thought that Biarne had not been very curious to get

* Laing's *Heimskringla*. The land is the present Massachusetts and Rhode Island.

knowledge, as he could not give any account of those countries." But the passion for adventure once kindled in the Norsemen's breasts is not easily extinguished, and shortly after Biarne's return, Lief, a son of Eire the Red, bought Biarne's ship, sailed over to America, named and explored portions of it, and spent a winter there. This expedition was followed by several others, all of which succeeded in reaching the newly-discovered country.

The longest and most important saga in the *Heimskringla* is the Saga of King Olaf Haraldson the Saint. "This hero, coming to England to aid the Saxon King Ethelred in reconquering his kingdom, which had been seized and devastated by the Danes, sailed as far up the Thames as London Bridge. King Ethelred was very anxious to get possession of the bridge, and King Olaf determined to take it, so he ordered great platforms of floating wood to be tied together with hazel bands, and for this he took down old houses; and with these, as a roof he covered over his ships so widely that it reached over their sides. Under this screen he set pillars so high and stout that there was room for swinging their swords, and the roofs were strong enough to withstand the stones cast down upon them. King Olaf, and the Northmen's fleet with him, rowed quite up under the bridge, laid their cables round the piles which supported it, and then rowed off with all the ships as hard as they could down the stream. The piles were thus shaken in the bottom, and were loosened under the bridge Now as the armed troops stood thick of men upon the bridge, and there were likewise many heaps of stones and other weapons upon it, and the piles under it being loosened and broken, the bridge gave way; and a great part of the men upon it fell into the river, and all the others fled, some into the castle, some into Southwark."* Ottar Svarte composed a poem on this event which reminds one of a well-known nursery rhyme; the skald's verses are as follows :—

> " London Bridge is broken down,
> Gold is won and bright renown,
> Shields resounding,
> War horns sounding,
> Hild is shouting in the din ;
> Arrows singing,
> Mail-coats ringing,
> Odin makes our Olaf win."

Other sagas of none but historical importance have reached us, but with the *Heimskringla* all that is best and greatest in the old Scandinavian literature comes to an end.

With the introduction of Christianity at the end of the twelfth and beginning of the thirteenth centuries, skalds and saga-men ceased to sing, Latin superseded the vernacular tongue amid the learned, and monkish legends took the place of the old Scandinavian traditions.

* Laing's *Heimskringla*.

> "All the old gods are dead,
> All the wild warlocks fled,
> But the white Christ lives and reigns!"
>
> LONGFELLOW.

Such is a brief sketch of the grand old poems and chronicles in which Denmark, Sweden and Norway have a common inheritance.

Denmark, with which country only we are concerned henceforward, claims for herself the great and learned historian, Saxo Grammaticus, who was a co-temporary of Snorre Sturlason, but who wrote in Latin. His work is characterised as "the greatest intellectual effort of Denmark in the Middle Ages," and as "a treasure-house of truth and falsehood." In it he frequently mentions England and English history, and one of the reasons of its interest for us is that in the pages of Saxo, Shakespeare found the plot of *Hamlet*. The poet has entirely changed the conclusion of the narrative, however, for the historian relates that Hamlet, after killing the king, became his successor, visited England and married a queen of Scotland.

Ballads constitute the most interesting portion of old Danish literature. In 1586 Sophia, Queen of Frederick II., having gone to visit Tycho Brahe at his observatory in the island of Hveen, was detained there by stress of weather, and to pass the time entered into a discussion with the astronomer on the unpublished ballad literature of the country. The result was that five years afterwards Anders Sörensen Vedel, who had been present during the conversation, edited, by desire of the Queen, the first hundred Danske Viser. A hundred years afterwards, Peter Syv, the royal philologist, published a new edition with the addition of another hundred ballads, and these again have been added to. They have much in common with our own ballads in "The Percy Reliques," and with the old Scottish ballads; they lend themselves to translation into the Scottish dialect with much more facility than into the English language. Longfellow, Borrow and Scott have each rendered a few of them into English, but there is no complete translation of them as yet.

At the present time, under the title *Gamle Danske Viser*, or *Kæmpeviser*, are included about 500 epic and lyric poems belonging to the Middle Ages, which relate the adventures and exploits of the old warriors—enchantments and the power of supernatural beings, remarkable historical events, and happy and unhappy loves. They are not all of Danish origin; some were written in Norway, most in Sweden, and part in Germany, England and Scotland. The names of the authors are unknown; what is known is that they were written in mediæval times, and that they lived on the lips and in the memories of the people for many generations before any-one thought of writing them down. They may very well have belonged to the epoch between 1300 and 1500, though the language at first glance points to the sixteenth and seventeenth centuries, for their age is not to be judged by the language. In the different copies which followed each other the form of the language was changed by the progress of time; many expressions were distorted so as to be incomprehensible or completely senseless, because the copiers themselves no longer understood the text, and it is exactly the last and most distorted copies that have come down to us. As we now possess these old Danish songs, with their errors in language, often with lines without sense, terminations without rhyme, and refrains not at all in harmony with the context, they did not come from the lips of the poets, and did not sound to the people of an epoch to whom they were a joy and consolation. However, we still have the essential spirit of them, though attired in an unbecoming dress. Their subjects show that they were made in the days when nobility and knighthood flourished, when monks and clericals were powerful and the power of the king weakened, when the peasantry was sunk in misery, and the bourgeoisie had not yet begun its development.

These songs were decidedly not only to be sung, but also to be danced to.* The melodies, of which a great many still exist, are usually melancholy and in a minor key, even if the subject be light and mirthful. The refrains are not something irrelevant, or late additions; they form parts of the songs and dictate the fundamental ideas, the sources from which they spring, or, as in the

* "What has been called the ballad-dance is said to be the beginning of literature. The emotions of the soul expressed themselves in movement, in music, and in speech."—W. CARPENTER.

Greek tragedies, the voice of fate. Besides their poetical value they are of the greatest historical importance, relating events on which the chronicles of the time are silent, and describing the daily life of the mediæval ages, especially that of the higher classes. I have endeavoured to render into English one of the most popular of these *Danske Viser*, "Aage and Else," which, among much that is droll, contains, I venture to think, elements of the truest poetry, and which may be taken as a fair specimen of the whole:—

AAGE AND ELSE.

There sit three maids in bowers,
    the two twine gold,
The third one is weeping her lover true
    under darkest mould,
For she has the knight or true-lovèd. *

It was the knight Sir Aage,
    through the isle did fare,
Engaged he maiden Elselille †
    a maid so rare.

Engaged he the maiden Elselille,
    so rare a maid,
All on their wedding evening
    he did lie dead.

So sorrowed much maiden Elselille,
    her hands she wrung,
That heard the knight Sir Aage
    far off and long.

---

* This refrain is repeated after every verse, which is a characteristic of the *Folke Viser*.

† "Lille," little, is used in Denmark as a term of endearment. I have endeavoured to retain the characteristic changes in the rhythm, the occasional absence of rhyme, and simplicity of the original poem. Its minuteness of detail is worthy of the efforts of some of our most modern novelists.

So sorrowed much maiden Elselille,
    her hands she clasped,
That heard the knight Sir Aage
    under black dark mould.

Upstands the knight Sir Aage,
    coffin on back he puts,
Thus takes his way to his best beloved's bower
    with very much pain.

He knocks at the door with his coffin,
    he had not a skin,*
"Stand thou up, thou proud Elselille,
    let thy lover true in."

Long time lay proud Elselille,
    to herself thought she,
"Can it be truly knight Sir Aage
    who cometh to me?"

Then outspoke maiden Elselille,
    t' weep she did begin,
"If thou can'st Jesu's name utter
    so cometh thou in."

"Stand up, thou proud Elselille,
    open thy door,
I can as well Jesu's name utter
    as I could before."

Upstood proud Elselille,
    t' weep she did begin.
Then did she shut the lifeless man
    the bower within.

Then took she up a gold comb,
    she combed his hair.
For every lock she combed
    she shed a tear.

---

* The word in the original is *skind*, which signifies "fur cloak." In olden times, when people knocked at doors with the hilt of a sword or a gauntlet, it was the custom to interpose the corner of a fur cloak that the noise might not be too loud.

"And list then, knight Sir Aage,
    ever dearest of mine,
How is it under the black dark earth
    in grave of thine?"

"So is it there under the black dark earth
    in grave of mine,
As in the joyful Heaven's land,
    so do not pine."

"And list then, knight Sir Aage,
    ever dearest of mine,
May I not follow you in black dark earth
    in grave of thine?"

"So is it there under the black dark earth
    in grave of mine
As in the veriest depths of hell,
    make cross's sign.

"For ev'ry time thou weepest for me
    sad* is thy mood, †
Then is my coffin inside full
    of clotted blood.

"Above there at my coffin's head
    the grass grows green,
Beneath there are my cold feet
    with serpents beset.

"But ev'ry time thou singest
    thy mood is glad,
Then is my grave within hung round
    with roses leaves.

"Now croweth the cock, the black one,
    in darkest nook,
Now ev'ry gate must be open,
    now must I go.

---

* His, ancient Danish, obsolete.
† Mod, ancient Danish.

"Now croweth the cock, the white one,
    in the highest hall,
To earth draw nigh all the spirits,
    go now I shall.

"Now croweth the cock, the red one,
    in hottest place,
The dead to the earth now must hasten,
    I must with them."

Upstandeth the knight Sir Aage,
    coffin on back he puts,
Then goeth he to the church's yard
    with very much pain.

That maketh proud Elselille
    so sad in mood,
Then followed she her lover true
    all through darkest wood.

When they came all through the forest
    in churchyard there,
There faded the knight Sir Aage,
    his yellow hair.

And when they came to church's yard
    the church within,
Then faded the knight Sir Aage,
    his rosy cheek.

"And list thou, proud Elselille,
    ever dearest of mine,
Now weep you no more ever
    for true lover thine.

"Look thou up to heaven high
    to little stars,
Then shall you see how joyfully
    how night doth fare."

Looked she up to the heaven high
    to little stars,
In earth then slipped the stark dead man,
    no more she saw.

So quickly slipped the stark dead man
    the earth within,
So sadly walked proud Elselille
    to bower again.

So sadly wept proud Elselille,
    God she did pray,
That she might not live longer than
    one year and a day.

It was proud Elselille
    sick she did stay,
And it was but a month before
    on bier she lay.
For she had the knight so true-loved.

Folk songs may be called the wild flowers of poetry; they come from the hearts of the people and shed beauty over their rude lives, as wild flowers adorn the rugged earth from whence they spring. As Longfellow tells us:—

> "Once more ancient Skald,
> In his bleak ancestral Iceland,
> Chanted staves of these old ballads
> To the Vikings.
>
> Once in Elsinore,
> At the court of old King Hamlet,
> Yorick and his boon companions
> Sang these ditties.
>
> Peasants in the field,
> Sailors on the roaring ocean,
> Students, tradesmen, pale mechanics,
> All have sung them."

I have in a former chapter sketched the re-awakening of the literary spirit in Denmark and its progress to the present day.

CHAPTER XXV

THE DANISH LANGUAGE

> "Old Denmark was our mother earth,
> Each cottage there is still our home,
> 'Twas there our manly speech found birth,
> Whose accents now so world-wide roam."
> GEORGE STEPHENS in *Dagligt Allehande*.

THE Norse tongue, which was formerly the language of Scandinavia, Denmark, Jutland and Slesvig, of the kingdom of Northumberland, East Anglia, and of parts of Mercia; of Normandy, of the Hebrides and Isle of Man, and of the Orkney, Shetland and Faroe Islands, and which has existed for four thousand years, was undoubtedly of Asiatic origin.* About 1000 A.D. this tongue became broken up into four different dialects, which have since existed as literary languages, viz., the Icelandic, Norwegian, Swedish and Danish. Runes† are the Scandinavian alphabet said to have been invented by Odin.

A series of linguistic monuments in the Scandinavian tongue, dating from the Iron Age 450 A.D.,

---

* Laing. Preface to the *Heimskringla*.

† "Le mot *rûn* (pl. *runas*), Gothic *runa*, conseil, chose cachée, interieure : il indique un science occulte, et qui n'est point accessible a tous."—BOTKINE.

according to some antiquaries, but according to Laing "few can be placed before the introduction of Christianity in the eleventh century" have come down to us. These Runic inscriptions are for the most part found on stone monuments, as well as on metallic and wooden utensils, weapons and ornaments, and up to this time a thousand or more have been examined. One of the most important of these is on the golden horn of Gallehus, found on the Danish-German frontier, and dating, it is said, about 400 B.C. It may now be seen in the museum at Copenhagen.

When the Danish kings, Svein Forkbeard and afterwards Canute the Great, conquered England, scores of thousands of Danes emigrated to the British Isles; their kingdom of Northumberland lasted about 300 years. At the compilation of the Doomsday Book by William the Conqueror, the lands of Northumberland, Westmoreland and part of Lancashire were omitted as being Danish, not English. Thus was the Danish tongue, which forms a component part of our language, introduced, and thus it happens that Danish is still spoken with but little admixture in the north-eastern part of England, the old "Danelag."

A writer in the *Ethnological Review* tells us, "With a good stock of broad Scotch (North English) a dairymaid goes to Sweden, and in a few months she makes herself understood. The thing has happened repeatedly, as the author was informed at Goteborg, with English and broad Scotch, and some other tongues. The author himself had travelled in Norway and set off without an interpreter. From the first day he began to use familiar words picked up at the inn; and he was satisfied English with all its dialects is to be classed with Norse. Travelling from place to place, speaking always with peasants, passing rapidly from dialect to dialect, and learning by ear alone, he found that each language (so called) helped him to the next."

The same tongue has been common to Norwegians and Danes for centuries; one Bible and one Psalter are used by both peoples, and the same popular legends, proverbs and national ballads are current in both countries. Before the beginning of the century the use of French and German by the higher classes in Denmark was general, but now, thanks to the efforts of Erasmus Rask, of the Stockholm Congress of 1849, and the recent improvement in the spelling and printing of books, the Danish language is free from unnecessary alien elements. It may be said that only within the last few years it has been reduced to grammatical rules.

Björnson and Jonas Lie have tried to resuscitate the old Norwegian dialect, but Danes cannot read it, and have much difficulty in understanding it when read aloud.

What we are accustomed to regard as vulgar pronunciation of English is, it seems to me in many cases, merely a relic of the pronunciation of our Danish ancestors passed on by the uneducated from generation to generation. For instance, the Dane calls a certain mollusc a "snile" (sneyl) and rain "rine" (regn), and so does the man in the street; innumerable verbs, too, are the same as our own least-refined forms of expression, as "gaa op," literally go up, for advance; "staa tilbage," stay back, for remain; "slippe," to slip, for escape; "kaste op," cast up, to be sick; "hjœlpe," to help, for to assist, etc., etc. In the comparison of adjectives the similarity of the languages comes out strongly, as "ond, vœrre, vœrst," bad, worse, worst; "god, bedre, bedst," good, better, best, the comparative and the superlative being much more like the English than the positive degree. Many Scottish words, as for example, "bairn," child, "sma," little, are pure Danish; in fact, so many words are alike in English, Scottish and Danish that a mere list of them would half exhaust the vocabularies of these languages.

To these superficial notes it must be added that Danish is certainly not a beautiful tongue; to a stranger it sounds like a succession of sharp pistol-shots connected by a guttural monotone; its merits are that it is terse and expressive.

The Gothic alphabet is slowly becoming superseded by the simpler but less beautiful Latin characters.

Besides such proverbs as are common to all races, nearly if not quite all our proverbs are to be found in Denmark. I subjoin a few which are characteristic and which I do not remember to have heard elsewhere: "Tomme Tundere buldre mest" (Empty barrels sound most); "Hvor man ikke kan springe over, skal man krybe under" (What a man cannot jump over, he must creep under); "Krummer ere ogsaa Bröd" (Crumbs are bread also); "Sort ko giver hvid Mœlk" (A black cow gives white milk); "God giver hver Fugl Fœde men kaster den ej i Reden" (God gives every bird food but does not throw it into its nest); "Alle Vegne staar Solen op om Morgenen" (Everywhere the sun rises in the morning); "Paa glat Is ere alle lige stærke" (On smooth ice everyone is equally strong); "Hvor en Snog faar Hovedet ind, faa den snart Halen bag efter" (Where a snake gets its head in, its tail comes after); "Det er sœdt at drikke men surt at betale" (It is sweet to drink but sour to pay); "Ogsaa Paven har været en Skolepog" (Even the Pope was once a school-boy).

CHAPTER XXVI

FOLK-STORIES

IN a remote peninsula of Jutland live the Molboers, a people about whom quaint and droll stories, such as we attribute to the Irish and the French to the Gascons, are told. These folk-tales are well-known in Denmark, and I translate a few for the amusement of the English reader:—

THE LEGS.

Once some Molboers were in a great dilemma. Certain of them sat down in a circle on the ground, but when they wanted to get up again could not make out which pair of legs belonged to each of them, so, thinking they could never rise, they remained calmly sitting. At last they called a passer-by and asked how each of them should find his own legs? He first pointed out his legs to each and told them to draw them up and rise; but as this did not avail he formed another expedient, and took his stick and beat first one, then another, then the third and then the fourth, over the legs. That succeeded, for as soon as they felt the blows on their legs they quickly recognised which belonged to each and drew them up.

THE FISH CART.

That the Molboers are not very courageous about evil spirits they once showed when certain of them were driving some dried fish to a market-town. A couple of rogues saw the cart and thought they would like some fish, but as there were so few of them they were obliged to try if they could not, by cunning, drive the Molboers away. So they agreed that they would get a wheel, bind it round with straw, put fire to the straw, and in the twilight set the wheel running down the hill towards the Molboers. When the Molboers noticed the wheel, one of them whispered to another, "What can this possibly be?" To which an old Molboer replied, "That is the fiend himself." As all the Molboers now got frightened, one of them advised that they should sing a hymn, and they began singing—

> "Our God a city is so strong
> He is our shield and our defence," etc.,

but at the same moment the rogues set the wheel running down the hill. As soon as the Molboers saw the flames come running toward them, the oldest Molboer among them cried,—

> "He may defend as He thinks good
> But I will run into the wood."

And then he ran, and the others after him, into the thickest of the wood, while the scoundrels made away with the fish.

THE STORK AND THE SHEPHERD.

One summer, when the corn stood high, there came into the field of the Molboers a stork which often walked up and down to catch frogs. This they had an aversion to, as they were of opinion that it trod down a great deal of corn. They consulted together as to how they could drive it away, and came to the conclusion that the shepherd of the village should go into the corn and do so. But as he was about to go in after the stork they discovered that he had very large and broad feet, therefore they feared he would tread down more corn than the stork. Then they were again at their wits' end; but there was one among them who gave the intelligent advice to carry the shepherd through the corn in order that he should not tread it down. This advice they all approved. They went and took off the gate of the field, put the shepherd on it, and four men carried him through the corn, that he might drive away the stork. In this way the shepherd did not tread down any corn at all with his large feet.

THE BLACK PUDDING.

Once, when one of the Molboers had slaughtered a cow, and his wife had made black puddings, a large pudding by chance fell down behind a chest without being missed. When it had lain there for some time and become moist, it turned mouldy and was quite covered with mildew. Then one day the wife asked her husband to help her to remove the chest. When he drew the chest out from the wall he noticed the mildewed pudding, which he looked upon as a strange animal. Quite frightened, he let go the chest, ran to all his fellow villagers, told them a loathsome and terrifying beast had come into his house, and begged them to help him to kill it. The valiant men accordingly armed themselves, one with an axe, another with a hay-fork, and a third with a dung-fork, and went with the man. But when they caught sight of the horrid animal no one ventured to go within a distance of three paces from it; therefore they all remained standing outside the door of the room and struck at it with their forks. While they were thus standing, and perspiration was streaming down their faces with terror at this battle, the yard-dog entered, ran in between their legs straight up to the pudding, and ate it. Then they saw with shame that it was only a mouldy pudding they had fought against.

THE HEADLESS MAN.

One day some Molboers went into the wood to cut down trees. When they had cut into a tree so far that they thought it could be pulled to the ground, they discovered that they had forgotten to bring a rope with them. The wisest of them then proposed that one of them should be lifted up in the tree and put his neck in a cleft in such a manner that the others, by pulling him by the legs, should cause the tree to fall. This advice was followed. One of them courageously put his neck in the cleft, and the remainder pulled him by the legs with all their strength. But the enterprise completely failed; at the first pull the body fell to the ground, while the head remained lying in the cleft, where no one could see it. They were greatly astonished at seeing the headless man, and could not imagine how he had got into the wood and up in the tree without a head on his body. However, there was now nothing to be done. They drove the body home to the wife, and asked if he, like the others, had had his head on him when he went out. "Yes, by my soul, he had his head on him," said the wife, "for certainly he ate his cabbage soup with it this morning before he went out."

THE WATCH.

Once some of them found on the road a watch which someone had dropped. They picked it up and looked at it with the greatest astonishment, as not one could tell what such an odd thing was. At the same moment one of them became aware that there was a ticking inside the watch. No sooner had he heard this than he exclaimed that "the devil must be inside," and threw it away.

Not one of the others dared to touch it. At last the oldest among them took a large stone and cast it at the watch, so that it was quite smashed and left off ticking. When he had executed this heroic deed he stooped down and laid his ears to the watch to hear if it was still ticking, but as he heard nothing he said proudly to the others, "You see I have taught him to be quiet!" They all rejoiced that they had vanquished this dangerous enemy, went away, and left the watch lying there.

THE BELL-RINGERS.

When the Molboers had to ring their church bell in memory of the most blessed King Frederick IV., as is still the custom here in the country when a royal personage passes away, neither the bell-ringer nor the squire would give a rope for it, because it ought to be rung several times a day for some months, and that would wear out the best new rope. But as the Molboers were people who had learned what a beautiful virtue economy is, they found out how, nevertheless, they could ring with the little bit of rope which remained in the bell.

Accordingly they fetched the fire-ladder of the church and caused one of them to climb up and hang to the bit of rope; when he had got up another was to hold him by the legs, this man again a third one, and so on till they reached the ground where the lowest was to stand and pull all the others, and in this manner ring in honour of the King. But when they had all caught hold of each other, the hands of the upper one who held the rope began to smart. He then cried to the ringer, "Stop a minute while I spit on my hands!" Then he let go both his hands to spit on them, at which they all fell down and were pitifully killed in a heap.

THE SALT HERRINGS.

One year when salt herrings were rather dear it was difficult for the Molboers to procure this food which they liked so much to eat. They consulted together how to arrange in such a manner that in future they should not be obliged to buy them at so high a rate every year. One of them, who wished to be thought the most witty, wisely resolved that as fresh herrings could breed in water, salt herrings must also be able to do so. He therefore advised them that once for all they should buy a barrel of salted herrings in Aarhus and throw them in the village pond, that later on when these had bred, they might every year be able to catch in their nets as many as they needed. This advice pleased them all so well that some of them directly set out, bought the herrings and threw them in the pond, that they might breed there for years to come.

When the following year they came with their nets to fish for salted herrings they could not, for all their pains, get hold of a single one; after a long time they caught a large fat eel in their net As soon as they saw it they immediately concluded that this was the thief who had eaten their salted herrings, and so they agreed that it should suffer the hardest and most painful death, but they could not resolve on what sort of punishment they should give it. Some of them would have it burnt, others hanged, some would flog it to death, others cut it to pieces. Finally an old Molboer came forth who himself had once been about to be drowned, and as he had not found it to his taste to stay so long a time in salt water, he thought it must be the same with the eel; he therefore advised his countrymen to put out on the wild sea with it and drown it there.

This advice they held to be good, therefore they took the eel, got into a boat, and rowed far out on the sea with it that it might not be able again to swim to shore. When they had got as far out as seemed right to them, they put the eel into the water. The eel, which had so long been on dry land against its will, rejoiced at coming to its native home and wriggled its tail as soon as it reached the water. When the old Molboer saw this he said to the others, "Do you see how pitifully he writhes! Yes, death is hard to put up with."

THE POT WHICH BOILED WITHOUT FIRE.

Another time some Molboers came to Aarhus. They went into a merchant's kitchen, where the maid had just lifted a large iron pot full of peas from the hearth; the pot stood still boiling on the floor after it was taken off the fire. This seemed very strange to them and they much wished to have a pot which could boil without fire also. So they asked the merchant what he would take for the pot, and bought it from him at a high price. Thereupon they went gaily home with it and rejoiced that they would hereafter need no more fire to boil their food as this pot could boil without fire.

But they could not wait till they got home to try the pot, they wished to cook themselves a dish of peas in the boat on their way. So one of them took the pot and dipped it in the sea to get water to cook the peas with; but unfortunately it slipped from his hands and fell to the bottom. Now they did not know what to do to get it again; at last they agreed that one of them should go down and fetch it, and the others meanwhile remain quiet and wait for him. So one of them sprang out to go after the pot; but as it lasted somewhat long before he came again, the others began to talk about what the reason could be. Most of them were of opinion that the pot must be too heavy for him, so they resolved that yet another should go down and help him to bring up the pot. Then another sprang out of the boat, but he did not come back either.

As the others had now waited a long time for them, and could not imagine what had become of them, one of the company said to the others, "We will not wait any longer for them, they have gone away home by the bottom of the sea to get back before the others." They then rowed home with all their strength, and certainly came home before their comrades.

THE BELL.

Once a wag made the Molboers believe that enemies were in the kingdom and that they would soon come to conquer their country; they therefore resolved to save what they could from their hands. That which they were proudest of and wanted to save first was the church bell. They then worked so long at it that they got it down from the tower, but they took council for a long time as to how they should hide it so that the enemy could not find it. At last they agreed to sink it down in the sea. So they dragged it with all their force to a large boat, rowed far away to sea with it and threw it into the water.

When it was thrown down they began to consider and said to one another, "Now it is certainly hidden from the enemy but how are we to find it again when he is gone?" One of them, who thought himself wiser than the others, sprang up and said, "That is no matter, we can put a mark near it." He immediately took a knife out of his pocket, cut a large nick in that side of the boat from which they had thrown the bell, and said, "Here it was that we threw it out!" When this was done they rowed to shore quite calm and glad, persuaded that they would be able to seek their bell again, according to this mark, when the enemy had gone.

CHAPTER XXVII

SKETCH OF THE HISTORY OF DENMARK

> "See the shine
> Of Denmark's Dannebrog on high,
> 'God and the King!'"*
>
> GEORGE STEPHENS.

THE race of men who established themselves in the countries north of the Baltic was undoubtedly of Asiatic origin. Amid the mass of conflicting evidence and the contradictions of controversy which surround the whole question, we may, perhaps, accept the account of Snorre Sturlason as well as that of any other; he says that Odin was a real personage who migrated with his followers from a mysterious city called Asgard, on the borders of the Tanais, about seventy years before our era. Odin founded the empire of the Sviar, a small territory around the Maelar Lake in the present Swedish province of Upsala, and had five sons, one of whom reigned over Skania, the original seat of the Danes; another of them, named Skiold, led a colony into Seeland and became the ancestor of the regal family of Denmark, the Skioldungs. Like the other Scandinavian nations, Denmark has the most

* The motto of the Dannebrog.

exaggerated pretensions to antiquity, its list of monarchs, according to the *Universal History*, beginning with Dan, who reigned 1038 years before Christ. From Dan, who united a number of small chieftains under his rule, the country takes its name—Dan-mark, or the marches or border of the Dans or Danes.

Its history, until within the last thousand years, is a strange mixture of fact and fable, more fable than fact, however; piratical expeditions, fights of petty kings, mythological stories and songs of skalds are intermixed in inextricable confusion. Later on it reads more like a romance than a history.

The circumstances that come out most saliently about these old Vikings are that they extended their conquests in the west as far as Ireland, ravaged in the south as far as Sicily, and in the east fought in Palestine and captured Sidon. The Varangian guard at Byzantium was composed entirely of Norsemen.

A traveller from Marseilles, about three hundred years before the Christian era, is the first to mention a northern country, and this he does under the name of Thule, by which it is supposed he meant Jutland. The earliest authentic account of the Danes is to be met with in the writings of the Anglo-Saxon and French chroniclers, who furnish details of their repeated invasions of England, their descents on Scotland, and their conquest of Normandy.

In the middle of the ninth century, Gorm the

Old, subduing a number of petty chiefs, became the first king of all Denmark. His wife, Queen Thyra Dannebod (the Danes' joy), who, according to tradition, was an English princess, pitying the sufferings of her subjects from the constant incursions and plunderings of their southern neighbours, built the Dannewirke, a rampart stretching from the North Sea to the Baltic. Christianity was first preached in South Jutland in 822.

Gorm the Old was succeeded by his son, Harold Blaatand. (Blue tooth), his son Svend Tveskæg, the Sweyn Forked-beard of English history, commenced the conquest of England which was completed by Knud or Canute the Great, who became king in 1018, thus uniting the crowns of the two kingdoms. On the death of his son Harthaknud (Hardicanute) without male issue, the Danish dynasty in England came to an end.

Svend Estridsen (1047-1076), son of the powerful Jarl Ulf of Norway and of Canute the Great's sister Estrid, was a protector of learning and the Church, and founded a line of kings which occupied the throne for three hundred years. Through him both Queen Victoria and the present King of Denmark may trace their descent back to Gorm the Old.* He was succeeded by five of his sons, in whose reigns the Danish Church was brought under strict discipline, and sanguinary civil wars were carried on.

Valdemar I. (1157 - 1182), after vanquishing

*Dunham.

many rivals, secured the homage of the Danes. He made seventeen campaigns against the pagan tribes on the south of the Baltic, and cleared the northern seas of the Wend pirates; during his reign a regular constitution began to be formed, and Copenhagen was founded by Absalon, the warlike bishop of Sjælland (Seeland).

With Valdemar II. (1202-1241) a prosperous and glorious period set in for Denmark, and his many conquests gained for him the title of Sejr (the Victor). He conquered Holstein, Lauenberg, Schwerin and other north German provinces, and set out on a crusade against the pagans in Esthonia with a view to converting the inhabitants. At the battle of Reval, during this war, Denmark commenced to use the Dannebrog or national standard—a white cross on a blood-red field. It is said that, as the Danes began to give way before their enemies, this flag was miraculously displayed in the heavens, and the sight of the sacred emblem so much encouraged them, and so affrighted their enemies, that the pagans fled and were afterwards converted by thousands. In 1223 the King was treacherously captured, while hunting, by Count Henry of Schwerin, and only regained his liberty by ceding the greater part of his conquests. On his release he devoted himself to making and amending the laws of his country, an effort of more real service than all his military exploits.

Wars with the association of the Hanse towns as to the tolls to the entrance to the Baltic,

Sketch of the History of Denmark

violent contentions between the Church and State, the throne and the nobles, followed the death of Valdemar II., and brought the kingdom to the brink of ruin. But Valdemar III. (Atterdag) succeeded by the great energy of his administration in restoring calm. With him the race of Svend Estridsen, which had occupied the throne of Denmark for three hundred years, came to an end.

Valdemar III. died in 1378, leaving daughters only, and one of them, Margaret, called the "Semiramis of the North," on the death of her only son, was crowned, by consent of Parliament, "All-powerful lord and master of Denmark." This princess was married to Hakon, King of Norway; at his death, in 1380, his kingdom had devolved on her, and by the decisive victory of Falkoping she added to her two crowns that of Sweden also. But under her weaker successor the union was frequently broken. The "Kalmar Treaty," providing for the joint-election of a monarch by the three kingdoms, entirely failing of its purpose, King Erik succeeded Margaret, but at his death Sweden elected Karl Knutsson as its king, while the Danes chose Count Christian of Oldenburg, the founder of a dynasty which for four hundred years occupied the Danish throne. He succeeded in re-establishing the union, acquired Holstein, and inherited Slesvig by the death of his uncle, Adolph. But the Union, as regards the Swedes, was far from being cordial; alleging the extravagance and cruelty of the

Danes as a reason, they broke into open revolt, and under the able leadership of Gustavus Vasa completely routed their enemies at the Battle of Brunkebjerg, near Stockholm, and Sweden was never again under Danish yoke. The nobles of Jutland also disclaimed their allegiance to the King, and offered Duke Frederick of Gottorp the Danish throne; finally Christian II. fled the country. With him the line of the "Kings of the Union" came to an end; his cruel policy cost him all he had at first gained, for by his orders the Massacre of Stockholm ("Blodbad"), which so much exasperated the Swedes, took place, when a number of the nobility and dignitaries of the Church were executed in the market-place of the town.

In the reign of Frederick I. (1523-1533) the doctrines of the Reformation found their way into Denmark under the auspices of the Danish Luther, Hans Tausen. The King himself embraced Protestantism, and it was recognised as the State religion by the Synod of Copenhagen. This King gave the nobles absolute authority over their serfs, and for three hundred years "the Danish peasant was a slave on the land where he was born."[*]

Civil wars and dissensions followed the death of Frederick I. Frederick II. built the fortress of Kronborg to check the Hanse traders, encouraged learning and protected Tycho Brahe, the astronomer, to whom he gave the island

[*] Otté.

of Hveen for the erection of an observatory.

Under Christian IV. two disastrous wars occurred,—the commencement of the Thirty Years' War (1618), in which the King fought on the Protestant side, and the Kalmar war with Sweden, in which the Danes won the celebrated battle of Kolberg (1644), but at Brömsebro (1645) were forced to conclude a disadvantageous peace. Christian IV. is the most beloved and popular of the Oldenburg line of kings.

Under Frederick III. (1648-1670) Sweden recommenced hostilities. At the storming of Copenhagen the Swedes were repulsed by the citizens, headed by their burgomaster, Hans Nansen, and Svane, Bishop of Seeland, with great bravery; but King Carl Gustav forced the Danes to conclude a treaty of peace at Roskilde, by which they ceded Skania, Aland, several places in the island of Rugen, and a free passage through the Sound, to the Swedish crown. Frederick, by the Hereditary Autocratic Act, made Denmark an absolute monarchy, a change in the form of government to be explained by the repugnance of the Danes to the ascendency of the aristocracy.

Frederick IV. endeavoured to regain the Skanian provinces which had been seized by Sweden, and though Niels Juel obtained a brilliant naval victory in the bay of Kjoge, and Peder Tordenskjold well maintained the Danish reputation for courage in many a wild sea-fight, the King was not successful. His opponent, Charles XII., invested the city of Copenhagen; its inhabitants in alarm appealed to the Swedish king for mercy, and the result was the conclusion of peace with the payment of a sum of money to the Swedes.

Towards the middle of the eighteenth century a period of tranquillity for Denmark commenced under the ministry of the two Bernstorffs, and a peace policy was adopted, to which the country has ever since endeavoured to adhere. Frederick V., representing the House of Holstein-Gottorp, even agreed in 1767 to forego his claims on Slesvig and Holstein on condition of receiving in exchange the duchies of Oldenburg and Delmenhorst, this being called the "Oldenburg Deed of Exchange" of 1767.

Denmark, thus enjoying the blessings of peace under Frederick IV. and his successors, Christian VI. and Frederick V., settled itself to encourage arts and manufactures, reform the "Slavnsbaand," or feudal system of vassalage, which forced the peasant during a certain number of years to remain on the estate on which he was born, and to arrange the finances of the exhausted country.

A German adventurer named Struensee ingratiated himself into the favour of the dissipated Frederick V. and found means to get himself appointed his Prime Minister, in which capacity he instituted a number of excellent reforms, of which the best was complete freedom of the

Press; but his open contempt for everything Danish, and the relation in which he stood to the Queen, Caroline Matilda of England, wife of Christian VII., who succeeded Frederick, excited ill-will. He was introduced to the young Queen as her husband's confidential minister, and on this the Queen-Dowager founded an intrigue, which ended in the arrest of Struensee and the Queen after a masked ball at Court. Struensee was beheaded and the Queen exiled; her guilt has never been proved, and the sympathy of the Danes is still always on the side of the unfortunate Queen.

Owing to the imbecility of Christian VII. the Crown Prince Frederick was appointed regent in 1784: surrounded by such able men as Goldberg, Bernstorff, Reventloo and Colbjornsen, he instituted a period marked by salutary radical reforms and national progress. Among these are the reform of the Courts of Law, enfranchisement of the peasants, abolition of the negro slave-trade in the Danish West Indies, and the emancipation of the Jews.

Amid this prosperity the old controversy with England, which insisted on examining Danish merchantmen to see if they carried contraband goods, revived, and in consequence Denmark, Russia and Sweden concluded a treaty of armed neutrality, the upshot being that the English, under Parker and Nelson, attacked the Danish fleet in the roadstead of Copenhagen on April 2nd, 1801. The resistance of the Danes was in vain, and most of their shipping was destroyed, but happily the capital was little injured.

A treaty of peace followed, soon broken, however, by Napoleon's intrigues with Alexander of Russia to force Denmark to take part in the war against England; the latter country forestalled her enemies and for three days bombarded Copenhagen, where a great number of public as well as three hundred private buildings were laid in ruins and the fleet destroyed. After the overthrow of Napoleon peace was again restored. Denmark gave up Norway in exchange for Pomerania, and Pomerania was again exchanged for a sum of money and a small district in Lauenburg.

On the death of Frederick VI. (1839) Christian VIII. succeeded, during whose reign the Slesvig-Holstein question began to assume graver proportions. In addition to the disputes as to its rightful ownership the people demanded a more liberal constitution, and the Holsteiners objected to the use of the Danish language to the prejudice of the German. Christian died in 1848 in the very midst of these perplexities. His son, Frederick VIII., succeeded him. The Slesvig-Holstein party now demanded the establishment of Holstein as an independent state and the incorporation of Slesvig in the German Confederation, of which Holstein had formed a part for some time. The municipal authorities of Copenhagen petitioned the King to assemble round him only advisers who would make it their aim to preserve Slesvig to Denmark. The King answered that he had already anticipated the wishes of the people by dismissing his ministers, and he promised "that if they would repose the same confidence in him that he reposed in them, he would always be their faithful leader to honour and liberty." He then declared that he would consolidate the union of Slesvig, which so much desired it, with the rest of the kingdom, and give Holstein an independent liberal constitution.

The Slesvig-Holsteiners then broke out into open revolt, and a Danish army of 10,000 men, under General Hedemann, defeated them at Bov in the neighbourhood of Flensborg. The insurrection would then have been at an end so far as Denmark was concerned, had not the King of Prussia, with an army of 20,000 men, marched into Slesvig and joined the insurgents. After an unequal contest, sustained by the Danes with great bravery, an armistice was concluded at Malmö in August 1848. But the suspension of hostilities was of short duration. In April 1849 the second Slesvig campaign began, which was distinguished by the heroic victory of Fredericia, in which, after six hours' fighting, 2000 men were left dead or wounded on the field. The Slesvig-Holstein army then crossed the Eider, but was encountered by the Danish force of 39,000 men in the most bloody and important engagement of the whole war—it ended, however, in favour of the Danes, who marched south and occupied the Dannewirke.

On the death of Frederick VII., who was childless, Prince Christian of Glücksburg, by virtue of a new law of succession, succeeded to the throne; in 1863 and the following year, the Danish army refusing to evacuate Slesvig, the second Slesvig war began. The Dannewirke position being declared untenable, General De Meza, to the exasperation of the Danes, retired northward, pursued by the enemy, who overran the country, dismantled the Dannewirke, established the German language, and endeavoured to efface entirely the effects of Danish rule. England then proposed a conference to terminate this disastrous war, but terms could not be agreed upon, and hostilities recommenced. The Danes, taken by surprise, were defeated at Dybbel with a loss of about 8000 men; Sonderberg and Alsen fell; Vendryssel was evacuated, and it seemed as if the very name of Denmark was about to be effaced from the map of Europe. Germans overran the country as far as to the north of Jutland, and the hopeless struggle, sustained with such heroic courage, was over. The Peace of Vienna was signed in October 1864, and by its terms Denmark ceded Lauenburg, Holstein and Slesvig to Prussia and Austria.

Since then the little kingdom of Denmark has prospered and flourished exceedingly, and her people are contented and happy. The constitution has been revised, banking system rectified, decimal coinage adopted, railway, postal and telegraphic services organised, and education has reached a higher level of excellence than in any other European state.

The new line of Kings of Denmark which commenced with Christian XI. in 1863 is nearly related to the Oldenburg dynasty. The present King's mother was a grand-daughter of Frederick V., while the late Queen was a grand-daughter of the Hereditary Prince Frederick, a son of Frederick V. The eldest of their six children, Crown Prince Frederick, is united to the Princess Louise of Sweden and Norway; their eldest son, Christian, is the destined heir of Denmark. Princess Alexandra became Princess of Wales. Then follows George I., King of the Hellenes, Princess Dagmar, Dowager-Empress of Russia, Princess Thyra married to the Duke of Cumberland, and Prince Valdemar, married to the Princess Marie of Orleans.

CHAPTER XXVIII

AFTERWORD

It is ten o'clock at night but I do not need a lamp to write by, and the pale and infinitely tender green sky is clear and lustrous, with never a single twinkling star in all its wide embrace. The fjord beneath my window is one vast sheet of unbroken light, save where in one little bay the dark masts of the fishing-boats rise like the spears of a giant's army stuck upright in the sand; every leaf and every flower, indeed, every object, may be distinctly seen in a weird light that seems to suffuse them and to be something unreal, unnatural. The early inhabitants of the village have already retired beneath their feather beds, not a sound disturbs the silence; it is as if all things almost held their breath in order that weary Nature might go undisturbed to sleep.

My pleasant task is ended, the pen about to be laid down and the ink-bottle closed, the sketches hang drying on the wall, and I ask myself, memory looking back over the stained pages, "Is there, after all, any interest in what I have written? Have I succeeded in recording any definite impression of what I set myself to describe?"

Afterword

Nervously I answer in the negative, and then set to work to make excuses to that most indulgent of critics—myself. And I say—with the splendours of the East, with the romance of Spain, with the tender beauty of Italy, Denmark can bear no comparison, so it is but natural that my book should not possess the splendour, romance and beauty of such as describe those favoured lands. But Denmark nevertheless has a character of its own; it is honest, rugged, and saturated with the brave old Norse spirit which is its crowning glory and which to this day even seems to animate its lakes and forests, its people and its literature, therefore my book may be forgiven if it be only honest, rugged, and having the scent of the soil on which it was written clinging about it—in a word, characteristic. If we have here no superb Arab with flashing scimitar caracoling on a thoroughbred steed, we have an industrious farmer leading a simple life, occupied in the sacred task of wresting from the earth what it is capable of yielding for the maintenance of the human race; if we have no lithe Spaniard singing to a guitar under the "reja" of his lustrous-eyed inamorata, we have a flaxen-haired youth, with face deeply tanned by labour in the sun from which his light blue eyes look truly out, telling the healthy and strongly-limbed maiden of his choice his tale of love beneath the shadows of magnificent beech trees, or in a boat amid the lilies of a murmuring lake; and if we have not the romance of the Italian, to whom the poetry of Dante and Tasso are as cradle-songs and the glory of Michael Angelo and Raphael a proud inheritance, we have the noble sagas of Sæmund Sigfusson and the fame of Oehlenschläger and Thorvaldsen to boast of. So, reader, when you have read my little book, do not cast it down, but put it on your shelf beside your Murrays and your Baedekers, and when you are very worn out indeed, or more than ever *blasé* with the light and glory of countries more showy but perhaps scarcely more fair, then take it down and let it hold you gently by the hand and lead you to a land of shade and green trees, of flowing water and of grassy plains; there you may rest your overwrought brain and aching eyes, and see how the Danes, content with that they have, live without casting regretful eyes on those whose fortune places them on other and more gaudy shores.

REPOSE.

Sea slumb'ring softly in the summer sun!
   O, winds which cease from wand'ring and are still!
O, folded flow'rs whose daily task is done!
   Leaves hanging idly at the zephyrs' will!
Would the sweet influence of your gentle peace
   Might steal within the passionate hearts we bear,
And teach the strife and bitterness to cease
   With which our lives are saturated here!
And bid repose, the balm of those who mourn
   And labour, come to us and still the sighs,
The doubts, the fears with which our spirits burn
   Before the grandeur of your mysteries,
And teach us that if labour is divine,
Repose is also solemn and benign.

MARGARET THOMAS.

WORKS OF REFERENCE.

History of the Literature of the Scandinavian North	HORN.
Art Tour to the Northern Capitals of Europe	J. B. ATKINSON.
The Poets and Poetry of Europe	LONGFELLOW.
Studies in the Literature of Modern Europe	E. W. GOSSE.
An Account of the Danes and Norwegians in England	J. J. A. WORSAAE.
The Sagas of the Norse Kings	LAING.
History of Denmark, etc.	DUNHAM.
Literature and Romance of the North	WILLIAM and MARY HOWITT.
The Elder Edda	
The Younger Edda	
Denmark	H. WEITEMEYER.
Denmark and Iceland	E. O. OTTÉ.

Colston & Coy. Limited, Printers, Edinburgh

TREHERNE & CO.'S NEW PUBLICATIONS

Six-Shilling Novels

Athenæum says—"The publishers deserve praise for the quality, and paper and printing, in the novels they have issued."

THE RANEE'S RUBIES. By Dr HELEN BOURCHIER.

Irish Times.—"Distinctly interesting and readable."

Daily Express.—"A well-devised and well-told romance of Indian life."

THIRTEEN WAYS HOME. By E. NESBIT.

Globe.—"The reader who does not find much in the book to interest him must be difficult to please."

Spectator.—"Full of spirit."

Yorkshire Post.—"A sheaf of thirteen love stories, all unconventional and charming.

THE SIGN OF THE PROPHET. By JAMES BALL NAYLOR, Author of "Ralf Marlowe."

Daily Mail.—"Incidents of the war between Great Britain and the infant American Republic early last century are entertainingly told."

TATTY: A Study of a Young Girl. By PETER FRASER.

Athenæum.—"The book is well thought out and distinctly well written."

EAST OF SUEZ. By ALICE PERRIN.

Punch.—"Runs even the best of Kipling's tales uncommonly close."

DROSS. By HAROLD TREMAYNE.

Westminster Gazette.—"A daring idea is well carried out. . . . The book is more than readable."

Three-and-Sixpenny Novels

"MAD" LORRIMER. By Finch Mason.

County Gentleman.—"A very readable book."
Free Lance.—"These stories will be widely read."

THE WOMAN OF ORCHIDS. By Marvin Dana.

Bristol Daily Mercury.—"The characters are skilfully drawn."
Aberdeen Daily Journal.—"Mr Marvin Dana is a very clever writer, and his story is well conceived and worked out."

THE CASE OF A MAN WITH HIS WIFE. By Theo. Gift.

Birmingham Daily Gazette.—"Well told and pathetic."

Half-Crown Novels

A FREE LANCE IN A FAR LAND. By Herbert Compton.

THE STAR SAPPHIRE. By Mabel Collins.

LONDON IN SHADOW. By Bart Kennedy.

THOROUGHBRED. By Francis Dodsworth.

THE WARRIOR WOMAN. By E. Vizetelly.

Shilling Sporting Series

No. 1. LITTLE CHERIE; or The Trainer's Daughter. By Lady Florence Dixie.

Scotsman.—"Brisk, eloquent and animated."

People.—"The story is well told."

Country Life.—"A lively tale of racing."

Onlooker.—"Readable and interesting."

No. 2. REMINISCENCES OF A GENTLEMAN HORSE DEALER. By Harold Tremayne.

Sportsman.—"Shrewd wit and observation are scattered through the pages."

Sporting Life.—"The author understands his subject."

Yorkshire Herald.—"A most welcome addition to sporting literature."

Bailey's Magazine.—"Readable and amusing."

No. 3. A FURY IN WHITE VELVET. By Herbert Compton.

Pall Mall Gazette.—"One of the best shillingsworths we have of late come across . . . it is readable, well told and exciting from start to finish."

Liverpool Mercury.—"Full of exciting adventure."

Irish Times.—"Certainly there is a shillingsworth of incident and excitement."

No. 4. FROM DOWNS TO SHIRES. By R. Alwyn.

Scotsman.—"Will be enjoyed by any sympathetic sportsman who chances on the book."

No. 5. A TRUE SPORTSMAN. By Francis Dodsworth.

..Treherne's Coronation Series..

Same size as Tauchnitz Edition, handsomely bound in limp art cloth, 1s. 6d. ; limp leather, 2s. 6d.

No. 1. **JOHN HALIFAX, GENTLEMAN.** By Mrs Craik.

No. 2. **PRIDE AND PREJUDICE.** By Jane Austen.

No. 3. **LAST DAYS OF POMPEII.** By Bulwer-Lytton.

[Ready shortly

No. 4. **IVANHOE.** By Sir Walter Scott.

No. 5. **WESTWARD HO.** By Charles Kingsley.

No. 6. **DAVID COPPERFIELD.** By Charles Dickens.

Acme
Bookbinding Co., Inc.
300 Summer Street
Boston, Mass. 02210

CPSIA information can be obtained at www.ICGtesting.com
Printed in the USA
LVOW022205260213

321862LV00005B/74/P